Dear Rod.

GW00634681

With Love

M Tray x

(Steph)

Hope you enjoy it!

THE CUCKOLD

THE CUCKOLD

Madeleine Gray

Book Guild Publishing
Sussex, England

First published in Great Britain in 2009 by
The Book Guild Ltd
Pavilion View
19 New Road
Brighton
BN1 1UF

Typesetting in Baskerville by
Nat-Type, Cheshire

Printed in Great Britain by
CPI Antony Rowe

A catalogue record for this book is available from
The British Library.

ISBN 978 1 84624 320 2

For my honey

Chapter 1

Sophie

'The only way to get rid of temptation is to yield to it. Resist it and your soul grows sick with longing for the things it has forbidden itself.'
Oscar Wilde

My mother left when I was just six and I never really got to say goodbye. Not the way that you would say goodbye if you knew that you were never going to see your mother again. Not that type of goodbye. My father had gone long before I had even started walking, so I stayed with a neighbour and was collected not too long after by my maternal grandmother, clearly not impressed with my sudden and uninvited arrival. And so, it was in her begrudging care that I matured, left school and entered the big bad world. All the time wondering how everything had gone so wrong and wondering why I didn't seem to fit in anywhere. I was smaller than I should be with hair that was too fine, a nose that was too straight and breasts that seemed to just keep growing. At eighteen though, I started to grow into myself, I found a haircut that made my hair look thicker and grew hips and became slightly taller. I then ran headlong into the arms of the first man who paid me any attention at all. We were married just four months later and for the first time ever I felt almost like the right-sized peg in the right-shaped hole.

1

So am I mentally scarred? I am not sure. Isn't everyone nowadays? It seems fashionable to have some kind of hang-up, to be affected by some terrible past event. I'm not sure that even the experts know what is normal now. I find that I am left, however, with a terrible feeling of foreboding, that one day I will wake up and all the people I work with or have come to call friends will suddenly see straight through me. All of my fine layers of pretence will fall away and leave me exposed for the entire world to see. I will finally be laid bare as the fake that I think I am. But then, maybe, there are lots of people who feel this way, as though life is just a great charade and that no matter how hard they try they can never quite cut it, never really fit in. I am sure there is even a medical name for such a phobia somewhere. I am happy though, or at least as happy as I think I should be. Each day I just get by, nothing particularly exciting ever happens to me, but I enjoy my ordinary life as much as anyone and I suppose that is just how life is. I guess I must have trust issues as I am not so good at getting too close to people. I don't have a huge circle of friends and have never really been comfortable in the middle of a large gaggle of girls – or boys for that matter. I don't think that I was ever really cool or trendy enough to be accepted, and I never believed that I was interesting enough to deserve one special friend. So I kept moving, always friendly but ready to flee if anyone looked like they were getting to know me too well. I recall that someone somewhere once said to me that the definition of a true friend is someone you can call on in the middle of a rainy night when your car breaks down somewhere obscure (I don't think the AA counts here, and I'm not really sure that it has to be raining). But anyway, if you use that as a definition then my list of 'real' friends is depleted even further. Even the people closest to me perhaps don't know too much about me, but I kind of like it that way. Anyway, doesn't familiarity breed contempt or something like that?

I used to dream in a fairy-tale kind of way about how my life may turn out, but I suppose most girls do. I used to dream that my mother and father would turn up one day to rescue me, they would be dressed in finery and carry me away to my real home. They would have tears in their eyes and enough hugs and kisses to last a lifetime. Of course in my dreams my real home was a castle somewhere because, obviously, in my dreams I was really a princess hidden until my secret identity could be revealed. I was never really convinced by the whole feminist movement so I would also dream of the man that I would fall desperately in love with. (You see even that sounds romantic – truly I am a hopeless case!) In my mind I would compose a list of the fine attributes absolutely necessary in a husband. He would have to be tall, dark, good-looking (obviously), charming, romantic and passionate. He would sweep me into his arms and off into the sunset, where we would have at least three children and perhaps a Labrador. He would carry a linen handkerchief at all times (just in case I became tearful or grubby) and would open car doors for me and kiss me tenderly (but with passion) often. We would spend the rest of our lives in wedded bliss gazing into each other's eyes and playing with our beautiful children and dog.

Unfortunately I am still waiting for my parents to turn up and reveal my hidden identity, but I did marry my tall, dark, handsome husband. Again unfortunately, this is where any similarity ceases. But please don't misunderstand me. He is the kindest, sweetest man. His name is Simon. He is solid, reliable and consistent and has a good job at one of the banks. A catch really, I suppose. His job is to discover fraudulent banking transactions and ensure that all processes and staff are strictly compliant at all times. He is neat and tidy, rarely complains, doesn't drink, smoke, gamble or womanize and tells me that he loves me every day. Even after all this time. Everything a girl should want. Who needs passion anyway? I am sure it is overrated. After all this

3

time I don't think I would recognize true passion if it fell on my head. But then we never really had that kind of fervour, not even in the very early days. I don't recall being kept awake at night frenzied or crazed with ardour, excited or enthused with dreams of the next time we would meet or be together. Not even initially did I feel that I wanted to be taken roughly or even gently and tenderly anywhere. Our relationship was more about the practicable reasons that we should be together, our friendship, our easy compatibility and of course our mutual love of Labradors. So, our planned marriage, athough swift, was exactly that: planned. I felt that the whole marriage thing was expected of me, it became almost inevitable, and then when it happened it was all a kind of relief somehow. People imagine that if you marry within four months of meeting someone that such hasty nuptials must have followed a wildly tumultuous and crazed romance, that I would have arrived at the altar dazed and dishevelled in a whirlwind of emotion, with my knickers stuffed hastily in my handbag. Of course it was never like that but, when people ask now, I just smile enigmatically and sigh; after all, people love a romance and to shatter their illusion just seems cruel somehow.

So after all this time our sensible relationship still feels safe but it has grown comfortable as well now, and our lives, well, they are filled with everyday practicalities and responsibilities. The duties and chores that slowly ground us as we grow older, the everyday routines that cleave to us, snaking like vines around us, choking to death the wild fancies and the exuberance of our formative years, slowly, imperceptibly taming any undisciplined yearnings into submission. And it all happens so slowly that we cannot remember any pivotal date or event when we allowed this to happen. I am terrified sometimes that an indolent rot has set in between us, a kind of apathy, a slothful dependence on the notion that each day and month and year of our lives will be the same. That nothing will change. Some days, I find myself wondering if perhaps I have died, and no one has told me yet. I wonder if I have forgotten what it is like to feel, really feel. And as time has gone by I feel cheated that our shared mortgage and our countless household errands have failed to bring us any closer, in fact we kind of co-exist. Not unhappily, you understand, but in amicable companionship and nothing more.

Sometimes, I am scared that we are without that invisible but necessary binding that should hold us together in times of trouble. Thank goodness that in the time that we have spent together we have never really come up against any vast problems that have tested us. Not really anyway. Our only reliable underlying tension is that after nine whole years of marriage there is still no baby, nothing to show for our perfunctory couplings. Maybe I don't get pregnant because there is no real depth of feeling between us. Sometimes I can't imagine ever feeling that kind of heart-stopping (but pulse-racing) emotion for anyone. And Simon tries hard, he is endlessly sweet, he definitely does all those little things that a girl likes and it is all very pleasant and agreeable, nice even. But lately I have wondered that maybe I could be frigid. I have even checked the contents of my cereal to make sure the ingredients didn't include bromide or any other dubious ingredients that could be the cause of my extinguished enthusiasm. After all, you can't be too careful nowadays, what with all these additives and colourings. But there wasn't anything like that, just a few innocent raisins and some oats. And I haven't always felt so lacklustre, over the years there have been a series of other men, extra marital flirtations and associations. Brief frantic sex snatched in hotel rooms, all of which left me physically satiated but emotionally barren. Sadly there have been numerous liaisons, each finishing as quickly as it began, leaving me wondering, quite frankly, why I bothered. Each time the only memory I am left with is that of another sordid misadventure seasoned with guilt.

I try not to look at the new mothers in the park with their smug expressions and trendy pushchairs. They stand beside the swings, all grouped and huddled together, to discuss their latest sleepless nights and teething issues. Sometimes, in between meetings, I can be found masked by the anonymity of being in other towns and faraway cities, surreptitiously stalking the aisles of Mothercare. Reverently I find myself touching the impossibly small baby clothes, deep in thought, planning a nursery and dreaming of cute accessories. Each time considering how it would feel to have a new life growing somewhere deep inside me. I have yearned and prayed with my whole being, and cried endless tears over our inability to have a child. Such a seemingly simple thing to do, all the couples we socialize with now have at least one. But still we have no baby. Simon and I have, of course, discussed this, to the point where, at times I fear I have driven him quite to despair. He does want children but I think that perhaps he doesn't need a child the way that I do. For him I am sure it is on a 'nice to have' list, somewhere between a better stereo and a new car. For me, if I let it, my need becomes an all-consuming longing, an emptiness that just seems to get bigger and more desolate with time. I am becoming deafened by the ticking of my biological clock, and I am aware that I no longer mark my time here looking forward to holidays or the next Christmas, instead I mentally score through each month of my life as it passes, undistinguished once more, and unmarked again by the birth of the child that should be ours.

I wonder whether one of the reasons we haven't conceived is that I am actually scared of what a child could really mean. All along it has been me, not Simon, who has been reluctant to try IVF or even seek a medical opinion as to why it hasn't happened yet. As much as I long for a child, I find that I am torn, terrified even. I am scared that I might, deep inside, be just the same as my mother: fine for the first few years, happy to be a mother and all that, but then, when the baby starts to grow, somewhere deep inside me a switch will trip and then some everyday occurrence will tip me over the edge and I will leave. For no good reason at all I will just get up and go. No longer caring about where my baby is or who is looking after it. Maybe it won't even be a big thing that makes me leave, just something trivial, perhaps I will go out for sausages and never come back, or run off with the postman.

I read somewhere that children who are separated from their parents often struggle with parenthood, as they have no blueprint to refer to. So, what if I don't love my baby, what if I am incapable of that unconditional love, the type of love you should feel for your child? And then what if Simon were to leave? The potential and possibilities for disaster are just mind-boggling. I try to think logically, try to lose the fog which I can only think must have been created by some kind of hormone surge. After all, I know I really want a baby and I know that Simon would be a fantastic father, but even as I clarify this to myself I struggle to imagine it. Try as I might, I just can't picture us old together with grown children, maybe even grandchildren. I wonder if this is some kind of sign, an omen perhaps. Maybe I need to see some kind of psychic to sort through my tea leaves or read my palm.

Lately I have developed one hundred or more different reasons to avoid having sex (and not just because I have no sex drive any more) because now, it all seems rather pointless. It is just a constant reminder that we can't get pregnant. I have started thinking that maybe I married too young, I do think that perhaps I didn't kiss as many frogs as I might have done, maybe Simon isn't Mr Right. Maybe that's why we still have no baby. This thought is almost so secret that I don't even like to admit it is there, even to myself. Of course there is a part of me that is fully aware that I just need to grow up and face life and be happy with my lot, but I can't seem to shake off my dreams. Is it so wrong to have dreams?

So here I am at the grand old age of twenty-eight, still married (and they said it wouldn't last!) and working as a financial para planner. Sounds impressive I know, but it really boils down to being a Girl Friday and general dogsbody to a much more qualified financial consultant. I work long hours for one of the largest financial corporations in the world. We pride ourselves on having the ability to provide 'holistic' financial solutions. This really means that we can provide everything a client could need within our organization; therefore there is no need for any of them to approach any of our competitors who then might poach them. We mainly provide consultancy services to other corporate entities, which translates into long meetings (lots of minutes), long dinners and lunches (lots of wine) and many presentations (blagging it). Our sales director maintains that the true art of consultancy is the ability to think on your feet, to talk a good game when you don't perhaps have all the answers and to look sincere. We are reminded time and time again that people buy people, and sincerity (or the ability to fake sincerity) is the name of the game.

Generally I am wheeled out at client meetings so the clients can 'meet the team'. This exercise is designed to make the client feel at ease and help him (yes it's usually a him) realise that there is more than one person working his account. This is not always true, but enables us to charge our exorbitant fees (thus enabling us to meet our exorbitant targets) and allows the client to feel that he is getting something almost tangible for his money. I say this because a pension or an investment isn't something you can really touch, you can't polish it and place it on the mantelpiece, it is a purchase without substance, an instrument designed to fulfil a future dream. The trick for the consultant, therefore, is to invoke a need, to build the dream, to convince the client that his very future is dependent on him signing on the dotted line. My job is to aid the process, I ensure that the paperwork is in order and that the consultant has at her fingertips the answers to any questions that may be out there. It is not always clear in the client's mind that he needs another investment; it is not like insurance, a necessary evil. To convince a client of such a need is a great feat in the world of sales.

I guess I am seen as competent and hard-working, fairly quiet but definitely not ambitious. I think our regional or national bosses would struggle to remember my name and I prefer it that way. I would definitely not be the person asked to speak at our annual conference or work on a special project. I meet the goals I am given, finish my work, usually ahead of deadlines, and have enough qualifications to get by. I go in early if needed and often work late. Our clients like me and I am fair and professional with my co-workers. Sometimes I think that I don't really know what I would do if I didn't do this.

My office is near my house, probably ten minutes away, in one of the UK's 'new' towns. Whatever were they thinking of? Long roads in and out of town that enable you to see the snarled up traffic for miles and a serious of ultra modern parks to give you that 'living in the country' feeling. Each park is complete with thorny shrubs to deter plant thieves, some weedy saplings struggling against the traffic pollution and vandals, a few swings and a slide. There is a plethora of red brick buildings, housing office blocks and retail outlets, homes and schools all set out like a lab maze for rats. We are encircled by motorways packed with fast-flowing traffic, leading to the larger northern cities and ultimately down to London. I miss trees: beautiful, old, majestic trees, but these seem to have been uprooted and replaced by the weedy saplings, the real trees were apparently hacked down long ago, to make space for further housing estates and parks. But housing is cheaper here, which is good as I don't qualify for a bonus because I am not a consultant. My job is to make the consultant's job easy, so she can appear sincere, so she doesn't have to blag it too much; in short I make her look good.

Now, if I think about it, that's not too hard. I can't think of a time when Amanda didn't look good. She has all the necessary industry qualifications, Pensions Management Institute and probably every exam the Chartered Insurance Institute has ever dreamt up. All this, and she has an excellent degree, a logical, commercial brain, and of course the gift of the gab. Sorry, did I forget to mention that she is also tall, slim, elegant and attractive? Definitely attractive, I think, with her long brown hair and hazel green eyes. Perhaps she is too assertive to be beautiful, but then maybe all that confidence is attractive in itself. Sometime I wonder if all those years of making sure her opinions are heard and duly noted at meetings have made her harder than she set out to be. All that constant striving has got to take it out of you. Maybe working in such a testoserone-fuelled industry in the end makes you less female. It doesn't seem to have held her back any, she is happy with her job, her marriage and her six-year-old son. Life seems to be so much more black and white for her.

Amanda is also my really good friend, possibly my best friend nowadays. I seem to spend so much time at work these days that all my previous friends have kind of drifted away. Amanda and I are together a lot, either travelling or working late, so that over time she has become my confidante and ally. We laugh together, sneak off and shop together, plan our diaries and lives together and over many a glass of wine discuss the choices we have made and our dreams and desires still unfulfilled. We work on deadlines and client projects. We bitch about the management and at weekends we see each other socially. Our husbands are good friends (her husband Pete is a landscape gardener) and, despite working together, we manage to go for whole evenings and not discuss work once, amazing really. Pete is an excellent father, simply adores their son, Max, and is a real hunk in a Lady Chatterley's Lover kind of way. Amanda and Pete tend to clash, as I think Pete finds it hard that Amanda is the main breadwinner. He is quite old-fashioned like that and sometimes Amanda with her strong opinions and superior attitude can just drive him crazy. You can tell he adores her though. From the outside it looks as though their relationship is all high maintenance and volatility, but when you get to know them you can just tell that they are still crazy about each other. Sometimes I wish that Simon and I would fight, perhaps that's what we need, a good old-fashioned argument or two.

We work well as a team, Amanda and I. She deals with the clients and I do the stuff behind the scenes and process the infinite minutiae which are financial services. Amanda has an amazing ability to sound as if she knows exactly what to do even if she doesn't have a clue. She really cares and it shows. I did try the consultant role once but I guess it isn't for everyone. There is huge pressure to meet targets and you are constantly assessed to make sure that the advice you give is relevant and up to date. I didn't mind any of that but I was undermined by my lack of confidence. I remember walking up and down a client's car park swallowing bottles of Rescue Remedy to calm my nerves just so I could walk through the door. In meetings I would start to stutter if not armed with the correct information. I couldn't just make it up as I went along and I was sure that everyone would see right through me. Everyone said it would get easier with time, that I would become more confident, but I just didn't have that practised charm and natural way of diffusing a fraught or tense situation. I have seen Amanda freeze aggressive trade union leaders with one icy stare and hand tissues to grieving widows without turning a hair. For me, despite all the training courses and role plays, I felt like an actor playing a part, desperate for the show to be over. In the end I realized that I didn't need to do this. I didn't have to prove myself any more, and I now know that I made the right decision. I am much better as an assistant. Much poorer, perhaps but happier.

Chapter 2

Amanda

'One may have a blazing hearth in one's soul and yet no one ever comes to sit by it. Passers by see only a wisp of smoke from the chimney and continue on their way.'
Vincent Van Gogh

It's Wednesday morning, 6.30 am and I am late again. Too much red wine and too little sleep, I am groggy and my whole body aches, again. The whole house is still asleep, so I am trying to be quiet. I bend down to reach for a Bionicle lunchbox, which seems to be wedged behind numerous convenient plastic containers. Where do they all come from? I remember buying two but they seem to be multiplying, I can hardly wedge them all into the cupboard now.

As I lean forward to try and dislodge the box, that familiar woozy feeling rises up and I lurch forward, banging my head painfully against the cupboard door. 'Shit.' Ouch, that hurt. I sigh and try again. More haste less speed. I need to get Max's lunch prepared before I leave and his football kit packed and in his school bag. I need to take some Ibuprofen or something; my head is just killing me. The kitchen is a mess, littered with take-away boxes containing congealed leftovers of last night's Chinese. I try to survey the mess but my stomach

13

seems to turn right over and the room reels away from me. I take a deep breath and try to control the queasiness. I make a mental note to cook and freeze some food at the weekend and make use of some of those handy plastic containers. I systematically sweep cartons and bags into the bin by the door. Pete is just no help. Would it really hurt him to throw something together for us to eat? Where is it written that being a wife is synonymous with being a slave? Surely if I have to be the one making the money around here he could at least make himself useful around the house? As I resentfully stuff football kit straight from the dryer into Max's bag the cat snakes herself around my legs mewing for food. I hastily throw kibble into a bowl and remember that the dustbins should go out today. Right now, with a steel band closing in on my brain, this seems an impossible task so I scribble a note to Pete pleading for some help and shove it on the table. I grab a piece of cold pizza (leftovers of another meal of convenience), check it for signs of expiration (it looks OK), and dump it unceremoniously into the Bionicle box with a yogurt, a packet of crisps and, oh God, I need something else that looks healthy. I know, a banana will do, in it goes and I shut the lid with a snap. Surely Pete can put the rubbish out, he can do it as he leaves the house to drop Max at school.

I grab my laptop bag, the client's files and my handbag and run for the door, noticing on the way the half-dead plant (must remember to water it), Max's school shoes (surely Pete will clean them), and a dead mouse (yuck, another gift from that bloody cat). I *so* don't do dead animals. Pete surely will see it – and hopefully before the cleaner – I think desperately. I snatch yesterday's unopened post and shove it into my bag. If I get stuck in traffic I will get a chance to sort through it. With a bit of luck I will have time to grab a coffee on the way as well. And hopefully my trusty assistant, Sophie, will brief me on the agenda for today's meeting and will have the figures I badly need to explain the fund's shortfall to the client. Perfect. We need this meeting to go well; the client was a bit of a hospital pass really, completely cocked up by some idiot working out of one of our southern offices. So I need to make the right impression.

Sophie and I have a good two-hour drive ahead of us and we need to hit the motorway in good time so that we can be ahead of the rush-hour traffic. Out in the street I sigh despondently when I take in the dark morning. The cold stings my cheeks and my breath billows around me, swirling and disappearing into the ether. I struggle to operate the car alarm on my key fob whilst wrestling files, coping with 5-inch heels on gravel and trying to ignore the pounding in my head. Damn; maybe there are some Ibuprofen in the car. It is absolutely freezing; and the windscreen is opaque with ice. I impatiently scratch and scrape at it with half a CD case until I have a space roughly the size of my head to see through. After five minutes I am so cold that I abandon the scraping and jump in the car. I switch the heating on full blast to try and thaw the sub-zero temperature within and switch on the headlights. I put the radio on loud and light my first cigarette of the day. Nasty. I toss it after about three drags, maybe I should try again when my hangover subsides.

As I wait for the life in my fingers to come back I curse once again our decision to buy a house with a drive rather than a garage. We picked up the house at an auction. Neither of us had any experience with auctions but thought the house looked nice and better than anything we had looked at for a long time. With Max on the way the house, built in the 1920s, seemed perfect with its larger than normal garden and four bedrooms. It needed some renovation but, not only was there room for the baby but we could also have a proper guest room. I remember Pete just staring at the pictures of the garden. The agent's description was 'mainly laid to lawn', which was true enough. There was nothing at all apart from grass. No bulbs to surprise us in the spring, no trees, shrubs

15

or anything climbing anywhere. 'A complete blank canvas,' Pete had declared excitedly, something for us to really get our teeth into. What he meant was 'his teeth' rather than ours. Pete had just finished horticultural college and was desperate to start his own landscape gardening business. The course had taken him four years to complete. Four years of living on just my income. As soon as we moved in Pete threw himself into the garden design. We now have great landscaping but crap bathrooms. Luckily his business seems to be thriving now and, at least as his own boss he can't be made redundant again. Fortunately, I am paid well and we can afford for one of us to follow their vocation. I must say, as time goes by, I am thinking more and more of leaving my job and perhaps starting a business of my own. Perhaps I will become a florist or open a small bakery somewhere near the sea. Perhaps I will take Sophie with me, now there's a thought.

I pick up Sophie outside her house. Despite the ungodly hour she is looking calm, relaxed and focused. She too has a briefcase of files, and an A4 plastic folder of notes to go over in the car. I think it is important that she meets the clients, it gives her a sense of worth and it is a lot harder to let a client down if you have met them. It also helps to keep her focused. I breathe a sigh of relief and turn the music down. She walks over to the car and places her briefcase on the back seat. Smiling, she hands me a freshly brewed cup of coffee in a small thermos cup, complete with lid. The coffee is black and strong with no sugar, just the way I like it. She glances over at me, taking in the air of frenetic tension and my ruffled demeanour. 'Late night?' A rhetorical question with no need of an answer, she knows me too well. She flicks back her hair and laughs. I smile ruefully in response, taking in her blonde carefully highlighted and straightened hair. Even at this time in the morning Sophie has one of those pink and white complexions that just seems to glow. Her face is bare of make up save a smatter of mascara and lightly glossed lips. Somehow she always appears to have an all-over healthy natural sheen. Quite petite, definitely under 5′4″, she has much bigger breasts than may ever be seen as fashionable. Sophie, therefore, spends most of her time trying to cover them up. She is always hiding herself under voluminous floaty blouses and worrying about her height to breast ratio. Oh, to have such a problem. She turns to the passenger window and waves to Simon. I can't believe after all these years of marriage he still gets up to see that she is OK, that she has some kind of breakfast and is picked up safely. She really doesn't know how lucky she is. Simon is a real rock, absolutely reliable and infinitely helpful and accommodating. I couldn't somehow see Pete getting up to support me. He will still be deep in slumber until Max wakes him around 8.00 am. They will breakfast together (with their beloved cat) and then amble to school (followed most of the way by the cat), telling jokes and playing tag. After the school run Pete will make his way to whatever gardening job he has on the go. I don't think we have ever started the day together, not even in the early days before Max arrived. We don't even manage breakfast together at the weekends as I like to get to the gym early before it gets too crowded.

I gratefully drink my coffee and I immediately feel calmer. Sophie has that effect, she understands me, I think. I have little time for incompetence – people might say that I don't suffer fools gladly and they would be right. Customer service is incredibly important to me, if I say I will do something I will and it has to be done correctly and checked and double-checked for accuracy and presentation. I have worked hard to build a good reputation in one of the most chauvinistic industries I know and I intend to keep it.

Sophie kicks off her heels, slurps at her coffee and we head off. Already the roads are busy. A hazy sun rises and glares unrepentantly through my windscreen just at my eye level. I squint and snap down the sun visor. Sophie rummages through her handbag and pulls out a bottle of Evian and a packet of Nurofen. She checks the road ahead to make sure that there are no sharp bends or roundabouts ahead, and then passes me the water and two of the pills. I take them gratefully. I swallow and shake my head, partly to clear the pills and partly to shake the nagging concern that I may have omitted a spoon for Max's yogurt. Did I put one in? Not sure, I hope so. He tends to go into meltdown if he thinks he is missing any vital equipment. I glance at my watch, we are thirty minutes ahead. We arrive very early, in fact early enough to nip into Tesco for a quick look at the files and a fried breakfast. I fill up on eggs, bacon and sausage and avoid anything that even faintly resembles a carb. Sophie nibbles on an apple and chases it with a yogurt. I grab another coffee and we head back to the car.

We park and enter the building. Our client is a long established manufacturer of shoes. Not the kind of shoes that I would buy, their market is top end, middle-aged women who want a shoe built for comfort and style, nothing frivolous or too fashionable. The building is designed for functionality, located on a sprawling industrial estate with handy burger vans at almost every corner. The smell of onions and hot dirty oil permeates the air. This isn't perhaps one of our better paying clients. The whole building (and some of the staff as well) has a musty, tired, lost in the past kind of feel. You can almost imagine a white-haired lady with a metal tea trolley touring the office at 3.00 precisely, handing out rich tea biscuits and bourbons with afternoon tea.

We don't have to wait in their drab reception area very long. A small, pale, balding, middle-aged man comes bounding quickly down the stairs. He has a concerned look on his face. I have met him before, so he smiles at me, waves and practically bounces off the last stair to greet me. He looks all at once relieved to see me and then even more concerned, if that is possible. I know he is worrying about why the company pension fund has failed to make the returns that it should have done. He is not just the owner of the company but a trustee of the pension scheme as well. It is his responsibility to all the members to ensure things are run correctly and that the onerous trustee responsibilities are met. The law states that the trustees should be informed of the law regarding their pension scheme, understand the rules that govern their scheme and meet regularly to assess progress. This is where I come in. I advise on legislation and basically provide some hand-holding throughout and all for a massive fee. There is nothing like a little healthy fear of the law to keep the fees rolling in.

I smile into his eyes and shake his hand in greeting. I turn to introduce Sophie, who again smiles and shakes his hand. We pass pleasantries and make our way to the boardroom. We are to address a board of eight people, all men. The boardroom is dimly lit, and the table has seen better days but there is a welcoming pot of coffee on the table and a plate of assorted biscuits. Again we meet and greet and Sophie tables graphs and further papers detailing the funds movement since the last meeting. I glance behind me and notice a flip chart. I love a flip chart. In fact I love this part of my job. I grab some coffee and we work our way through the agenda. These people make shoes. They are not financially minded at all, so I speak as simply as I can and try to keep the meeting moving. Sometimes I believe that this is my vocation, and I really do feel as though I was born to be a consultant. Put me in front of a group like this and it is as if someone else takes over. I feel in complete control, my hangover has utterly disappeared, words and explanations just come to me and I am on top of the world. I feel an excitement wash over me when I know that they understand a technical point because of my explanation or I receive affirmation that they trust what Sophie and I are doing. I look over at Sophie and we smile at each other, all is going well. At 11.30 on the dot there is a knock at the door and the investment manager is brought in as I arranged. After all, consultancy isn't about what you know but who you know, and who you can bring to the table. I sit back, smooth down my skirt and relax now that the bulk of my job is done. I listen with the group to the investment manager's explanation. Every now and again I ask informed questions to aid the trustees' comprehension of what can be quite a daunting subject. When he leaves I ask permission to use the flip chart and draw a few diagrams to further illustrate and expand their understanding. I know that by the time the next meeting comes around they will have forgotten most of this but I throw myself into it anyway. All the while Sophie takes minutes, nods or shakes her head when appropriate and lists action points.

The meeting draws to a close and we once again shake hands, promise minutes within ten working days and make our exit. We get into the car and drive back out of the city; I light a cigarette and inhale deeply as soon as we are far enough away from the clients so as not to be spotted. The adrenalin departs slowly, relinquishing its embrace with the passing miles, leaving me light-headed, happy and hungry. We drive out into the country looking for a place for a late lunch. Sophie spots a sprawling country pub and we pull in. We order food and a large glass of wine each. I turn on my mobile to check for messages whilst Sophie visits the ladies.

Six messages. I grab a pen and make some quick notes. The first call is from the office, the next two from a consultant from another office. The third is Pete. The fourth is Pete. The fifth and the sixth are all from Pete. His tone becoming more and more agitated. Just listening to the messages puts my back up. I replay the sixth message in disbelief.

'Amanda, are you there? Pick up.'

'Amanda, it is now 3.00 pm, are you there? I need to know that you are going to pick up Max today.'

Pick up Max? Of course I'm not going to pick up Max; I am over two hours away. Does he not listen to me? I told him that I had a meeting today. For God's sake, what is he doing? I listen incredulously as he finishes with an instruction to call him 'urgently'.

I pick up the phone and speed-dial home. No answer. I then try his mobile, he picks up after the second ring.

'Where are you?'

'Hello to you too. I have just finished my meeting,' I respond testily.

'You need to pick Max up,' he says.

I can't believe we are even having this conversation; Sophie has returned from the ladies and is looking at me quizzically, trying to guess who I might be talking to.

'Why, where are you?' I try to sound calm but irritation is creeping into my tone. Surely no gardening job is that important.

'I am still at the Stevens job, the crane has just turned up and I can't just leave'

'Well you'll bloody have to,' I stand my ground and grab another swig of wine. I wedge the phone between my shoulder and my ear and rake around in my bag trying to find a cigarette. I find them and light one, moving the phone into a more comfy position.

'Amanda, I am paying by the hour for this thing, you will just have to go and get him.'

The phone goes dead. I stare at the display in disbelief. I am angry, frustrated and butterflies of panic start to flutter through my system. He has to get Max. Only Pete can make me this angry.

I swear and then pick up the phone again and speed-dial his number; there is no response and the phone clicks in to an answer machine. I leave a message explaining slowly and precisely that I am too far away to help and that I wouldn't get back in time even if I were to leave now. I finish by adding that it is a sad day when the price of a bloody crane is more important than picking up his son. I hang up and throw the phone back into my handbag; I fume for a minute more then grab the phone again. I phone the school and in my sweetest, caring parent voice inform the school that Max's Daddy is due to pick him up today as I have been delayed on business. I provide them with Pete's mobile phone number just in case there is a problem. I thank them, hang up and take another large swig of my wine. I think of my little Max standing all by himself waiting for Pete. He so better turn up or I will kill him. I wonder briefly how Max's football training went today but then get side-tracked by the menu.

Sophie looks at me with concern as I replay our conversation. I mean, how ridiculous, as if a crane can't wait another hour. Pete knows how important today was for me. He really is just hopeless. Sophie looks anxious so I explain that of course Pete will pick up Max. Obviously, once he picks up my message and starts thinking clearly, he will do what any sensible person would do and collect Max and reschedule the bloody crane for another day. How hard can it be?

I laugh the whole thing off but deep down the butterflies are still circling. I start to dread going home to another scene. I am so not going to back down on this one. He is absolutely in the wrong and if he has any sense he will realize and apologize.

We pay the bill and leave the restaurant, somehow we kind of got talking and it is now well past 5.00 pm. Shit. That means it will be nearly 8.00 before we get home, and I will miss Max's bath time and I won't get to read him his bedtime story. Even more annoying, Pete will think I have stayed out just to wind him up. Why does he have to think that it's always about him? Sophie and I pile back into the car and make our way back to the motorway. It is dark already, the traffic is horrendous, there is freezing fog and it will be slow going to say the least. Sophie falls asleep beside me and I start to think about how I should play it when I get home. I could just go to bed; I am too tired to argue tonight. I will walk in and be pleasant but if he starts I will just go upstairs, shower and go to bed with a glass of wine. Maybe he'll have calmed down. I suppose it is conceivable that I was a little hard on him, but he knows that anything to do with Max will get me going every time. Perhaps I should just apologize and put it down to work pressure. I glance over at Sophie; she even looks tidy when she's asleep, no twitching, fidgeting or dribbling there. I wonder if I can crank the music up a bit without waking her. Next time I think I will get her to drive then I can have a nap on the way home.

At last the traffic starts to move and as the miles slip by I start to think about Pete. Without realizing, I appear to have bitten down three of my nails. Why do I do that? I peer at them in the gloom with disdain. I could really do with a regular manicure; perhaps I should just forgo a lunch break once a week and get it done properly. Then I could treat myself to a really nice ring, something outrageous and sparkly. I sigh and think again about Pete. Last night had been great, a family game of Scrabble with Max and several bottles of wine. Later with Max safely asleep and another bottle of wine on the go, I had gone to the fridge to find something to nibble on. We had eaten copious amounts of glutinous Chinese but I needed something sweet. As I stood up Pete was behind me, and in one swift movement he encircled me. Pushing my head to one side, he slowly grazed his lips down the side of my neck and down to my shoulder, sending shivers all the way down my spine. With my back to him I was pretty much unable to resist. So I leant back and relaxed into his warm hard body and snaked my hands up behind me to touch him. As I leant back he grabbed my wrists playfully, and then held them easily, pushing me forward towards the worktop. With one hand on my hip he worked the other up under my shirt and undid my bra, slipping his hand over the swell of my breast teasing my nipple with his fingers, all the time relentlessly sucking and kissing my neck. Tingles of pleasure ran up and down my body, stealing my very breath away and robbing me of any strength I may have had to protest. I swear when he touches my neck like that I can feel the very core of me swell, every nerve ending tensing, prickling and standing to attention.

I tried to turn to face him but he kept me turned away from him. I could feel his amusement at my weakness. His touch becoming more teasing, almost playful, enjoying his dominance. I wriggled against him almost pleading him to touch me again, and again, longer and harder. He increased the pressure of his tongue and teeth on my neck, pressing his hardness into my back. I started to moan and squirm, still trying to gain control of the situation and face him. But still he held me firm. His hand slipped down, demanding and insistent, roughly tugging my skirt up around my hips, running his hand up the flat of my back forcing me forward, his fingers entwined in my hair, his breath on my neck. He must have undone his fly but I have no memory of it, by then I was wet and urgent, I needed him, needed release. He shoved me against the worktop and entered me swiftly; I ground my body back against him, pushing against the worktop for leverage, feeling him hard and slippery, deep inside me. We panted like animals, moving together frantically, aware of nothing but sensation and each other. Then suddenly, release. I remember my breath catching in my throat for what seemed like an eternity, time and space disappearing as I was lost to the feelings pumping through me. Pete's cry seemed almost distant as he shuddered, panting, against me. I could feel his legs trembling and his heart thumping in tune with my own. We were both breathless; a sheen of sweat coating his face as he turned me round and pulled me to him. He kissed the top of my head and we smiled at each other, me with my whole body loose, like someone had disconnected my vertebrae and stretched out all my limbs. Him tousled and glowing, pleased with his show of dominance and power. I felt amazing, beaming, contented as a cat. And that was just last night, I think wryly. It just goes to show what a difference a day makes.

I am brought back from my reverie by the loud monotonous wailing of a police car hurtling past; I hear other sirens and sigh deeply. This is not a good sign. I pray to the traffic gods and cross my fingers. Hopefully it's not an accident otherwise we could be stuck here for a very long time. Sophie stirs beside me, stretches and sits up. She runs her fingers through her hair and peers groggily about her.

'Where are we?' she yawns.

'We're not even close yet,' I reply, 'and I think there may be an accident ahead, the traffic is definitely slowing up.'

She groans and reaches for her phone, checks her text messages and smiles.

'I should send another message to Simon just so that he doesn't worry.'

I nod in agreement, feeling sad that there is nobody out there concerned for my wellbeing, sending me text messages and waiting for my arrival.

All of a sudden the traffic speeds up again and within a few minutes it is as if nothing had happened, no sign of any emergency services anywhere, no flashing blue or red lights on the horizon. I put my foot down and accelerate into the fast lane.

It is 8.45 pm when we reach Sophie's house. All the lights are on and as we pull up Simon opens the door to greet us; Sophie rolls her eyes at me and collects her things from the car. It has been another long day. I refuse Simon's offer of coffee, telling him that I should really get home. I am absolutely exhausted now. We say our goodbyes and Sophie reminds me that tomorrow our new hotshot sales consultant should start. The new guy has been the talk of the office. No one has met him as yet, not even our manager. He is one of a new team of super sales people, head-hunted from our competitors and brought in to work up and down the country. Someone somewhere has decided that we need to find new business, double digit growth is now the name of the game. Apparently this new guy managed to negotiate a huge salary to move from his previous position (this is a feat in itself knowing our management) and the rumour is that he has managed to win some pretty big clients in the past. I think it will be interesting to see how he gets on with our team. We are quite close and fairly particular, let's see if he is as good as they say he is.

I yawn again and try and find a comfortable driving position. I have been driving now for hours and my right knee is killing me, it feels like my patella is about to explode into a million tiny pieces; I try to bend my leg slightly to relieve the pressure. Not long now. I light another cigarette when I hit the last roundabout before our estate, partly to keep me awake and partly to calm my nerves, that way I can just hit the shower when I get in and dive into bed. Not far now. I try to concentrate, vaguely aware of reading somewhere that the majority of traffic accidents happen just a mile away from home. I shake my head to help me focus and as I pull up on the drive I notice that Pete's car is not there. My mind flits back to our earlier spat and tiny flutters of nerves start to appear in my stomach. I turn the key in the lock, dump my bags on the kitchen table and walk into the lounge. I am met by Maria, our neighbour and emergency babysitter. All at once I am on edge, and a little scared. I was expecting Pete to be here.

'Hi, is everything OK?' I say. My mouth has gone dry, I feel like I am speaking through a mouth full of sawdust.

Maria smiles and I relax a little. Maria explains in her

broken English that Pete has gone out to meet some friends – perhaps I had forgotten? And so she offered to babysit until I returned. I apologize profusely, blaming my late return on a meeting that had overrun, I pay her, and as she leaves I go upstairs to check on Max. I take the stairs two at a time, my footsteps cushioned and silenced by our fairly new honey beige carpet. I must remember to pick up some groceries tomorrow, I think idly, I am sure we are nearly out of milk, but then all practicalities and daily chores are forgotten when I see him. He sleeps, my little angel, all blond hair and freckles, hunched up in the middle of the bed with his favourite panda discarded on the floor below. I pick up Pandy and tuck him in close, kissing Max's head and taking a minute to breathe in the fresh, clean, sleepy smell of him. My heart contracts and I fiddle once more with his blanket, making sure no draughts can touch him. Then I turn and hit the shower, wanting to be in bed and asleep before Pete comes home, as least that way I can claim a moral high ground if needed.

Sometime after 2.00 am from somewhere in my dreams I hear a door slam. Pete. I hear him tiptoe up the stairs and sneak into the bedroom. Obviously drunk, I think. And to think I was worried. I fume quietly, not wanting to give myself away. I close my eyes tight, concentrating hard on regulating my breathing, pretending sleep to avoid having to make any conversation. Pete, obviously too far gone to notice anything, stumbles over something in the corner (probably his shoes) swears and staggers into bed. I would guarantee that he hasn't even looked at me. It takes him two minutes to discard his clothes and settle himself in. Forcefully he turns over, nearly taking all the covers with him, and in exactly five minutes he is snoring at full volume. How does he do that? I wait until I am sure he is fast asleep and then I furtively try and get him to change position to stop the snoring so I can get some sleep at least. As soon as I touch him he moves as far away from me as he can, it is as if even in his sleep his whole body is reverberating and bristling with indignation at the unresolved issues between us. I lie still again, waiting for his breathing to ease and subside into the peaceful sleeping rhythm that I know so well. I don't have to wait too long. All at once he is deeply asleep and very slowly inch by inch I move closer, tentatively stretching myself out along the warmth of his long back, breathing in the smell of alcohol and stale smoke, relishing the warm familiarity and the comfortable fit that is my husband.

Chapter 3

Gareth

'Those who restrain their desires, do so because theirs is weak enough
to be restrained.'
William Blake

8.45 am. It's Thursday morning and after six months' garden
leave I am finally going back to work. Feels kind of strange
after all this time, but I guess I am ready for a new challenge.
There should also be some fresh totty to look forward to, one
of the benefits of office work; there are always a serious
amount of babes knocking about in pencil skirts and stilettos.
What's a man to do? I ask you. I smile and stretch out my limbs
languorously, feeling myself harden at the thought. After all,
perhaps it was beginning to get just a little boring going to the
gym and hanging around the house watching porn. But you
just have to love garden leave, six months of being paid not to
go into the office. They couldn't take the chance that I
wouldn't take all their precious clients with me to my next job.
So I get to stay at home on full benefits and I even get to keep
the company car for the duration. Classic! All this and I will
still take their best clients anyway, maybe not straight away, I
usually bide my time, lay low for a bit, just to ensure my name
won't be linked with any dubious activities. And then bingo! I

have got it down to a fine art now. I usually keep up some friendly contact with a few of my better clients, you know, nice, select firms, no difficult cases, and then bang! After about six months I take the cream with me, a few big names, or companies with some big projects or potential mergers, and nobody can prove anything. I then get the credit for the same clients again at the new company. Easy. I swear I have one client who has followed me to my last three jobs! The CEO there just loves me, I can't do anything wrong.

This must be my fourth garden leave in about six years. You see, I am one of the best financial consultants around. It's like a gift, a natural talent. I have that hidden factor, you know, call it charisma; well, I have it in spades and trust me, I know how to use it. And I also know the business, so that combined with my natural flair and ability makes me one of the best. Honestly, I am so good it almost isn't fair. I win the business almost every time, and then before you know it another company wants me and they offer me even more money! Hell, I can even dictate how and when I work nowadays. But then jobs are like women, there is always a better one around the corner, and it doesn't pay anyone to be overly loyal these days. You have to remember that it's all about the money. The number of times I have worked with these sad guys, constant, trustworthy, dedicated to the company types who spend their whole life playing the good corporate citizen, working overtime, giving up their weekends, for what? To be made redundant after twenty years? No thanks, I take the money every time. I get the job done and move on. But, like I said, I'm a natural, and you can't teach aptitude. I'm pleased to say that I have built up quite a reputation in the industry and I work hard at keeping my name out there and my network sweet. Mind you, even without the reputation I reckon I could still swing it, I am just one of these guys that other guys love to be around and women, well, women just love. No, seriously, women seem to find me irresistible, if there are ladies around the table I soon have them eating out of my hand, they just lap me up. It's all in the delivery; really it never ceases to surprise me how successful I am.

Age doesn't seem to be an issue either; all women, regardless of how many miles they have clocked up, seem to respond to the same tried and tested routine. They all want to feel attractive, even if they are complete mingers (in fact the really ugly ones are sometimes the easiest). Women seem to need the whole romance thing like guys need football, and I have been around enough women (if you know what I mean) to know what I am talking about; in fact, maybe I should write a book or some kind of self-help manual for shagging. Normally it doesn't take too long to get a few juices flowing, unless of course they are raving lesbians, and I have even had a few of those. I know straight away if a woman fancies me and I don't mean to sound like I'm boasting but, usually they do. I spend a lot of time keeping the body beautiful and frankly I am so good in the sack I could shag for a living. I go out of my way to make the ladies feel special, you know, romance them a bit, I do the whole champagne and chocolates routine, it always hits the spot, and you only really need to do it once. After you've had them they'll always come back for more. Seduction is definitely my forte. And if they go away happy you never know, they might put in a good word with their mates, there's nothing like a referral, after all, and stranger things have happened.

It never ceases to amaze me, but I reckon in this industry I could still get laid at least a couple of times a week if I want. And, of course, after all that I still need to service the wife; good job there is enough of me to go round.

I take another look in the mirror before I go downstairs; I sweep my thick brown hair off my forehead and turn my face to get a look at my profile: yep, looking good. I have a strong face with almost chiselled features and blue eyes. Despite being nearly forty, I have been using a good moisturizer for a while now and it has really made a difference, I don't have too many lines and my skin is clear. I am tall, just over 6'3" and right now I am in even better shape than usual. Six months at the gym have seen to that. My shoulders are broad and you can catch the outline of my pecs through my shirt. I stretch my shoulders back to get the full effect. Very nice indeed, even if I do say so myself! I haven't worn a suit for a while now and I must say I do look quite magnificent. A quick squirt of one of my favourite colognes to boost up the old pheromones (women love a man who smells nice) and I am ready for the game. I grab my jacket and join Suzie and the boys in the kitchen. She smiles at me as I appear in the doorway and I can see from her face she is appreciating the new suit, and the close shave. After all, she's only human. She hands me a coffee and stretches up to kiss me. Her hair is still sleep-tousled and she is devoid of make up but she is still a fine-looking woman. God, when we met she had the best body I had ever seen. She swam for the county and had the most amazing tits and arse ever. Nowadays she is softer but still a fantastic lay and she gives great head, all the attributes you want in a wife really. One of the reasons why we are still married, I often think. You see, I reckon that it's all down to foreplay. I really try to put in some extra time early on. When I go down on a woman I do it properly, and before you know it she is gagging for me. I play her like a fine instrument and, believe me, if you play the right notes, after a while she will do anything you like for as long as you like. Add in a few candles and set the ambience with some suitable music and, frankly, the world is your lobster. I have this amazing CD (in fact I have a couple), which is purely songs guaranteed to make the ladies whip their knickers off. Works like a charm every time. I keep one in the car just in case – after all, you never know when you're going to get lucky and just that little bit of extra groundwork pays dividends every time. Anyway, must be doing something right as we have been married for nine years (actually it might be ten) and we have two boys and now a dog as well. The boys are seven and five, Toby and Tristan. They are good kids, a bit high-spirited at times, but I guess that's the nature of boys. The dog, a big hairy Collie, lies at Tristan's feet gazing adoringly at his toast. He is just eighteen months old and was bought as a present for Suzie. One of the best things I ever did.

I was shagging a really cute blonde a while back, not great looking but a really appreciative shag, very energetic. Anyway, Suzie started getting antsy, asking questions and acting suspicious, damn nearly walked in on us one day. It was all a little too close; she obviously had way too much time on her hands. And in the end my mate Luke suggested getting a dog. I think he had played this card as well at some point as they have a rather similar hound, which, from memory, was also purchased at a sensitive time. Well, it worked like a dream. For as long as I can remember she had wanted a dog and it turned out to be a fantastic distraction. He's managed to shift her attention no problem, so he really has turned out to be man's best friend in more ways than one.

So now she has to walk the dog (Collies need loads of exercise), take it to the vet (dogs always need some kind of vaccination or special shampoo) and go to dog training sessions. Perfect! Recently she has even started talking about agility training. Fantastic. A dog walk is also a great excuse for an outdoor shag as well, which is always a nice diversion. Anyway, Suzie was absolutely thrilled with the dog, and he is quite sweet really. I put him in a box and tied it with a big ribbon. The boys called him Harry as we wouldn't let them call him Megatron, Batman or Pingu. He was a really cute puppy as well, great looking, fantastic pedigree, all soft hair and big brown eyes, there was no way Suzie was ever going to stay mad at me. I got a whole heap of brownie points; in fact we had one of the best shags ever that night. Anyway, between her job (she is a part-time nurse), the dog and the boys she keeps herself quite busy. Suits me perfectly; marriage is great but you do need your own space from time to time.

By the time I get to the office it is around 10.30, perfect. It is never good to look too eager on your first day and I firmly believe that you should start as you mean to go on. I take a slow tour around the car park, checking out where the best spaces are and, after carefully avoiding the reserved spaces, park the car, check my hair, and register with reception. I take a seat in the glass-fronted reception area and check out my new surroundings. There is a central island that is home to a front desk set-up. A pretty little receptionist speaks discreetly on the phone and a security guard, inflated with his own importance, checks out the parking via a CCTV monitor. Casual armchairs are dotted around coffee tables and potted plants, and I notice that each table has a very precisely organised assortment of financial papers and magazines. I usually go out of my way to bond with the security guys and receptionists – after all, you never know when you are going to need a favour, a parking space closer to the building, for instance, is always a bonus, and it is always great to have an alibi on site if you are late back from lunch. I grin at the girl on the phone when I notice her watching me and she grins back conspiratorially. Looks like I haven't lost my touch then.

I pull out some notes from my briefcase. I have spent the last few days catching up with changing legislation and industry stuff and it never hurts to do some last-minute cramming. In my experience there is always some wise guy trying to test your knowledge on your first day, looking to catch you out. All my interviews for this job were done centrally, so I have no idea what the team are like or who my boss is. Anyway, it looks good to be reading some technical stuff, first impressions are always important. After about

34

fifteen minutes my new boss comes to greet me and I groan inwardly. I have met him before, well perhaps not him exactly but I know his type. This is a guy who obviously showed talent at some time, perhaps won a few new clients, maybe even one of the big names, but it was all a long time ago. Now after being PBC'd (promoted beyond all competence) he is all hot air, singing the company song and so committed to double digit growth that he has lost all sight of real life. Probably can't even get it up any more. This is the way with these large companies. As soon as someone shows promise in sales they up and move them into management. Completely absurd if you ask me, as sales and management require completely different competencies, but they do it anyway.

The guy is nice enough but is fundamentally a muppet. I bet if you cut him he would bleed company blood. He's not someone that I could ever respect but I play the game, look interested in what he is saying and laugh at all his jokes. I think I have the potential to do well here. Weak management is always a boon. It is a large company with many probable links to new business, great for building up your network. There are lots of departments as well: over the years I have found that it's always handy to have somewhere to disappear to if things get too boring, and there is nothing better than totty on another team to liven your day up. After all, you don't want to play too close to home.

We go up to the fourth floor and I survey my new department. Nice views, all open plan, no corner office though. This is not necessarily a bad thing. It means I get to sit with the team to find out what is going on, where the prospective business is, get to know the gossip, learn the dynamics of the office and basically have a laugh. I was lucky enough to be born with an innate talent for summing people up and quickly, so I know it is not going to take me too long to work out who are the movers and shakers and who are the numpties. I am hoping to meet some people I can actually learn from as well; surely there must be some talent around here somewhere.

The team are conscientiously beavering away, heads down or speaking into telephones whilst scribbling notes. The air is filled with the muted hum of industry, hushed telephone conversations and the quiet clatter of multiple fingers striking keyboards on identical looking laptops. A mild and pleasant middle-aged lady introduces herself as Brenda (team secretary) and runs off to get me a coffee. There is a lady polishing plant leaves and in the corner a photocopier diligently spews sheet after sheet of duplicated structure charts onto a tray, all sorted and stapled and ready to go. You have to love modern technology, at least when it's working. I take a deep breath in and smile, it's nice to be back in the real world again. I am walked around the dozen or so desks and introduced to each of the team in turn. Our first stop is three guys, all consultants, who seem friendly enough. From what they tell me, it seems as though they have been with the company years, one of them having survived four different mergers. How tedious I think. I look at his grey pallor and waxy skin, this is a man who spends far too much time in the office, even his eyes seem to have lost their shine. Next I meet a hard-faced girl called Amanda (nice body, obviously fit but frosty), definitely feisty (could be worth a tussle if you could thaw her out). Then there are a few administrators, all very nondescript but, as it is totally essential to win the affection of the admin team, I spend at least half an hour talking football with the guys and getting to know the girls. These are the people who will be making sure my presentations are put together on time and accurately, they will also unfortunately get lumbered with all the crap jobs which, frankly, I can't be arsed to do. Making a friend here will be well worth the time and effort and a few shy smiles and blushes from one of the girls (I think she said her name was Emma?) definitely confirms that I might have struck gold. I have been around long enough to know that when things get busy it is the popular consultants who get their work done fast and first. I make a mental note to spend some extra time with Emma over the next few days, just to make sure she is feeling the love. As I walk away, I turn and give her a wink so that she knows she has made an impression, and then I stroll nonchalantly over to the corner of the office.

Here is where the other girls on the team sit. One is pregnant and the other is sadly a total moose. Even her complexion looks rough. I try to be pleasant (after all, you should be charitable to the less fortunate) but I find myself wondering if that is what happens to you if you don't exfoliate regularly. I am mesmerized by the blackheads between her thick, chaotic eyebrows and try and focus my gaze somewhere else. I move around the office and try and spend some time chatting with everyone; I talk to the ambitious, the gossips, the feckless and ineffectual. I briefly meet some people in the team next to ours and then spend some more time with my new boss, Stuart, getting some inside knowledge on how the company are tackling the latest challenges and opportunities in the industry, and finding out who the local competition are. Then suddenly I see her. A blonde with the biggest breasts I have seen for a long time. I am still trying to work out if they are real, without obviously staring (I wouldn't want her to get the wrong impression), when she comes over to meet me.

I am finding it increasingly difficult to make eye contact, in fact it is taking all my strength not to look down at her chest, and I realize that I have become extremely conscious of every breath she takes and that I seem to be breathing in tandem with her. Suddenly, as if she senses my preoccupation, she folds her arms over her chest, smiles, and picks up some paperwork from a table in front of me and turns to face the frosty one. I realize I am now gazing at her arse and look up quickly to find Amanda (who I think I have started to impress

37

with my industry chat) regarding me, one eyebrow raised with, what is that? amusement, understanding, sarcasm? – well, a strange look in her eye anyway. She looks as though she has me all worked out and, furthermore, she looks intrigued, like she understands the game and is up for the challenge. She keeps on staring then suddenly drops her gaze to my mouth where it lingers for the longest time, perhaps just a little too long before turning to talk to the girl with the breasts. I watch the small smile playing on her lips as she flips back her hair. I realize suddenly that I have been holding my breath and I exhale deeply and lean back against the desk. As they both turn to look at me, I smile and flex my shoulders, making sure that I give them both the full glorious view of my chest and shoulders. With a flick of hair they turn back again and continue their conversation. As she is talking, Amanda sneaks sideways glances at me and chews her lip in what I must say is quite an endearing and rather saucy manner. I guess that they are talking about me, as they are now giggling, and then they both look at me and giggle some more. I try to ignore the heat in my blood, and concentrate on a conversation with the guy next to me. I find out the object of my desire (the girl with the breasts) is called Sophie and from where I am standing it looks like she has a great arse as well. Things are definitely looking up.

I am called back into the office for a chat with the new boss. There is always lots of boring first day stuff to get through but luckily it is nearly lunchtime so I suggest that we head out for lunch. Stuart seems a little thrown by this, I think he probably has a pack of sandwiches and a yogurt somewhere, but after suggesting that perhaps we could extend the invitation to the rest of the team he visibly brightens and goes back outside to rally the troops. I laugh inwardly at his sad attempts to be Mr Popular around the office. After rounding everyone up we make our way down to a small village pub quite close to our base; the team are greeted warmly by the landlord so I guess that this must be quite a regular watering hole. There are gaudy, metallic Christmas decorations festooned gaily everywhere and the polished wooden bar houses a miniature Christmas tree at each bend. A larger and more tastefully decorated tree stands towards the back of what I guess is the restaurant section in a large bay window. The whole effect is quite homely and a roaring fire in each section adds to the atmosphere.

I sit at the bar next to one of the trees as the team start ordering drinks. As I sit, I let the buzz of conversation wash over me. We are the first customers of the day and there is an underlying yeasty aroma of alcohol with undertones of pine disinfectant. I glance sideways and notice that the small tree beside me is adorned with miniature female elves, all of whom appear to be topless with pointy Barbie-doll-type breasts. Each elf has tinselled red booties and a tiny tinselled Christmas hat. Quite bizarre, I don't even know where you go to buy anything quite this crass. Amazed and fairly bemused I take my drink and follow the rest of the team down to one of the tables. We sit at one long table, and I manage to break the ice further by cracking my head fairly hard on a long, low ceiling beam. God that hurt. I smile and laugh (even though my head is bloody killing me) at the resulting good-natured ribaldry and comments and, rubbing my sore head, sit opposite the admin team and beside Amanda. The drinks and conversation seem to flow quite well. All being said, they seem like quite a nice bunch. I get talking to Amanda, who seems to thaw out even further with a few drinks under her belt. This is a girl who knows her stuff and seems to set and expect quite high standards for the rest of the team. I realize that unwittingly I must have impressed her with my newly swatted up technical know-how and industry network. I have already got the impression from Stuart that she is held in high regard by the National Sales guy and the regional boss, which is not bad for a girl. She is a smoker and I wander outside with her and a couple of the guys for a cigarette. I don't smoke but sometimes the best gossip can be picked up outside with the smoking crew.

It is absolutely freezing outside and I try not to shiver, don't want to look like a wimp. I try to make some impression on a completely frozen puddle of water with my heel as I listen to the banter and general chat. The ice-covered patch beneath my feet is frozen solid but I manage to make a slight crack at the very edge. The air is bitter, cold and frigid. We stand huddled together, mainly to try and trap some warmth between us, and I find out that most of the team also think that Stuart is a muppet. Very ambitious but clueless seems to be the general opinion. Apparently he came from a very different side of the business and doesn't really add much value on a day to day basis. The team all seem to agree that, although Stuart is as much use as a chocolate teapot, he shouldn't really give me too much grief. Surprisingly the general consensus seems to be that Amanda should take on the managerial post for the office. I glance curiously over at her but she just shrugs in a non-committal gesture and drags on her fag. As we walk back in, Amanda explains that the managerial position was offered to her but she has no interest, she wants to be out there at the cutting edge, meeting with clients and prospects and resolving problems. Besides, it's not a role she thinks she can do justice to with a little one in tow. Amanda has really started to open up now, and she begins to discuss animatedly the prospects and projects she is working on. I am quite surprised to see how passionate she is, after all, employee benefits are a tough subject to get steamed up about, but, hey, whatever floats your boat. We have agreed that we should meet up tomorrow to discuss all the current opportunities further and perhaps make some appointments. As she relaxes further with the effect of the alcohol she becomes more tactile, touching my arm to get her point across and at one point leaning against me. She really has the nicest hazel eyes, and there is definitely an attraction between us. I can feel it fizzing, electrifying the air between us and if I didn't know any better I would swear that she was challenging me. When we were talking earlier, I leant over and brushed a small tendril of hair off her face. Worked like a dream. She stopped in mid sentence, and for just a moment our eyes met. Fantastic.

Not only is she thawing but her friend Sophie with the colossal tits also looks like a goer. I was quite disappointed to notice that Sophie had not joined us for lunch. But then, just when I had written her off as a no-show, she breezed in looking fabulous, all windswept and rosy and sat herself down right next to me. So now I have Amanda on one side (I am sure she keeps pressing her leg against mine) and Sophie on the other. It turns out that Sophie is Amanda's assistant, and as luck may have it they work and play very closely together (Amanda's choice of words by the way). Magnificent! It just gets better! Perhaps there could be an opportunity to have them both, maybe even together. I think I am going to love my new job.

We are all now getting on like a house on fire. A local serving wench has brought us huge platters of sandwiches with bowls of fries and coleslaw and we all get tucked in. Sophie leaves the table to get some more drinks and when she returns she sits almost opposite me. She is not a classic beauty by any stretch of the imagination, but the heat of the room and the drink have given her quite a sexy glow. Her eyes are shining and she has stopped self-consciously trying to hide her chest. Which I must say works for me. She doesn't say too much but the lights are obviously on and she laughs easily, throwing her head back and exposing her wonderful bouncing cleavage. You could get lost in there for a month at least. She has very blonde hair and every time she moves her head or leans towards me I get the faintest scent of apples (shampoo? some kind of spray?) and I find that I am drawn to her – she is completely natural right down to her perfectly shaped and buffed fingernails and there are no false airs or pretensions about her. She seems to have a kind of innocence about her as well; she blushes easily and gazes at me openly, beguilingly. Shockingly, I am overcome with a mad urge to protect her, to gather her into my arms for a while. This is fairly unusual, to say the least, not normally the reaction I get when I am this close to a blonde with enormous breasts. I'm sure it will pass. Must be something to do with the time of year, all these Christmas carols and roaring fires (not to mention the topless elves) are enough to turn any man's head. I must be going soft.

I find out that she's married (no wedding ring, unusual, normally women love a bit of jewellery) but no children, obviously something going on there, as she coloured up quite dramatically when I mentioned kids. Amanda is also married but she has one child, a boy. It is really strange, I just can't imagine Amanda with kids, however Sophie looks like she would be a natural. And for one second, I have a fleeting glimpse of her laughing and gathering a brood of children into her bosom. I realize I am staring at Sophie in a drunken and dazed kind of way, so I smile at her (hopefully in a non-lustful, I haven't been trying to look at your breasts kind of way) and start to turn away, then, to my delight, she blushes enchantingly and smiles back. Looks like it could be my Christmas.

Some of the team start to head back to the office but we stay put. Amanda moves the subject back to work so it looks for all the world as if we have a bona fide reason to stay. We are joined by Will, one of the other consultants and as soon as everyone else goes back to the office we order another bottle of wine and get stuck in. I find out that the office Christmas party is just six weeks away, it will be held in a local hotel pertinently named (well, one can only hope) the

42

Spread Eagle and it will be work employees only, no wives, husbands or incumbents of any kind. All at once a myriad of exotic sexual possibilities spring to mind and all the blood in my body seems to rush to one point. I cross and uncross my legs, surreptitiously manoeuvring myself into a more comfortable position. I sling my arm across my middle and try to look casual and indifferent. Of course if the venue is a hotel there will be rooms. Magnificent! I make a mental note to book a room just in case, after all, even if I don't get lucky it will save me driving home and I can have a drink. According to Amanda the company usually puts on quite a good bash with copious amounts of alcohol, some decent food and a live band. Will adds that the whole of the fourth floor are invited and last year things didn't wind down until around 3.00 am.

The girls then go on to discuss outfits, so I drift out of the conversation not quite able to believe my luck. I would lay money on both the girls showing some interest. OK, so they are married, but somehow I don't think that will stop them. Sophie is definitely quieter so may be more reticent but I am quite sure that underneath that shy demeanour she is a complete vixen. I have visions of those big doe eyes looking up at me as she sucks my swollen cock and I feel myself harden again. Don't they say it's the quiet ones you have to watch? As for Amanda, well, I am sure if I get enough alcohol down her she will be quite open to suggestions. This is a girl who likes a drink and has already said that she is up for a good time. Honestly, I can't believe that some people actually think fidelity is still important in a marriage, so out-dated. I always say a little bit of what you fancy does you good, and actually I'm sure it stops the whole marriage thing becoming stale. The best thing about getting it on with someone else's wife is that they have to go home to their husbands at the end of the day. This in my experience stops all sorts of problems occurring. There is nothing worse than some bird getting all soft and clingy on you. No, you have to play your cards carefully, shag them and move on.

When I get home Suzie has prepared a veritable feast, complete with champagne. I start feeling just a little nervous, could it be her birthday, our anniversary, her mother's birthday? She wraps her arms around my neck, kisses me, grabs my hand and leads me upstairs as I frantically try and remember what I may have forgotten.

'How did your first day go?' she enquires. She looks fantastic.

'Er, fine, really good,' I am still not quite sure where I am being led and what the occasion is.

'Er, you look amazing, your hair is lovely,' I manage to stammer. Even to my own ears I sound guilty, must be the lunchtime drink, never did agree with me drinking at lunchtime, really must try and rally.

'Thanks, hon, I had it done this afternoon,' she says looking at me quizzically. 'Have you been drinking?'

Fair question I guess.

'No, not really, well, a little – went out with the team for a lunchtime bevy.' I say. Great, she is still smiling. This can only be a good thing.

'I thought we would celebrate your first day in style. I just knew you would blow them away and the kids are having a sleepover so we have the whole house to ourselves. You can tell me all about it and then I'm going to shag you senseless.' She smiles at me then, completely guileless and I know in a flash that she has spent most of her afternoon off shopping and cooking and making herself look fantastic, all this to make me feel good, to celebrate my first day. All at once I feel almost humble. She really has worked hard. The food smells amazing too. Well, I'd better make the most of it. I excuse myself and dash to the bathroom. I swish some mouthwash around and spray on some cologne – at least that will go some way in hiding the alcoholic aroma I am sure I must be carrying around with me. I run one of the children's flannels (Thomas the Tank Engine) under some hot water, add a little squirty soap and whiz it over the old man. Well you never know just how lucky you're going to get! Having been a boy scout I always try and be prepared and you don't have to be Einstein to read the signs tonight.

The next six weeks at work fly by and I am introduced to all sorts of people: staff, brokers from insurance companies and clients. I also have to sit through many compliance tests to make sure that I am up to standard. Really, compliance is just taking over. Seriously, when Maxwell went overboard, any sanity in the pensions industry went over with him. Even the clients complain about the amount of regulatory paperwork and they are the ones who are supposed to benefit from it all. Anyway, it's been a time of learning the company line, shaking the right hands and ticking all the right boxes. During the month or so since I started I have also become closer to Amanda as we are now working on several clients together. We are definitely working well together, she is great to spark ideas off and has the contacts I need internally. She definitely likes me as well, I can just tell. Every now and again I see her sneaking glances at me and there is a real chemistry in the air when we are together. By the end of the month, Thursday in fact (there is definitely something about Thursdays), we decide to jack it in early and hit the bar. Sophie is on a training course of some kind so it is just the two of us.

We leave the office at about 4.00 pm. Already it is dark, the air is crisp and the sky is heavy, brooding with the potential for snow. Every day this week snow has been forecast but so far all we have seen are a few desolate flakes that vanish as soon as they are spotted. The world seems so bleak, cold and grey, with everyone wrapped up against the chill and scurrying off to somewhere warm. We leave in our respective cars and as I drive away I glance again at the sky and can't help thinking that a really good snowstorm would be a great excuse for a day off work. I could spend some time with the boys in the garden. I smile to myself as visions of snowmen, sledging with the boys and playing with the dog fill my head. I get to the bar and notice that Amanda's car is already there, she must know a shortcut. I take a folder of paperwork out of the car and into the bar with me. Always good to have some paperwork with you, it is a great alibi; after all you never know who you are going to meet. Amanda has already ordered the drinks when I get in, and a bottle of white sits on a corner table with two full glasses beside it. Amanda is texting, her fingers flashing over the keys; I watch her as she presses send and throws the phone on the table. She takes a giant swig of her wine and smiles at me, watching me get settled.

'So, you never told me how much they are paying you,' she stares at me, her bearing and body language almost daring, defying me not to answer.

I stare right back, trying to gauge her mood. God, women can be tricky. Is she just being provocative to see how I will react or is this her idea of fun?

'What have you heard?' I counter. I love to hear that I am being discussed around the office already.

'Well, you know what it's like, I heard they were paying you £80k but that you also get a hundred per cent in the first year of any new income you bring in.'

I nearly choke on my drink. 'I wish! Is that really what they are saying?' I can't believe it; nobody ever gets one hundred per cent of new income.

'So it's not true?' she asks, one eyebrow raised.

I explain my deal briefly: that I get fifty per cent of any new business that I bring in that is then retained for one year. I don't mention the golden handshake I got or the credit I know I will get for the clients I will bring with me. She relaxes a little and explains that her deal is less bonus and a higher basic. Her role is more about keeping existing clients happy so it kind of makes sense. She seems to relax a bit more and thankfully changes the subject.

'So, tell me about Suzie,' she says.

This is always a leading question. A sure sign that she is interested, I just know it. I take off my jacket and watch her watching.

'Well, she is a nurse, she works in orthopaedics, but only part time since we had the children,' I reply.

'Have you ever been unfaithful?' she looks at me intently, trying to ascertain if I am squirming internally.

God, I hate it when they ask this. My mind races. Definitely don't want to be too up front. Not sure I could even remember how many times I have strayed. After all, we have been married for that long. Perhaps I'll tell her about Debs, I think. I must have had too much to drink as I start by explaining that Suzie and I have been married for nearly eleven years, which is a long time in anybody's book. I tell her that we have a good marriage and that Suzie is a great lady, one of the best. And then I tell her about my search. I tell her that perhaps I am looking for something that I just haven't found yet. I try and describe my theory that everyone has a soul mate and that if you haven't met yours yet then perhaps you have to keep searching, maybe even for ever, until you find that special someone. I pause for effect and look at her to check that she isn't looking too sceptical before I go on. But I see that she is nodding and so then I explain that perhaps we don't even consciously realize that we are looking until one day we meet someone at the coffee machine, or in the supermarket or in the park and in that one moment the whole world will just stop. And everyone and everything else will just disappear, and all at once the world will seem brighter. And then I tell her that when you meet the right person nothing in the world will be able to keep you from

47

being together, and that you will know without a doubt that you have met that one person designed to be with you for all of time.

All the time I am talking, Amanda is just nodding so when I finish I take a deep breath and then I tell her. 'A few years ago I kind of got caught up with a girl, I didn't mean it to happen,' I add hastily, trying to gauge Amanda's reaction.

'We met at work; actually, she was my assistant. Straight away we just knew there was an attraction, I swear when I met her, the rest of the world just ceased to be important somehow. We both tried to fight it but in the end I felt like I had some kind of fever, as if I really couldn't be without her.'

Amanda is looking at me completely absorbed and all of a sudden it feels right to explain how it happened, and before you know it, maybe it is the alcohol or the slowly falling snow, but I start telling her how much I had loved her, how she went from being my assistant to being my whole life. How just dancing with her was the most erotic and sensual experience of my whole life and how we used to lose hours just kissing and talking. And then I tell her about how even now after all this time I still miss her.

At some point in the story I kind of sober up a little and realize that I seem to be pouring my heart out and I suddenly wise up and add in bits like, 'well, of course, Suzie and I were kind of on a break at this time, you know what it's like, we were going through some difficult times ...'

But when I look at Amanda, far from judging me she is looking positively misty eyed, she holds my hand in hers and tells me that she is sorry that it didn't work out. She asks me whether I still love Debs and I tell her that it was all a long time ago, and that it would not have been right for us to be together and that we would always be friends, and that when it came down to it I owed it to Suzie to try and make a go of it with her and the boys. I sigh then and pour another glass of wine.

I tell Amanda: 'Suzie and I after all this time, if nothing else, we are good friends, and we have always said that if either of us were to fall in love with someone else then we would just let go, after all, don't they say that love has no truer test?' And then I add something like '"if you love something you should let it go ..."' She nods in recognition. I know that this is a practised line but I say it as sincerely as I can, as this, as you can imagine is not strictly true. I think Suzie would in all honesty come for me with a blunt fork if she ever found out about any of my indiscretions. But it is a great line, sounds profound every time and provides me with a kind of legitimate loophole to explore any opportunities that may be out there.

We finish our drinks, pay our bill and leave. I notice that Amanda sways quite noticeably as she puts on her coat. I put my arm around her (just to steady her, as any gentleman would) and we walk out into the spiralling, swirling snowflakes. All at once the world is beautiful again and we stare upwards with the wonderment of children. Then all at once our eyes meet and all of sudden we are kissing, passionate, frenzied and desperate. I manoeuvre her against a wall that has been overlooked by the harsh security lighting and we cling together in the darkness with her hands in my hair pulling me closer and the snow falling all around us. I swear I can feel her heart beating as I push my hands inside her coat, frantic for the feel of her. We fall deeper and deeper into each other, losing track of the time and space around us, lost in that amazing heady excitement of a first kiss. Then, just as quickly, we are apart gasping for air. 'Oh my God,' she says and stumbles away from me. She has her hands on her hips and she is walking around in small circles like a runner trying to steady her breath. 'Oh my God,' she says again. I smile. 'Maybe,' I say, 'but you can call me Gareth.'

She laughs and I pull her to me and kiss her again, slowly this time and with more finesse. I take my time to taste every inch of her, breathing in her subtle spicy fragrance tinged with the scent of Marlboro, revelling in the feel of the snowflakes falling down on us, melting quickly on our heated skin. I nuzzle deeper into her, but she stops me this time, her breathing ragged. 'Look, I really should go,' she says, 'I have to be home for Max's bath time. I'm sorry,' she says, walking backwards as she talks, 'all hell will break loose if I am late home again.' And with that she rakes her hands through her long brown hair and looks at me one long last time, all desire and indecision, and then turns and runs to her car. And there I stand with the falling snow dancing all around me, still slightly breathless, just watching her tail lights disappear into the thickening snow.

Friday drags on for ever, neither Amanda nor Sophie are around today. I think Sophie is still on this course and Amanda is out with clients. I have tried to call Amanda several times but there is no answer. It's been a week now since I kissed her and she has had back to back client meetings every day so we have not had any time at all to talk. I really want to talk to her, see how she is feeling about the other night, but there is no reply. I daren't send a text as I don't know how exclusive her use of the phone is. The last thing we need is someone else picking up her messages and getting the wrong end of the stick. I idly wonder if she might have got an attack of the guilts, sometimes this happens with the married chicks, it is all very boring but not insurmountable. And now she has had a taste she will find it even harder to resist next time. I smile to myself as I imagine her begging for me. I just need to play it cool right now and give her some space.

At lunchtime I walk aimlessly around the shops, I grab a steak sandwich at the local deli and after delaying my return to the office for as long as I can I head back. Still no one around, everyone seems to be out today. I trawl around the floor making idle conversation with the staff who are in, and surf the net. At 3.00 even more staff leave, mainly secretaries and female support staff. They are all off to hair appointments because tonight is the night of the staff Christmas party. At least I will have a chance to talk to Amanda tonight and if I play my cards right I might make use of the room I booked. The clock drags round to 4.00 pm and I close down my laptop and shove it in my desk drawer. I lock the drawer, grab my coat and bag and walk out. It is so good to be out I take a deep lungful of the cold crisp air and stretch out my legs as I walk to my car. Last night's snow has all but melted and heaps of grey slush, now compacted and frozen, lie in woeful clumps in the corners of the car park. The sky is a deep velvet-indigo colour already and the car park is now almost deserted. There is nothing like a good excuse to get home early, I think, as I unlock the car and shove a briefcase of technical updates in the boot. The traffic is awful so the thirty-minute drive home takes nearly an hour.

When I get home I am bombarded by boys and the dog, the youngest winds his legs round my waist and clings onto my neck like a spider monkey. I wangle myself free of his grasp, set him down and ruffle his pale blond hair, listening all the while to their excited chatter and tales of the day. As I hit the bedroom, removing office garb on the way, they bounce up and down alongside me, all energy and exuberance. I change into some jogging pants and a thick jumper and beat the boys down the stairs. They jump the last three stairs and hit the floor together, where the dog, pleased to be part of a game, barks happily, charging around between them. Happy for the diversion I slip into the kitchen and greet Suzie, who looks tired and is trying to stir something that looks a little like a bolognaise sauce. We exchange the usual evening greetings and I steal a tomato, then I take the kids and the dog out into the dark evening to expend some energy. We hit the park and spend at least thirty minutes running round the deserted, floodlit field chasing the ball like lunatics, the boys giggling and scrapping, our breath spreading out around us, eddying and whirling before vanishing into nothing. All the time our excitable Collie charges round and round barking gleefully, trying desperately to round us all up. By the time we return our faces are scarlet with the cold and exertion. Tristan riding on my shoulders has torn his trousers in a spectacular fall over the dog and onto the frozen ground, and he has a small cut that will need some attention. I shepherd all of them in and send the boys to their mother while I hit the shower to get ready for the party.

The dress code is black tie, which is a bit of a pain, but I must say with my physique I was made for black tie. I appraise myself after dressing and sweep back my hair one more time. I stand in front of the full-length mirror and pull out an imaginary gun. James Bond eat your heart out. I am looking seriously hot tonight. I think of Amanda and then of Sophie and smile, they don't stand a chance. I kiss Suzie goodbye and she fiddles a little with my tie and my hair. Women are like that, they just like to think that they are leaving their mark.

'It's such a shame I can't come,' she says a little petulantly.

'I know, honey, perhaps next time.' She looks a little dejected so I give her a hug and promise to take her to her favourite restaurant on Saturday. She rolls her eyes at me good-naturedly and I can't help but smile.

'OK,' she says, a little bit happier. 'But I really miss you when you are gone, the bed just seems so big without you.' This last bit is added with a coquettish flutter of her eyelashes and I smile and kiss her.

'Honey, it is only for one night and I will miss you too, but I really can't get out of it; all of the team are staying and it will look a little odd if I don't. Anyway, saves the worry of trying to get a cab so late at night,' I say.

'Where is it again?' she asks.

'Do you know, I am actually not sure,' I lie. 'I'm getting a lift with one of the guys, but you can reach me on the mobile if you need me.' I answer her with a kiss on the top of her head. She shrugs in agreement, kisses me back and waves me goodbye. Will, who is turning out to be a really good mate, is picking me up. I hear him sound his horn as he pulls up, obviously eager to get there. So I smile apologetically, kiss her again, and disappear out into the night.

We arrive at the Spread Eagle and a couple of local teenagers divert us across the road to a nearby field for parking. I am quite taken aback by the sheer number of cars already parked efficiently in lines. As we get out I notice each car by now has a light coating of white frost, gently iridescent in the light of the moon. Delicately we pick our way across the field, over the hardened troughs and furls beneath our feet, turned and hewn when the field was ploughed on some earlier hazy autumn day. Actually it is bloody hard work when visibility is dim (in fact non-existent in some places) and it is quite icy in places. It doesn't help that we are mincing around in dress shoes. I shudder to think how the girls will get on in stilettos.

We get to the door with our breath short and rising in billowing clouds around us. But then all is forgotten as we are greeted from all sides by friendly faces and a glass of champagne is proffered. I make my way across the foyer and cannot help being impressed by the towering Christmas tree (and not a topless elf in sight) sheltered by the not un-impressive sweep of the stairway. There are ornately trimmed topiary bushes and miniature green trees all around, each one trimmed tastefully and decorated with small blinking white lights. And all the guests just look stunning. I am acknowledged and welcomed by everyone, which is really quite a revelation as I didn't think in my short time at the company that I had met half these people. Just as I spot Amanda and Sophie a bell is rung and we are called in for dinner. I just get the chance to wave and then we are ushered into a dining room, a conspicuously new addition to the older, more traditional building. I look over at the girls again. Amanda looks amazing. She is wearing an ankle-length dress that clings, well, just everywhere and incredible high heels (how did she cope with the field, I wonder?). Her brown hair is all kind of swept up with long tendrils gently curling around her neck. She looks incredibly sexy. But Sophie, oh my God. Sophie. She just lights up the room. In contrast to all the black and the occasional red dress, Sophie is wearing an incredible pale gold number with some kind of swinging fringy effect at the bottom. The dress is also a lot shorter than most of the other dresses around, kind of over her knee but definitely not too short. She too is wearing amazingly high shoes that with the short dress make her look cute but as wanton as hell all at the same time. To make matters worse she is wearing some kind of necklace thing that hangs right down, I mean right down, almost hanging between her breasts. I can't help but stare. As Amanda turns and walks towards the dining area, Sophie raises her glass to me and smiles, and the candles and twinkling lights shimmer on her hair and her dress and lend her a luminosity that is almost ethereal. I must say I return the toast suitably entranced.

I wonder, not for the first time, whether Amanda has told Sophie about our passionate interlude in the pub car park. I guess I will know soon enough. I look at the seating plan and realise the whole team have been split up. I guess that this is to make sure that everyone socializes and that people don't congregate in their own teams only. Somehow, though, Sophie and Amanda have managed to stay together on the same table. How annoying. I look at the list of names for my allotted table and groan inwardly. None of the names sound familiar and I shudder at the thought of the next few hours making small talk with a whole table of strangers. I walk to my table, find my space and start to introduce myself. The dinner party gods are obviously smiling down on me because I find that they are not a bad bunch at all. And after a couple of drinks I must admit that the whole set-up works remarkably well, everyone is in good spirits and wine is flowing freely. The food is really quite good considering it is a fairly small hotel and they are catering en masse tonight. Not a piece of rubber chicken in sight.

Straight after dinner someone (no idea who) stands up and praises everyone for their efforts for the year and speaks a little of the company's aspirations for the New Year. There is a little bit of heckling but mostly people are respectful and after a rousing round of applause the usual after dinner quiz begins. This seems to be a tried and tested formula and every firm I have ever worked in has had the same idea. Each table is issued with a sheet of trivia questions and the table with the most correct answers wins. It all starts off fairly amicably but as each table exhaust their trivia knowledge the whole thing really kicks off, with people texting friends for the answers and massive cheating between tables. Sometime around question six a fairly inebriated Sophie totters over, clutching her table's list of questions. She stands with her back against the table and conspiratorially leans in to me. She smells of something fresh and fruity and I try very hard not to notice that her breasts are just inches from my face. Suddenly she realises that her posture is perhaps putting me in a difficult position. 'I'm sorry, they really get in the way sometimes,' she giggles, leaning back against the table.

'Honey, they can get in my way any time you like,' I quip.

'You are really quite bad, aren't you?' she admonishes, making a playful swipe with the question sheet somewhere near my nose. She leans over me and whispers in my ear, 'Do you have the answer to question eight?' I can feel her breath in my ear and her hair on my neck. She leans back fluttering her eyelashes seductively. She doesn't need to bother, I am as hard as a hard thing and it just gets worse when I notice her glance down.

'What's it worth?' I counter.

'Look, how about I show you mine and you show me yours,' she teases, looking pointedly at my crotch. She looks like she is enjoying this immensely and she is now teasing massively. This is no longer just harmless banter. Her tone is suddenly far lower and she appears to have sobered up remarkably. She is now gazing at me boldly, suggestively, almost daringly as she rubs her ankle against my calf. Then, just as I think I am imagining it, she leans over and whispers quite clearly, 'I think I would quite fancy my dessert outside, how about you? How about in ten minutes, by the oak tree?'

All of a sudden my tongue appears to have swollen in my mouth and to confound matters I seem to have lost the power of speech. I nod and she laughs. 'See you soon then, noddy,' she says and drifts off back to her table.

Then the panic sets in. Then the paranoia. What if this is some kind of female prank? Maybe Amanda has said something, maybe this is a form of planned revenge and if I turn up they will both dismember me slowly with some piece of blunt ancient farm equipment. I gulp and make a grab for my wine. With one swift movement I down the lot. It doesn't help. I try and think rationally. I suddenly feel very hot. Then a moment of clarity. Maybe Amanda has said something, and perhaps they both want me! Now that could be interesting.

Well, in for a penny in for a pound. I excuse myself and head for the gents. I check my teeth for stray vegetables and shake the snake. Then I am out of there, I rapidly crunch on two mints as I stride purposefully out towards wherever this oak tree may be. I open the door and, with a quick glance around, slip silently into the night to meet the lovely Sophie. I find I am in the garden but there is no tree in sight so I saunter round to the side of the building and there it is. A huge majestic oak adorned with hundreds of tiny sparkling lights, the tree is so large that it almost dwarfs this side of the garden. I stare up at the branches into the lights until I start to feel a little dizzy. Nothing. I start to wander around the tree, I sidle up near the trunk and peer furtively around. Nothing and then all of a sudden, out of the dark, there she is, all breathless and giggly. She comes to a stop and starts fiddling nervously with her hands.

'I feel really scared now,' she says almost haltingly.

'So you should,' I say, stepping towards her. I slowly, very slowly, trace a stray tendril of hair over her face and hook it behind her ear. I leave my hand there just very slightly stroking the back of her neck and the side of her face.

'So, did you bring dessert?' I ask with an air of innocence.

She giggles again and shakes her head nervously.

'I guess I will just have to make do with you then,' I whisper. Her breath is now coming in shallow panting gasps and she is staring at me with those amazing eyes. Time starts to move really slowly and all I can hear is the pounding of blood in my ears. And I don't know who moves first but suddenly we are kissing and panting like bears. She rakes her hands over my fly, struggling and grasping for an opening, seizing at the length of me. With one hand I free myself and then, like in all the best movies she drops to her knees on the frozen ground with my engorged cock straining in her hand and takes me into her mouth. She caresses me so tenderly with her tongue that I think I am going to shoot all over her. I groan audibly as she slides me up and down greedily, my hands are in her hair and it is all I can do to stop myself from ramming my cock further into her warm wet mouth. I lift her up onto her feet and feel her shaking, and then with all the care and restraint I can muster I kiss her deeply, and with her arms around my neck and her back against the tree I pull her dress up and pull her panties to one side and thrust myself into her. Her legs are tight around my waist and it feels so good. I try to bury myself deep into her, all the time mindful of not scraping her too hard against the tree, but I am fast losing control. All too soon I am spent, and she cuddles into me. We are both breathing hard now from our exertions. We fall against each other and I kiss her tenderly and help her fix her dress and her hair. We are both starting to cool down and I notice that she is shivering. I wrap my jacket around her and tell her she is amazing. Then all of a sudden she starts to cry. I am alarmed and a little worried; I don't usually have this effect. But then she sniffs and apologizes.

'I am so, so sorry, I just haven't felt like that before, well, actually like this for ... well, really, I have never felt like this. I just wanted to touch you. I'm not really like this, I don't really know what came over me,' she is laughing and crying all at the same time now, snuffling and sniffing all the while.

I tell her to blame me and that I think she is incredible and that if we don't go back soon I may have to have her again. She smiles at this, dabbing at her nose with my hankie.

'Look we had better get back in,' she says.

All the time she is sniffing and talking she is trying to tidy herself up, smoothing down her dress and trying to pin her hair back up. Finally she rubs down her knees and after giving her eyes another dab, smiles up at me and turns to go.

I grab her hand and try and keep her with me. 'Stay just for a while, I'm not ready to let you go yet and anyway they will be dancing by now and they will never miss us,' I say.

She falters, looking at me as if I have the answers to all the questions in the universe, and I swear I start to unravel just a little.

'You can't just shag me and wander off,' I state incredulously.

She giggles now and turns to go again.

'Look, that was amazing, you are amazing, no really, truly magnificent. When can I see you again? I haven't stopped thinking about you since I met you,' I say, trying once more to keep her here with me under this beautiful tree under this beautiful sky.

'Please will you just think about it?' I chance.

She looks at me and smiles. 'Yes' she says. 'I will think about it, but not now because now I just want to dance,' she says laughing.

And so I watch her sashay her way back in through the door and after about ten minutes of freezing my nuts off I follow her in. As I walk through the door I come face to face with Amanda, hand on hip.

'So where have you been? I have been looking all over for you.' Her voice is cold, stone cold.

Surely Sophie wouldn't have told her, would she? This could be the shortest time I have ever worked for a company. Can you imagine? This kind of thing sure doesn't lend itself well to great working relations. I reach out to touch her, to pacify her somehow but she pulls back sharply.

'Don't. Touch. Me. How could you?' She is so cross now she is almost spitting the words at me, her face inches from mine.

'I know all about you. How dare you think you can come in here and add us to your list of conquests? I know all about you. Do you think you are the only one with a "network"? You see, I've got friends in the industry too,' she spits. 'I know all about your games. I can't believe I nearly fell for it. Don't, even, think about coming anywhere near me again. Oh and stay away from Sophie as well.' And off she stalks with not even a look behind her.

I am gobsmacked. Quite unbelievable. She must have seen us. That means she will definitely go shooting her mouth off to Sophie about that bloody kiss. I cringe at the thought. And what is she talking about? She must have heard something from somewhere. It doesn't matter how many times you change jobs your past has an uncanny habit of catching up with you. I mean, hasn't everyone got a few skeletons hanging around? Amanda hardly looks as pure as the driven snow herself, who is she to criticize me? I need to find out what she knows, diffuse the whole situation before it gets out of hand. I try and find her, try to spot her in the crowd as I head to the bar. I wonder what she thinks she knows?

Chapter 4

Sophie

'For it was not into my ear you whispered, but into my heart. It was not
my lips you kissed but my soul.'
Judy Garland

I can't believe it, and I just can't stop smiling. Every part of
me, every tiny millimetre of my skin feels precious now. I just
keep touching myself because somehow it feels like it brings
him closer.

Last night was the most amazing night ever. Not only did I
totally and brazenly seduce Gareth in the garden of the
Spread Eagle but then, when the whole party was over and
everyone had gone home, I snuck back and spent the rest of
the night with him – four more amazing hours. I think he was
as shocked as I was. I didn't think I had it in me to be so
sneaky or so daring. I kissed everyone goodbye, even Gareth,
and then got into a cab by myself. I asked the driver to head
towards the centre of town and then told him I needed to go
back to the hotel as I had left something behind. I paid him
(really well, I think, because all my cash seems to have
disappeared) and then told him I would have another drink
before going home. It was really late by then, probably
around 2.00 am, and Gareth had literally just got into the

61

room. Despite the late hour, he had showered and all he had on was a white fluffy towel wrapped around his hips. He didn't say a word, he just stared at me and then, before I knew it, I was in the room, in his arms and he was kissing me again. Surely anything that feels this amazing can't be wrong. I didn't leave again until nearly 6.00 am and, despite the lack of sleep, every little bit of me feels alive; my whole body feels as if it is singing. And I am actually bruised! Can you believe it? I thought that was just the stuff of romantic novels but I am actually sore in unmentionable places and my lips still feel swollen from his kisses, my face grazed from his stubble. I never ever thought I could feel like this. I mean, it is not as if I'm some young girl that could be easily swept off her feet, I am a grown woman, rational and sensible and married, for goodness' sake. But I feel for all the world like I am seeing clearly for the very first time, it is as if the air is fresher and colours are brighter. Sometimes it seems as though all my life I have struggled to work out where I fit in, to work out why I am even bothering to struggle even. But now it is as if all of the pieces of my puzzle have connected, it is as if all of a sudden I have found all the answers I have been searching for. I feel almost as though he is my reason for being here. How can this be happening?

Something happened the very first time I saw him. I am sure of that now. It was as if I was drawn to him somehow. Like he was supposed to be the one. My stomach would just flip every time he looked at me. This has never happened to me before, not on this scale anyway. I mean of course I meet men every day, all different shapes and sorts of men and occasionally I will find one or more of them attractive. Amanda and I have often sat in bars playing shoot, shag or marry. But this is different. I have never ever felt such a strong attraction to someone before. It is as if he holds some strange power over me, or he has some sort of weird magnetism that I am just powerless to resist. Wherever he is that is where I want to be. All I want to do is think about him. I just want everything to stop so I can escape into this dream of him, because that is how it feels – like a dream. I want to remember every single minute of our time together and etch it deep into my memory so that I never forget. But this wasn't supposed to happen; I didn't mean to fall for him, not like this. At one point last night we just sat and talked for nearly an hour and he said he felt the same as me, that he had felt irrepressibly drawn to me. He said I was beautiful and for the first time ever that is how I feel, I feel young and beautiful and daring and passionate. He told me that he hadn't kissed anyone except his wife in over eight years and that when he met me he felt as if he just had to be with me. He told me that he had a brief affair about eight years ago but it never really amounted to anything and it wasn't at all serious. It is so rare that you meet someone who feels that they can and want to be so honest. I feel strangely like I could trust him with anything.

I have never in my life seduced anyone, not really, not even Simon. Of course, I have imagined it but I have never ever taken control like that before. There is just something about him that makes me feel empowered, almost dangerous even. I don't think I will ever get tired of hearing how beautiful he thinks I am or how soft he thinks my skin feels. I know he is married but then so am I, and if we had perfect marriages then this wouldn't have happened, would it?

He has sworn me to secrecy and asked me not to say anything to anyone, not even Amanda. I told him that Amanda was kind of like my best friend and she wouldn't tell a soul, but he was absolutely adamant that I don't even confide in her. He said he wants it to be our secret and that for the time being we should just enjoy our time together. I think he is worried that if anybody finds out it will just taint this amazing thing we have found. And you know, he is probably right, people are just interested in gossip, something to discuss over coffee and lunch. They wouldn't, couldn't possibly understand how we feel. We would be labelled as just another office romance, something sordid and ridiculous.

It has been really hard not telling Amanda. When I disappeared halfway through dinner I think she got a little concerned and apparently looked everywhere for me. She was acting really strange when I went back in, really moody. I swear she is psychic because she asked me straightaway if I had been with Gareth. She was really aggressive and my first instinct was to deny everything. It was far too soon then for me to tell her anything anyway, I just wanted to be on my own, keep the whole thing to myself, and just find some time to think and sort myself out. She means really well and I know she really cares about me but sometimes she can be a little controlling. She asked me whether I had been crying, and really quickly I made up some story about going back to the car and having an argument with Simon on my mobile. I hate lying to her and she did look at me suspiciously at first but then she calmed down and gave me a hug and asked me if I was all right. She knows that Simon and I never argue so I guess she thought it must have been serious. I told her that it was just something silly and we had made up in the end. She kept saying that she had been scared that I had gone off with Gareth and that I should be really careful of him and that he was a real player.

I can't believe she said that, just because he is a good-looking guy does not mean that he is easy. She can really jump to conclusions sometimes. In fact I could tell he was really struggling with the whole fidelity issue when we were together. Why else would he have mentioned this woman he had an affair with so long ago? It appears that some friend of Amanda's at one of the insurance companies has told her all these stories supposedly about Gareth; I wouldn't put it past her to have made it all up. Maybe this 'friend' had tried it on with him at some point and was turned down. Gareth was telling me how difficult it can be to be so attractive to women. This must be just the kind of thing he was talking about. Of course, he would be too much of a gentleman to mention anything like that anyway.

I just can't wait to see him again; minutes just seem like hours when we are not together. We have arranged to sneak off on Wednesday, straight after work. I wonder what I should wear; I might go into town and buy some underwear.

I hate to say it but I think Amanda may have developed a bit of a thing for Gareth as well. After all, he is easily the best looking guy any of us has seen around the office for a long time, and I know that he took her for a drink the other day. I bet she does, I bet she fancies him. She will just die when she finds out about us. I must tell Gareth to be careful, as it could be quite embarrassing for the poor man if she throws herself at him.

Chapter 5

Amanda

'I envy people who drink. At least they have something to blame everything on.'
Oscar Levant

Saturday morning, I go to move and every bit of my body is stiff and sore and my head is just swimming. I try and sit up but the room and the floor seem to move in opposite directions around me, so I lie back down, hold my aching head and wait for the world to stop spinning and the nausea to cease. I listen tentatively for sounds of life in the house but thankfully all seems quiet, and I thank God for Pete, he must have taken Max to the park or something. I lie back down again and listen to the silence, well, nearly silence, as I appear to be able to hear my heart beating in my head. My hair feels disgusting; it reeks of stale smoke and seems to resemble straw. I feel ghastly. I lay and fiddle absently with my tangled frizzy hair, thinking of all the plans that I had made for today. I need to get some food in; Max has a birthday party to go to; I really need to phone my mother as well. I gingerly touch my head. There are parts of my scalp that are actually sore from the pins and effort of such a glamorous updo. Sophie and I had joint hair appointments yesterday;

we had our hair put up and our nails done. It had all looked amazing but after several cans of hairspray and more than a ton of hairpins to hold it in place, it now feels like a very large scraggy nest. I lick my lips and swallow. My mouth feels as though a small furry animal expired in there some time ago and my lips are dry and flaky. Nice. Very attractive. No wonder Pete disappeared rather quickly this morning. I wonder how Sophie is feeling today. I groan as I think of Sophie and then groan again when I remember what I said to Gareth. I try desperately to remember exactly what I did say. I try and piece together the snaps of conversation, but there seem to be lots of missing pieces.

The night was going so well; my dress (found in a sale in Oxford Street some seven months ago) still looked amazing and I actually felt good for once. Max had told me that I looked 'delicious' when I left home, my sweet, wonderful son. But then, even Pete had looked at me admiringly (unusual for him to notice) and when I walked out of the door he had patted my bottom quite proprietorially, as if I was a prize horse or something. Men are so funny. I peer over the side of the bed. Yep, there it is, my beautiful dress, in a heap on the floor, and is that a wine stain? I start to see stars so flip back quickly onto the bed. I was exhausted when I left the house last night. Typically I had been rushing about most of the day and had tried to fit in a fleeting visit to the gym as well. As a result I can't remember eating much more than a banana and a couple of Max's chips all day. Fatal. And how much did I drink? I remember having at least two glasses of champagne when we got to the party (maybe it was three?) and then a vodka redbull to wake me up a bit and then wine with dinner and then I guess I hit the vodka again. Nasty. No wonder I feel horrendous. And vodka as well, I can pretty much drink anything but vodka. For some reason it has a particularly bad effect on me. In fact, Pete has banned me from drinking it when we are out together as it just makes me obnoxious and angry. Once after a particularly vodka-fuelled evening, we had a full-scale row in the street, and I was screaming at Pete so much that a passer-by asked us if I needed help. Very embarrassing. I should *so* know better by now. Aren't you supposed to get older and wiser? I swear at this rate I am off alcohol for at least a week. Maybe a nice detox would help. I could drink just lemon and water or pomegranate juice or something. Perhaps I could even take some of those vitamins I keep buying.

I sigh and move to a more comfortable position in the bed and stretch out in a star formation, feeling the cold sheets against my body. I must be ill, I don't even fancy a cigarette, my chest feels tight and heavy as if a very large dog is sitting on me. For a while I just lie, staring at the ceiling and enjoying the space and the quiet. My stomach rumbles ominously and I realize that I'm hungry, starving in fact, I really must get up in a minute. But then as I go to move it all comes back to me again, last night, Gareth, me shouting like a fishwife. I really had just meant to speak confidentially with Gareth and tell him that what had happened had quite obviously been a mistake. I wasn't even going to mention all the stuff I had heard about him. I was going to be very professional and friendly. Very adult about the whole episode in fact. I don't really know what went wrong. It didn't help that he turned up looking so incredibly sexy. I mean you can see how women would be attracted to him. And black tie makes even the biggest geek look good (even Kelvin from IT looked respectable) so it was bound to make him stand out. Not that I am at all attracted to him, he just caught me by surprise that's all. There is definitely something about him that you can't trust; he is so sure of himself, overly cocky, overly self-assured and absolutely self-possessed. Oh and vain, did I mention vain? All that and one whiff of a shandy and I start acting like a bitch on heat. After a couple of drinks I started thinking about that night and how exciting it was to be kissed like that. And, my God, he can kiss; you have to give him that. I guess I felt flattered. Ridiculous, I know. It is not even as if I'm unhappy, far from it. I am a very happily married woman. I think the whole snog in the car park thing was just a spur of the moment incident that should just be put down to experience, stress at work and too much alcohol. We just got carried away, that was all. Anyway, I had resolved to tell Gareth straight after dinner, get it out of the way before either of us had too much to drink and before the party really got going. That way I could still have a nice time without it hanging over my head and I would be sober enough to fight off any further advances.

It all started to go wrong when Sophie disappeared. The last time I saw her she was trying to find the answers to that stupid quiz but then I got talking to Marie from accounts and lost track of time. When Sophie didn't surface by dessert, I thought she had just got chatting to someone somewhere, but then, when everyone left the tables and moved back to the bar area, I still couldn't see her. I started leisurely wandering around the hotel, I remember looking in the ladies and then I must have meandered outside but there was still no sign of her. Then somehow (probably helped by the vodka) I started putting two and two together and making five. Because I noticed that I couldn't see Gareth either. I started thinking that both of them must be together somewhere and that just made me crosser and crosser. I think it is the fact that he thinks he can just waltz in here and start picking us off like sitting ducks. I mean, how dare he? The thought of him laughing it up behind our backs just makes my blood boil; he is just so bloody arrogant. And I do feel as though I need to look out for Sophie. I really do think that she is quite vulnerable. She can also be annoyingly naïve. I think some stuff went on in her childhood, things she has never really spoken about but alluded to after one too many. I hate to think of someone like Gareth, importunate and

69

evidently a real player, getting hold of her and seducing her just because he can.

I spoke to a really old friend yesterday, we used to work together and occasionally we still have lunch and catch up on old times. We got talking and she tells me that she knows Gareth really well, in fact he is quite famous for putting it about, shall we say. Quite the ladies' man. The worst part is that according to her he is certainly no gentleman and it seems that he is well known for bragging about his various conquests to anyone who will listen. I obviously had a lucky escape, who knows what could have happened? I groan at the thought. How could I have been so stupid? What if Pete found out? What if anyone else from the office found out? I pull the covers back over my head and hide. Surely he wouldn't say anything, he wouldn't be that stupid, would he? Anyway soon it will be Christmas and it will all be forgotten by the time we go back, just a few more days to get through. I have worked so hard to get on in this industry but it is sadly still a man's world, and all a girl has is her reputation. And I cannot, and will not, have that compromised.

When Sophie finally did show up, I am embarrassed to say I gave her a really hard time – almost accused her of getting off with Gareth. She had obviously been crying. That's the trouble with being so fair, it's a real giveaway. Her eyes were red and puffy and her face still looked a little blotchy. I started to feel a bit bad for giving her a hard time, especially when she went on to explain everything. She told me that she had received a call from Simon during dinner and that they had argued and to get some privacy she had finished the call in her car. I can't believe I had even thought that she and Gareth had. Well. You know. Thank goodness anyway. And to think that I had actually felt a little jealous as well, God knows why. He is definitely trouble, there is no doubt about it.

Chapter 6

Simon

'We did not change as we grew older; we just became more clearly
ourselves.'
Lynn Hall

Something is different, I can't quite put my finger on it, but
something has changed. I guess I'm a simple man really, I
enjoy my job, well, most of the time anyway, and things are
going well for me. I love my wife and, despite the challenges
we have had in that department, would love nothing more
than to have children one day.

Neither of us came from money, but we both work hard. I
have been at the bank for ten years now and Sophie works for
a huge financial company. We have a nice house – nothing
too flashy, but it's in a fairly desirable area just on the
outskirts of town. We manage to have at least one nice
holiday a year and if we are careful we should pay off the
mortgage early. We married young, but it felt right. When I
met Sophie I just knew that we should be together, and we fit
together perfectly. Neither of us is massively ambitious or
passionate or mad for travelling or clubbing or anything like
that but I like to think we are happy. In fact I am sure some of
our friends think that we are positively boring in our

happiness. However, I prefer to think of us as settled, contented and comfortable. Not so comfortable that we have given up, you understand, or even that we take each other for granted. In fact, not a day goes by when I don't think how lucky I am or I forget to tell her that I love her. I think the whole fertility thing has been hard for her. Nowadays she doesn't say much about it, but I watch how her face falls every time a pram goes by or how she visibly stiffens when we are asked if we have children. It is not that people are cruel, but if they don't know they go right ahead and ask. And when I see her hurting, I suppose I hurt even more. I just want to make it right for her. It is different when you are a man though; we feel pain just the same but we learn to bury it deep inside of us, perhaps in the hope that without air or light it will just wither and finally disappear altogether. I watch her physically flinch when the baby thing is mentioned and I know that no matter how nice our curtains are or how exotic our annual holiday, she would give it all up in a heartbeat if she could just get pregnant.

First of all, when things seemed different, I wondered if it was the whole pregnancy thing again, you know, I wonder if she's thinking, 'well, here we are again, another Christmas without a baby,' so I tried again to talk her into seeing the fertility doctor. It seems to me that this is the only subject in the world that we argue about. Surely it wouldn't hurt to just go and talk to someone? It is glaringly obvious that this is not something that is going to happen by itself, and who knows why it hasn't happened? This is nobody's fault, this is not fate or because we don't deserve a child, it is not because we don't love each other enough or that this is some kind of divine retribution from God for something we did in the past. This is just life. And fertility problems seem to be on the rise, everyone seems to know someone who has had some kind of help to get pregnant. I read somewhere that maybe it's because huge amounts of women have been taking vast amounts of contraception for years, and then all of these drugs are then being passed into the sewage systems. Apparently all of these substances then just hang about and cannot be completely removed by the water treatment companies. The water is then returned as drinking water or sent back into rivers and streams. They say that some of the rivers in the world are now so polluted with drugs that male fish are changing sex! Very slowly we are unknowingly sterilizing whole populations of people. There was even an article in the paper the other day suggesting that certain types of ear phones should be classed as 'toxic to reproduction' because they contain phthalates, chemicals that have the ability to interfere with sexual development.

I remember we went to a dinner party once and met a couple who believed that infertility was linked to all the junk food we eat, and so for ages we tried to eat organically, avoiding E numbers, and chemicals, caffeine and mono-sodium glutamate. For months we didn't even look at a sausage or a frozen burger. And maybe they are right, maybe all this stuff that is added to make food look more wholesome and last longer is actually mucking up our systems. Or maybe it's something to do with global warming or the amount of mercury in salmon. But then maybe one of us has a medical issue. Perhaps we are overweight or underweight. There seem to be a thousand different reasons out there. Maybe a quick tamper with a stethoscope and an injection will sort the whole thing out and we will go on to have six children. You hear of it all the time, infertile couples that have treatment and then they have twins or triplets. They can even impregnate sixty-year-old women now. I don't know what she is so scared of, if we just went to see a doctor then at least we would know.

Sophie had just the saddest childhood (although you would never know). Her mother left when she was tiny, and she lived with her grandmother, who was as tough as old boots. I reckon if you sliced her open she had a core of solid steel or maybe even ice. When I think of my Sophie in that cold cold house there is a part of me that wants to grab her up and protect her. She is tougher than she looks though, that kind of upbringing would have really affected some people, but not Sophie, she is as sweet and as kind as anyone you could ever meet, but with a tenacity and resolve that you don't often see. If she sets her mind to something then there isn't much that will get in her way. She never really says much about her mother but she has one picture tucked away in a box, and every now and again she looks at it. I try and tell her that it can't be inherited, that it is not some congenital condition that has been stamped into her psyche. Then I look at her and I see the fear in her eyes, and on some days there is nothing I can say that can convince her that one day she wouldn't just up and leave her child.

I just can't quite work her out. Women, they can be a complete mystery. She doesn't seem ill or particularly worried about anything. She's definitely not pregnant, I know that for sure. She says work is OK and she has even taken up an evening class to study painting and a body pump class as well. And I love this about her, I love the way she sees each New Year as a fresh beginning. I watch her shed her old self as the old year disappears, and then I watch her start each New Year with a list of resolutions and declarations a mile long, of all the things she will do differently or change. But now, well, she seems so distant, and it is as if there is an ocean of space between us. She just seems so remote and almost vague. In fact, all over the Christmas period that would describe her perfectly, it is as if she is with me physically but her mind is a million miles away. We did all the usual stuff, we exchanged presents and we cooked Christmas dinner and all the time she seemed happy. She played with my nieces and chatted to family and at times she almost seemed to be the old Sophie again. We decorated the tree and went to church and watched the Queen's speech.

74

Everything was just the same but somehow it was different. She has recently bought some new clothes and maybe it's this new weight class, but she looks better than she ever has, in fact everyone has noticed. But somehow now, when we are together, when we are alone, I feel as though I am all by myself.

Today is Saturday, my favourite day of the week, we are halfway through January now and I am washing up after breakfast. After a week spent rushing around trying to get us both out to work on time, at the weekends we slow things down a bit. Sophie tends to make breakfast and then I wash up. I quite enjoy the tidying up part; I like to have everything back in its place and all spick and span. It doesn't take long and it gives Sophie some time to herself to shower, choose an outfit and do her hair, etc. Then we both go out, maybe into town or sometimes we will go walking or go and have lunch out in the country. The last few Saturdays have been different though.

Sophie was up and showered well before breakfast again this morning and she is going to meet up with some old friends in town; I think the plan is that they will shop today and then go and see a show. She wants to stay in town overnight so that they can go for a drink and something to eat after the show.

I think this is the third Saturday in a row that we have been apart. Sophie has become, over the last few years, my best friend and I try and ignore the nagging feeling of resentment. Ridiculous, I know. She works hard and I feel all at once selfish and self-centred for wanting her here with me. It will be nice for her to spend some time with her friends. I think there is some rugby on later and maybe I can catch up with some jobs around the house, maybe Pete will be up for a drink a little later. Well, the kitchen is tidy again. I stand at the sink and look out at the garden; we have a beautiful garden, a real haven. Pete has done a terrific job. It was quite pricey (considering it was supposed to be a mate's rate) but I lose hours just looking at it or wandering around tentatively touching flowers that seem to appear from nowhere. Even at this time of year, in the thick of winter, I still feel drawn. I should really try to get to grips with it myself, especially now that Sophie seems to want to spend more time with her friends.

I am still staring out at the white, frosted lawn when suddenly I see her. Sophie is outside, standing almost hidden to the side of the house. Her blonde hair is caught up in the breeze and I watch her struggle to control it while laughing with someone on the phone. She is talking animatedly, unaware that I am watching her. I wonder why she is not using the landline. I wait until she comes back in, her cheeks bright pink with the cold and her hair dishevelled.

'What on earth are you doing out there? It's freezing,' I chastise.

She looks at me and tries to flatten out her hair, 'Oh, I think there is something up with my phone, I keep losing the signal, and it is freezing!'

She puts her phone in her handbag and places the bag on the table in the hall and runs upstairs, probably to do her hair again. I don't know why but I walk into the hall, rummage through her handbag and pick up her phone. The signal indicator bars look fine. I can feel my heart beating. I press the green telephone key which will instantly bring up the number last dialled. Amanda2 the display reads. I flick the display back and shake my head. Those two, I don't know what they find to talk about, they are together every day for work then they do all these classes together. Women. I am relieved despite myself. I am not really sure what I was expecting to see, it's just that she has been acting so strange lately. Can't believe it actually crossed my mind that there might be someone else! Sophie would never do that. I shake my head; maybe I'm the one with the problem. It's not until she has gone and several hours later, that I realize that I forgot to ask her why she didn't use the landline. Why stand outside in the freezing cold with a mobile when you could just as easily use the phone in the hall?

Chapter 7

Sophie

'Love is merely madness.'
Shakespeare

I usually hate January and February. I despise the cold, damp, grey days when it doesn't snow but feels like it should. I don't know which month is more tiresome. January, I think, when everyone is fed up after Christmas. Work is also usually a nightmare, with the team trying to build up some enthusiasm to start on their business plans and all of our clients wanting meetings in the first week back. Amanda always tries to give up smoking in January and spends the first week back at work practically biting my head off every two seconds, so that I am virtually praying for her to light up again, anything to restore some peace. Each year she has tried a different method: hypnotism (twice), patches (three times now), gum, boiled sweets and meditation. This year she tried some herbal concoction from the Chinese medicine shop that she had to drink three times a day. That lasted all of a day. In fact, I think she abandoned it at lunchtime.

Then there is the annual conference, which is always in January as well. It tends to be at some really nice swanky hotel. Which all sounds great but company policy is that only the consultants are allowed to go. So Amanda usually swans off leaving me festering in the office making sure all the clients are happy. The office is just dead when they all go and it is made all the worse because you know they are off having a great time while us admin staff get left behind, fending off anxious and complaining clients and sorting out all the boring things the consultants should have finished before they left. It really is dismal. February is usually a little better, and at least you can count the days away until Valentine's Day, when you know the evenings and the mornings will start to get a little lighter. There is something depressing and unnatural about going to work in the dark and then getting home in the dark, day after day after day.

This year was different though, this year I had a different reason for looking forward to the fourteenth. It was our first Valentine's Day together. Over the years I had long forgotten the thrill of receiving illicit gifts covered in hearts or sending carefully selected love tokens. I had forgotten the delicious excitement of knowing that you are the object of someone's affections. And somehow, knowing that nobody knows, and that it is our secret makes it even more thrilling. When I got to the office I found a single red rose, tied with a satin ribbon and placed on my desk, on top of my diary. In one of my desk drawers, hidden beneath the multitude of stationery and envelopes there were heart-shaped chocolates, and in another drawer a card. Everyone just assumed that the rose was from Simon and a few of the girls commented on how romantic Simon was to have gone to so much trouble. They assumed that he had bought the rose and done some deal with security to get them to hide this stuff all over my work station. I smiled and nodded, agreeing that Simon really was very sweet, but inside I was bursting with excitement. I couldn't look at Gareth just in case I gave the game away. All morning I just fizzled with anticipation, wishing the minutes and hours away until we could be together again. And it really didn't matter that we couldn't meet that night, because right now every night we get to spend together is like Valentine's night. And for the next few days, every time I looked at my beautiful rose with its velvety petals slowly unfurling, I smiled, and not only because he loves me. I am sure that this happiness (although to describe how I feel as happy seems quite lame, really, as I am jubilant, blissful and ecstatic) is something to do with the fact that in this magical time that we have spent together, like my rose, I have opened up as well. I feel as though I am blossoming, becoming the person I always thought that I could be. And I am trusting and loving someone for the first time in my life without reservation, loving him wholly and utterly. And for us to be together on Valentine's Day, well, it would have been wrong, and Simon would have definitely become suspicious.

All that evening when I was out with Simon I thought of Gareth. If he had turned up unannounced and uninvited I don't think I would have been surprised at all. I would have been quite sure that I had conjured him up, that somehow my soul, bereft without him on this night of lovers, had left my body and gone out into the night to search for him. There were times that I tried so hard not to think, not to imagine his evening without me. I didn't want to think of him at some candle-lit restaurant with her, or think of him at home with her, slowly undressing her, making love to her. Instead I concentrated my efforts on Simon, dutifully playing the role that I accepted so long ago. I watched almost detached as we both slipped effortlessly into character once more. Our body language comfortable and our lines considered, as we moved sedately through the evening. I can't even say that I felt uncomfortable, constantly aware that our relationship had become a pretence or a sham. Instead, I was aware of how easy it all was, like a practised charade or a well-worn performance. And I wonder how we managed to typecast each other like this. How both Simon and I could have become so confident in our parts that we stopped imagining that either of us would ever want to try out for something different.

It is not always easy though. I have actually made myself physically sick thinking of them together. I torture myself with visions of what she looks like, of how they look together. I imagine her with him, touching him, caressing him, loving him. And I have to stop myself before I go quite mad. It is worse at night when I lie awake, not able to sleep, tossing and turning, wondering whether he is sleeping or whether he is thinking about me too. I know that Gareth told me that the physical side of their relationship died years ago but I still can't help but torture myself. I wonder how she expects to keep a man like Gareth trapped in a loveless marriage. Does she really think that he will stay with her just because they have a couple of kids?

About a month ago Amanda and I finished a client meeting early and I went home 'to write up minutes' and I couldn't resist, I just wanted to see where he lived, perhaps get a glimpse of her even. So I drove to his address, thinking that I could park the car and perhaps unobtrusively observe the house and maybe spot her with the children. But when I got there I found that he lives in a very small cul de sac and, apart from private driveways, there was hardly anywhere to even turn round let alone park unnoticed. So the only sighting I got that afternoon was of the house as I reversed. And it seems like a nice house, the garden appeared tended and the windows looked clean. But there were no real clues as to their life together. I don't really know what I was expecting or hoping for, perhaps obvious signs of her neglecting her housewifely duties as well as her marital ones. I desperately wanted indications of obvious slovenliness, perhaps a filthy front porch, overgrown garden or copious litter. I wanted to catch her looking shabby with bad hair and a thick midriff, shuffling around in slippers and an ill-fitting tracksuit. I think maybe I wanted to find reasons to despise her, to ease my jealousy perhaps. I am usually quite even-natured and I can't really think of too many people that I really dislike. But here I am feeling an almost intense hatred of someone I have never met, someone whom by rights I should pity. And I wish I could say that I felt bad about what we are doing but I don't. It is as if my conscience has taken leave.

Whenever Gareth and I go out I can't help but look around us. I watch the other couples dining together to see how we stack up. I watch the obvious newly-weds in wonder of each other, discussing the menu and their life plans, holding hands and each other's hearts almost shyly. And then there is always the couple who struggle to say two words to each other, hard pressed to even make eye contact, as if even speaking to each other has become too much of an effort and breathing the same air stifling. They simply eat and then leave, seemingly stuck in some parallel universe that they are not strong enough to leave or overcome. Gareth and I have always said that we would shoot each other rather than become like that. But then, deep down, I worry that perhaps it is inevitable that after spending a lifetime practising and trying hard to attain the perfect relationship, you lose spontaneity, maybe you stop laughing when you have heard all his jokes a thousand times before and you think that that trick that he does with the fork, the spoon and the cocktail stick is not amazing any more, just mundane. When does the world of new lovers start losing its colour, its passion, its glory? And how do you retain that first flush of romance? The heady, exhilarating, dizzy brilliance of those early days.

I have examined my memory, trying to think back to any time when I can honestly say I was swept away by Simon. And I don't think I ever was. There was never this heart-stopping passion that Gareth and I have. In fact I have never before felt so complete. So it is not that I had all this before and I just let it go. I didn't stand by and watch our love and our marriage slip through my fingers like sand. And I know now that I am not fickle, not inconsistent in my affections. And after all these years of trying to conjure a love and a passion from what I now recognize was only ever a friendship, I understand that perhaps I just married the wrong man and that is not his fault or my fault, it is just life. So, with this new appreciation and understanding, I have stopped worrying that at some point I will look at Gareth and take that glint in his eye and that heart-stopping smile for granted. I know that there will never come a time when I will listen to his voice and not feel shivers up and down my spine. I know that whenever he kisses that special place on my neck it will always feel as though my brain has melted and slipped out of my ear. In fact, I know now in all certainty that this isn't some obtuse crush and that I am in love with him. Head over heels, rapturously and euphorically in love with him. Every little bit of him.

So this year I have hardly noticed the cold or the rain or grey skies above me. It's as though being with Gareth has changed everything. I live for our times together and can't wait to see him. At the office we slip away unseen at every opportunity. We volunteered to work on a 'project' reviewing business opportunities in our local area, so it is easy for us to just sneak off together. Sometimes we just talk but I don't think there are many places left now that we haven't christened. I have got it so bad now that I hate being away from him. Five minutes can seem like an hour when he is absent. I struggle now to remember what my life was like before we were together, how I managed to get through each day, and live through each monotonous year. And we have started talking about the future. Our future. About being together and leaving our old lives behind us and starting again. We have talked about us both getting a divorce and getting married, perhaps in the Lake District with just some close friends with us.

We have also talked about having children and how sweet our babies would be. One day we were talking and Gareth was telling me about a friend of his whose wife had trouble conceiving. Apparently after having acupuncture and reflexology she fell pregnant within weeks. She now has three children without IVF or surgery or anything. I was so excited when he told me that I couldn't wait to get home. I went straight on to the internet to see what information I could find. I was amazed to see that something like sixty per cent of the infertile women surveyed went on to have completely normal pregnancies after having acupuncture. I just couldn't believe that I had never heard about this before. When I rang to make the appointment I was shaking with excitement. I actually booked to see a holistic practitioner, someone who specializes in alternative health as well as acupuncture, and on our very first meeting she told me that she thought she might be able to help. She examined me and then sat me down and explained. She told me that my Qi was blocked. She explained that Qi was the flow of energy around my body and that when the body's energy path is blocked all sorts of problems could occur, infertility being just one of many. And I think from the moment she said she could help me I started to cry, huge sploshy tears from so many years and months of pent-up, repressed emotion. And instead of handing me a tissue she held me and comforted me while I wept, and afterwards she told me that it was a reaction she saw often and that she understood how isolating infertility could be.

She gave me lots of information in the first couple of sessions and I learned that your energy paths could be blocked by trauma, stress or imbalances within your body but, most importantly, that this could be cured. Every session left me feeling drained emotionally but empowered as well. And we really got on well together; she advised me on nutrition and diet and recommended that I take up Yoga.

And the treatment was actually not painful at all. The needles looked quite scary, they were thin and hollow and very long, but I actually came out feeling wonderful, not sore at all. Even when she inserted one into my head I just felt relaxed, really peaceful. And now? Well, now I feel stronger, more alive somehow. I no longer feel so anxious about the whole pregnancy thing either. For the first time ever I have even started to think about adopting. I am sure Gareth would consider adoption. I could imagine that he would love any child; he is such an amazing person with an enormous capacity to love. In fact we have talked about this a lot and Gareth has told me that it really doesn't worry him in the slightest that I don't seem to be able to have children. This to me is just so refreshing. I really do feel as though a weight has been lifted.

And it is as if sex is fun again. I have even been sleeping with Simon. It isn't that Simon has been pressuring me. In fact quite the opposite, but I think he would start to get suspicious if I ignored him totally. At the moment he really hasn't got a clue and I need to keep this quiet for a little longer yet. I need to buy time, I need to stay until Gareth and I are both ready to be together. It's strange but Simon doesn't even mention us having children now. It's kind of been swept under the carpet along with any other discrepancies he might have noticed. I guess he must be a bit relieved that he no longer has to put up with my monthly tantrums and moods. But even though he doesn't say anything about the baby any more I can tell there is something worrying him; it doesn't seem to be work and he won't talk about it, but it's there all the same. Like a large grey elephant sitting on the couch between us.

In February Gareth and I managed to get away for a long weekend and we stayed up in London. On the Saturday we went shopping and then went to see a show in the evening. We woke up late the next day and just never got up. We ordered room service all day, watched old movies and porn and just relaxed. And I have never felt so loved. He really is addictive; the scary thing is that this doesn't seem at all wrong any more. Gareth has found this great chain of member-only hotels called Club Quarters. And it is just like joining a private members' club. You elect which hotel you want to use and then everything is done over the internet. Each member is then given a card for entry and the whole thing is uncomplicated, tasteful and discreet. The desk has all Gareth's information so there is no standing around posing as Mr and Mrs Smith or embarrassing form-filling. Even better there is no chance that his wife could turn up unexpectedly (always my nightmare) because without a key card she can't even get into the reception. It really is perfect. We chose the London Gracechurch because it is so central, right near the Tower of London and a stone's throw from Monument tube. And it really is a gorgeous old building; it used to be the Hong Kong and Shanghai bank so it has all that lovely Edwardian architecture, and a great bar. Surely it doesn't get any better. We try and go there at least four times a month now. It is bliss; I get there and never want to leave, it is like our secret hideaway. The awful thing is that I really have turned out to be such a natural adulterer. I find that I have become accustomed and adept at deceit. I am ashamed to say that I can now look Simon straight in the eye and mislead and deceive him. It is so easy to think up reasons why I need to stay away for the night. And not once has he questioned me. I tell myself that any dishonesty is unfortunately a necessary evil. It would be irresponsible to just leave Simon without even knowing Gareth properly. And if Simon doesn't know, how can it possibly hurt him?

In March we stayed in London for four nights in a row. I told Simon that we had a series of presentations to do and Amanda was on hand to back us up if anything went wrong or Simon became suspicious. And now our whole affair has taken on a routine, we see each other on regular nights of the week, and I tell Simon that I am working late or doing a class. Gareth has a friend called Luke who is also a great alibi. He has a girlfriend as well (in addition to his wife) so sometimes we meet up in London for dinner and drinks. On these nights it is very easy to believe that we don't have other lives, other partners or obligations. We exist in our own time only, pursuing hedonistic pleasures and our own version of happiness within our own manufactured rules. And we are not hurting anyone; we are just flouting the rules until we are ready to make our move. Sometimes I get home looking obviously dishevelled but Simon never questions me. Very occasionally I imagine that he looks a little sad, but that is just me being ridiculous, as there is no way he has any idea of what is going on. Anyway, Gareth has me well versed in what to say if he ever confronts or accuses me. He says that we have to deny, deny, deny.

We have started going back to Gareth's house at lunch-time. No more skulking around in the street for me, oh no, now I just walk brazenly through the front door. We shag on their bed. At first it seemed weird but now I think Gareth is right – what she doesn't know can't possibly hurt her. And Gareth really gets off on it. It's a real turn on for him. I think he likes the thought that she could come in at any moment and catch us. And we have nearly been caught twice. But each time we've got away with it. The first time she came home early and I escaped out of the kitchen door and into the back garden. I had to wait for nearly forty minutes in the garden shed before Gareth was able to come and get me. The second time she walked in on us. We had only been in the house for about ten minutes and luckily we were still dressed so Gareth spun her a line about picking up some paperwork to take to a client meeting. Afterwards, when we were sure that she had left, we shagged like rabbits, not quite able to believe how we managed to get away with it, because for a moment I really thought we had been caught. Something about the way she looked at me, I could have sworn she was suspicious, but perhaps it was just that the whole meeting was so awkward and embarrassing.

Honestly, Gareth is so turned on by the idea of getting caught that we have taken the whole thing a step further. First of all he thought it might be fun to invite Simon and me for dinner. He thinks it would be hilarious having to keep a straight face through dinner whilst playing footsie with me under the table. I thought he was joking but now I'm not so sure. He seems really keen on meeting Simon. The thought of him laughing and lording it up behind Simon's back seems quite cruel really and I told him that I wasn't sure. I told him that the whole dinner party thing felt wrong. After all, this is not about hurting other people, it is supposed to be about us. But he wouldn't leave it. And so now Simon and I are going to attend an Easter party at his house. I must say I feel sick already.

Meeting her was a shock, too. Far from being the drab, apathetic, downtrodden housewife I had imagined she was actually quite pretty and tall as well. She really seemed nice and scarily she appeared to be quite affectionate towards Gareth. I think I physically recoiled when she hugged him. But later, when she had left, Gareth said that it was all for show and I shouldn't be fooled. Basically, he said, she would do anything to maintain her lifestyle and that when they are alone together they hardly speak. I think it must be so strange and so sad to put on a show like that every single day, but then I guess she couldn't really get away with publicly shunning him, that would be just too awful. I couldn't help thinking how little self respect she must have to live like that. How awful to depend on someone so completely because you are not strong enough to face the world alone. She lives a lie just so that she can have a facial and her nails done once a week.

Chapter 8

Gareth

'Any fool can tell the truth but it requires a man of some sense to know how to lie well.'
Samuel Butler

Easter weekend already! The year is just flying by. The weather has taken a turn for the better and it is a gorgeous 'anything could happen' kind of day. I have just finished my morning run and I couldn't feel better. Everything is going well and the first quarter at work really surpassed all my expectations. I stretch out slowly and think about the last few months. I am loving my job right now, and I am already making a name for myself with a few new business wins. Soon it will be time to start introducing a few of my previous clients and I will be recognized by all as the sales god that of course I am. I can't help grinning when I think about how gullible the company are. It is all about knowing how to work the system. The whole thing with Amanda turned out to be just a storm in a teacup as well, thank God and although I see her watching me closely, almost curiously sometimes, I think I have won her round with my natural charm – had to bend the truth a little as well, of course, but it all turned out for the best in the end. A rather lucky escape there, I think. I still reckon she would be a great shag though, but hard work, really high maintenance and frankly there is far easier sport to be had currently. I also can't shake the feeling that you might just find her one night watering cress seeds into your carpet and shredding your suits. She might even boil the bloody hamster (we don't have a rabbit) in that scary psycho kind of way. Maybe she is best left alone; sometimes you just have to trust your instincts on these things and she really is the kind of bird you don't want to get on the wrong side of.

Amazingly Amanda has absolutely no idea about my sideline activity with Sophie, which is just perfect. I think she still has suspicions about the Christmas party but both Sophie and I have denied everything. It really is quite astonishing that no one has noticed a thing; sometimes I think it must be obvious to the whole world when we are together. It never ceases to amaze me how people see only what they want to see. After our little dalliance in the car park, Amanda would never want to think that I could have moved on to her best mate. Women attach too much emotion to the whole thing, they just don't get it. The whole thing with Sophie (which just seems to get better and better, by the way) would come as quite a shock now to Amanda, so it has all worked out superbly. And Sophie is just so sweet and trusting, she would never question me. She honestly believes that I have only ever been unfaithful once before! But for all that innocence she is proving to be quite the diversion, wonderfully insatiable; we just can't get enough of each other at the moment. Sophie will have me just about anywhere, I swear. Dirty little minx as well. I smile to myself as I remember the stationery cupboard, various offices at work and the fire escape. We are so going to get caught if we are not more careful. She is such a little tease. Sometimes I think we both push it more than we should and we are dreadful at egging each other on. I can understand the whole Bonnie and Clyde thing now; there is definitely an excitement, a feeling that anything is possible when we are together. Sophie is a good laugh as well, really easy to be around; if I didn't have the boys I could almost imagine trading Suzie in.

I smile as I hear Suzie downstairs rolling boiled eggs around in paint with the boys. We have around twenty-five people coming over this afternoon and somehow she is not fazed by this at all. I walk downstairs and look around; the house looks amazing. There are spring flowers everywhere and the sun is streaming in through the windows. I stretch and yawn, suppose I should ask whether anything needs doing, although I know that Suzie worked most of yesterday preparing food and stuff. We invited all of my team as well as some close friends and some people Suzie works with for a barbecue. Amanda will be here with her hubby Pete (quite curious about him – apparently they are real opposites) along with Sophie and Simon, and some of the admin team are coming along with all their children. Must say I am quite pysched up about meeting the competition this afternoon, although not sure that he is really much of a rival – Simon must be pretty dim not to realize his wife is being shagged stupid at every possible opportunity. We are out together most nights of the week now, for goodness' sake, how can he not be suspicious? Yep, it will be quite an interesting afternoon. I think you can tell an awful lot just by checking out people's body language and the way they interact around each other. Sometimes you can learn more from non-verbal cues than you can from what people say. Every good salesman knows that it's all about gesture, posture, facial expression and eye movements. I will soon have him sussed. By the end of the afternoon I will have a pretty good idea how much he means to her as well. I wonder how many times I could feel her up before he notices.

People start arriving around 12.00 and my best mate and his wife turn up around 1.00 ish. I met Luke about ten years ago at some corporate bash at a real ale festival. Dreadful venue. Not being real ale lovers the whole thing was a complete wash-out. Some really odd characters hang out at these places as well; they all seem to have very long beards, ruddy cheeks, bulbous noses and beer bellies (and that was just the women) – enough to put you off real ale for life. All that and not a decent Cabernet anywhere. Luke and I soon hit it off and disappeared off to find something respectable to drink, somewhere with a bit of atmosphere. We found a great wine bar and got stuck in. We got on like a house on fire, both of us ended up missing the last train home and crashing in a hotel in London for the night with a couple of game hairdressers from Southend. Completely random. The great thing about Luke is, he is always game for a laugh and we are right there on the same wavelength. He is probably one of the only people on this earth I really trust. Always manages to have a great bit of skirt on his arm too. If all men are wolves, well, this guy could lead the pack, if you know what I mean. And then of course there's his wife, Rebecca. Nice enough, nice looking, kind of blondish hair, nice figure, not a real looker but there is definitely something about her. She used to be so sweet but then as soon as he got a ring on her finger she changed – almost overnight. And despite my many charms she hates my guts, well, I guess you can't win them all. And reading between the lines I think I'm perhaps a little too close to her Luke for her liking. Some women are like that, really possessive, would do anything to stop Luke going out and having a laugh. She's a little bit too prim and proper nowadays for my taste. She is always suspicious and asking questions as well. They have two children, a boy and a girl, very sweet, a lot younger than our two. And luckily they take after Luke's side of the family. Luke always falls on his feet though, over the years he has done quite well for himself, you know, nice house with a bit of land around it and he loves his cars. Always has a couple of sporty numbers in the garage, a hot car is always a real babe magnet.

Suzie has arranged an enormous Easter egg hunt around the garden and the house with hopefully enough eggs to go around. There is a more difficult hunt for the older children, with well-devised clues and all the eggs out of reach of the little ones. The smaller children have their own hunt, no clues, just a mad scramble to grab as many eggs as they can. Should be fun, hope the weather holds out. Can't believe that it won't, it is really hot now. The dog is lolling in the shade and breathing heavily. His large pink tongue is listlessly hanging out the side of his mouth and he looks exhausted already. There is a gang of children around him trying to coax him into playing ball but I think he's done for. I throw the kids a bag of sweets and tell them to go and play and let the poor hound have a break. I swear he looks grateful as he pounds his tail on the cool concrete and lays his head back down. I look around and check things out, everyone seems happy and the barbecue is lit. Luckily there are enough people here for me to give Suzie a wide berth. I mentioned to Sophie that we weren't all that close. I mean, we're not really, not compared to how Sophie and I are. But I imagine that I may have to smooth things over with Sophie a little if she sees Suzie and me together too much. As usual a huddle of guys have all congregated around the barbecue, drinking beer and occasionally turning sausages and the like. I wander off, wine bottle in hand to do my good host thing and make sure all the ladies have enough to drink. Beats me why anyone would want to hang out with all those hairy, lager-drinking blokes when you can have a decent glass of wine and spend some time with the lovely ladies. After all, it's not as if the girls want to spend time talking together, a man in the middle just spices the whole thing up.

I find myself cornered and talking to the wife of someone that Suzie works with. She has the most vividly highlighted auburn hair I think I have ever seen, vibrant streaks of gold and red and even pink sparkle artificially in the afternoon sun. Veronica or Vivienne, I think she's called. Well, whoever she is, she has an amazing outfit on, accented with quite eclectic but eccentric jewellery. She is a very tall woman as well, and it is really quite disconcerting to meet a woman who can look you in the eye. How the hell are you supposed to dominate someone like that? She looks like a bloody gladiator. I stand back slightly to give myself some space. She is quite broad around the middle now but was probably quite stunning in her youth. The more I look at her though the more I think that her youth was probably a very long time ago now. I try and concentrate as she describes her recent holiday but find my attention is diverted by her ambitiously painted fingernails, and my growing anxiety to see Sophie. I glance over at the door again for what seems like the hundredth time but still there is no sign of her. I take a swig of my wine and try to calm my nervousness but even after a few deep breaths the butterflies in my stomach are still turning cartwheels. How does she manage to do this, I wonder? It is always the same, she gets me as jumpy as a horsefly and it happens every time I know I am going to see her. We talked for ages about whether she should even come this afternoon; about how wise (or unwise) it would be for Suzie and Simon to meet and even whether it was prudent for Sophie and Suzie to meet at all. Sophie spent ages trying to tell me about the things I should and shouldn't say to Simon when we did encounter each other. I remember nodding and promising to say all the right things but, to tell you the truth, I'm really not that bothered, I mean, it's not as if I am trying to be his mate or anything, I just want to shag his wife. I try and tune back into the conversation with Violet (or was it Vera?) but find I have become mesmerized with her teeth, which are beginning to look stained by the red wine she is drinking. Her voice is forcefully jolly and overly loud and I am starting to think that before long her teeth will match her hair, when thankfully we are joined by Suzie, who sends me off to check on the food and I am saved from any further conversation. Then, I see them arrive, Amanda and Pete and Sophie and Simon, all together.

As I head across the lawn (not towards them, doesn't do to look too eager), I notice that Suzie has seen them arrive as well and is heading over towards them. I am intercepted by Viv, one of our admin girls, and as I pour her some more wine I realize it is taking all my strength not to look over at them, not to stare and gape and gawk at Sophie. It feels like a week since I saw her last, was it really only yesterday?

I sort out the food and then amble over to them, I greet the girls with a polite peck and shake hands and exchange pleasantries with the guys. Simon is a lot taller than I had imagined but otherwise he has that rather serious, geeky look about him, at least he doesn't have a beer belly or bad breath or anything. I notice his hands; they are office worker's hands with short, clean fingernails. He is wearing jeans and loafers and a rather nice Cartier watch. Not what I was expecting at all, had him down for being without taste as well as without spine. All the time he is talking to me I realize that he is appraising me as well. Nothing blatant but it is happening as we speak, very covert, a surreptitious examination of each other, man to man. I must say I am surprised to notice how sincere he looks, he is thanking me for inviting them and it feels a little strange to hear another man speak on behalf of Sophie. My Sophie, I think gloatingly.

Pete, on the other hand, is another story completely. With a slightly off-line nose and cauliflower ears this man was obviously a contact sport junkie at some point in his life and I am thinking more of rugby or perhaps boxing than any karate or judo. He has definitely been on the rough end of a scrum once or twice, I think. He has a very powerful handshake, and despite the thinning brown hair, this is a man who is confident in his own skin, happy with his lot. I have to contain a snigger as I can't help thinking that he

95

looks almost horizontal compared to Amanda who, despite the surroundings, is talking animatedly on the phone whilst trying to locate a car for Max in her bag and hold a glass of wine at the same time. Pete sees me looking over and immediately grabs Max up and holding him upside down introduces him. Max, who is as fair as both Amanda and Pete are dark, giggles and wiggles to be put down. As soon as his feet touch the ground he is off at pace to join the other children. Amanda sighs with relief, turns her phone off and smiles for the first time.

'I have decided that I am not answering the phone any more as people are just stupid today,' she declares as she swigs heavily on her wine and chucks her phone into the depths of her handbag. I have almost ignored Sophie to the point where the side of my jaw has started to ache with the effort of smiling politely. But as she talks to Amanda about Max I feel I have a reason to look at her. As we make eye contact for the first time she falters mid-sentence, blushes and hurriedly looks away. She looks beautiful. Correction, I think she *is* beautiful. Maybe as you get to know someone and find out about who they really are they become more attractive. I notice that despite the heat of the day she looks a little strained, she is very pale and she has the ghost of shadows beneath her eyes. I am sure it is just the strain of the day but can't wait to get her on her own. I am sure we could sneak away upstairs for a shag even if it is in one of the bathrooms. I have this urgent need to possess her, stamp my mark all over her. There are so many people here now that I am sure we wouldn't be missed.

All at once she looks straight at me and I can't stop myself. I ask her if she is OK. She nods and I tell her that she looks a little tired. She nods again and just tells me that she didn't sleep too well last night. She seems ill at ease, apprehensive. I watch her lower her eyes and turn in conversation to Amanda. It is as I watch her that I become aware that Simon is looking at me with the strangest expression on his face. I turn to him but he is already walking away towards the food, striding purposefully across the lawn. But as he walks he suddenly turns and looks at me, and for a moment I think I see his eyes narrow, but it is just a moment, and it could have been the sun in his eyes or maybe he got a pain somewhere, because in a blink of an eye he is smiling again.

I shake my head to dispel any guilt-induced paranoia I am feeling. Why should I feel guilty? If he was a better husband she wouldn't have to go shagging other men. After all, I myself am managing to keep two women quite happy at the moment. I don't see Suzie making any complaints. I walk over to Luke and Rebecca. Becky has the baby on her lap and after passing some pleasantries about how adorable the baby is and how much she looks like Luke (and she does as well, it is quite freaky), I manage to take Luke off to the end of the garden for a chat. We take a cigar each and wander off companionably.

'You lucky bastard,' he laughs, grinning from ear to ear. I laugh and we high-five each other, and I smile again at the understanding we have. After much back-slapping we return to the party and I notice that Sophie is standing alone outside the kitchen. I go inside and happily discover the room empty.

'Meet me in five in the study,' I whisper.

She giggles. 'You are nuts! We are *so* going to get caught.'

'You know that's exactly what makes me want you even more,' I whisper back as I start to head for the study.

After around five minutes she follows me in and hurriedly shuts the door behind her. I am relieved to see her flushed and happy after her earlier pallor. I am hiding around the corner and so she can't immediately see me, and when I suddenly appear I swear she almost jumps out of her skin. We both collapse into each other's arms giggling like children. I smooth her hair away from her face and kiss her deeply. We make love in a hasty, passionate flurry against the desk and then against the wall, and then I kiss her again and again. Suddenly I want everyone to just go and leave the two of us alone. But even as the words telling her not to go form on my lips she leaves me, sneaking back out and back into the sunshine. I run my hands through my hair and sit down at the desk. I have all of five minutes' peace to find composure, when at least ten children fighting over a piece of paper come bowling in, loudly searching for Easter eggs. I smile and leave them to it, smiling in wonder at the innocence and exuberance of them. Mind you, if they had come in just a couple of minutes earlier their innocence may just have been tainted somewhat.

Outside hordes of children are running everywhere. I try and stay out of their way and make my way over to Amanda, who is looking very relaxed under a tree. I go and sit down with her and we talk about work. I can just tell that she still wants me. As soon as she has had a drink she starts to talk about sex. A sure sign. But she is stopped as Rebecca joins us. I introduce them and I can tell that Becky thinks that I am up to no good. I laugh inwardly; she is way off the mark, but I lean a little closer to Amanda just to wind her up. She looks at me through calculating narrowed eyes as she asks (actually it is more like interrogation) Amanda how we know each other. Amanda, who is clueless, chats away amiably, but somehow still manages to peer at me in that 'come get me' kind of way. I swear the more she drinks the saucier she gets or maybe that's just me. This undercurrent of sexual tension is not missed by Becky, who pointedly pulls Suzie into the conversation and continues to glare at me meaningfully. Sharp as a tack is Becky, so consistent is her belief that I represent everything that is objectionable and repugnant in the male species that I swear she has made it her lifelong ambition to find proof that I am the aberration she believes me to be. Sad really, as actually I am what every red-blooded male wishes they could be. Sanctimonious bitch. She wouldn't be quite so confident if she knew about Luke's activities. In fact he makes me look like an amateur.

Around 5.00 pm, Simon comes over with Sophie, who is now gently sunkissed with grass all over her skirt, and tells me that they really should go as he has to fly off for some business trip the next day. He elaborates slightly, explaining that he received an email last night instructing him to go to Hong Kong as one of his colleagues was unexpectedly taken ill. I listen politely not taking in any other details apart from the fact that he will be away for most of the week. Fantastic. I daren't look at Sophie. I shake his hand and look him straight in the eye. He holds my gaze and I thank him and Sophie for coming, he leans over to kiss Suzie goodbye, and all the while I am trying to catch Sophie's attention. I fail miserably and have to watch and wave goodbye as Simon leads Sophie away from the house to the car. I think of our earlier fumblings and smile. Looks like my little Sophie mouse will have a chance to play while the cat's away. I lean against the door jamb relaxed and happy, planning our next meeting. I am feeling hard again already.

Chapter 9

Amanda

'Love is all we need of heaven and all we need of hell.'
Emily Dickinson

Don't you just hate blue alcohol? Seemed like a great idea when we got here, they serve it in huge glass jugs with frozen frosted glasses, really nice until you try and stand up and then, when you try walking, you find that somehow your knees have been replaced with some strange effervescent material, making standing up and walking quite a challenge indeed. I find that I actually have to think carefully about just putting one foot in front of the other. Could be time to go soon, I think. I weave my way to the ladies, trying to look as sober and as upright as possible. I look over to the lavatory signs and realize that I am going to have to negotiate at least one flight of stairs. I take a deep breath and will some energy into my limbs. They feel very heavy all of a sudden. Heavy and fizzy? I hear my heels clicking on the wooden floors and the sound seems like it's coming from somewhere far away. I really am in trouble. I giggle with the effort of being sensible and stifle a hiccup, God, I hate the hiccups. They seem so childish and girly, definitely not befitting my image as strong, successful career woman. Shouldn't you grow out of hiccups, sort of like ringlets, skipping and sucking your thumb? Oh, there I go again. I hold my breath and hope that they will stop soon. I make my way up the wooden stairs. Sophie and I have found a nice trendy wine bar in the city to celebrate the success of our latest business win. It was quite out of the blue, the company is a referral and have actually asked to work with me. It is a large company, a household name and will look very nice on my portfolio, thank you very much. Even better the fee will complete my target for the rest of the year so I should be able to slow up a bit and start taking things a little easier. Perhaps I can spend some quality time with Max.

I make my way gingerly back to our table where Sophie is looking annoyingly sober. She is driving later so has managed to be really good and keep to the minimum. Did I really drink most of that jug of blue stuff? Dreadful the way they hide these frankly lethal beverages under the cover of harmless looking blue slush that tastes completely innocuous. Shouldn't be allowed. No wonder all these kids nowadays have drink problems, I think, as I sit down and pour myself some water. That should do it.

'I'm having an affair,' says Sophie.

'What?' I'm not quite sure I heard her, maybe that drink is affecting my hearing as well. I take another long draught of water.

'No, really, I am. I'm having an affair.' This time her face has reddened and I can hear the tension in her voice. 'With Gareth,' she says.

And all of a sudden I feel as though I am falling and from somewhere that seems a long way away I hear her pleading with me not to say anything and telling me that she loves him.

Time passes and I just listen and stare, listen and stare. At some point I realize that I am now completely sober. No fizzing or hiccupping, all that has melted away in the face of this news. I am all at once careful not to say the wrong thing and confused at the feelings coursing through me. She tells me that it started at Christmas and that no one must know and that she has never felt this way before. She speaks honestly and wistfully as she describes a whorl of feelings that, like a tornado, have sucked her in, until she feels helpless and stripped of any defences. And while she is talking I am just looking at her, at this person who now seems a stranger. She is almost lit up as she speaks, and all I can think of is how that wily, womanizing egotist must be laughing.

We talk and talk and she pleads with me to forgive her for not telling me sooner. I tell her that I understand but in reality, I don't, I just can't understand how you can live a lie like that. And she must have lied to me over the last five months. And then it dawns on me. Five months. Incredulously this has been going on for five months. I think of Simon and the times he has phoned to see if she was with me. I think of the times that I have told him that I thought she had an aerobics or painting class. An unknowing alibi, why did I tell him I knew where she was? And then I realise it is because that is where she had told me she was. The level of her duplicity hits me and again I stare at her as she tells me that he loves her, that they are considering absconding together (she actually said running away) and starting their own family. He has told her that they would have beautiful children together.

'But he has beautiful children,' I say, 'do you not remember? You've met them, and his wife as well. What about Suzie?' I say in desperation to make her stop and think about the other lives around them that will be destroyed by their dishonesty.

'You don't understand, just let me explain,' she says.

'They don't really love each other any more, they are more or less just friends now and they stay together for the children. If he left maybe she would find someone, who knows, maybe she already has?' I look at her astonished, gullibility was always one of Sophie's foibles but this time she has been reeled in like a sucker.

102

'You can't honestly believe that,' I say in complete amazement. 'I can't believe that he has fed you all that "we are not really in love" crap. Did he tell you that she doesn't understand him as well?' I snap. 'How can you do this to Simon? He will be devastated,' I spit. 'And do you honestly think he will be faithful to you, with his track record? Or wait, I bet he told you it was different this time,' I finish.

'He told me all about his affair, it was such a long time ago, and Gareth and Suzie were on a break then anyway.' She says this coolly, as if rehearsed, as if she was expecting me to bring this up. 'And all that stuff you heard from your mate, well, that is all second-hand industry gossip anyway, you don't know him like I do,' she continues. And then, for good measure, she adds, 'It doesn't matter what he has done in the past, it will be different now. Maybe he was just looking for the right person.'

I shiver with foreboding as I remember the conversation that Gareth and I had that night before Christmas about how he thought that his previous affair was the one. And for the next hour I hear about their many trysts and assignations, and I hear about his declarations of love and how happy she is.

Later on we go our separate ways and I sit on a train, I stare out of the window, watching the fields and the trees whizz by, tunelessly serenaded by the rhythmic clatter of the train on its tracks. I sway with the motion, unconsciously trying to avoid bodily contact with the woman next to me. I swallow but my mouth is filled with a bitter, acerbic taste and I am annoyed with Sophie, annoyed with myself and I can't stop thinking that I should have told her about the night in the car park, the night I kissed Gareth. I keep trying to convince myself that I am not jealous or jaundiced, just a little taken aback by it all. I am positively reeling if the truth be known. If she knew that he had come on to me as well, surely she would rethink their relationship. I am still gobsmacked that she can trust him at all; he is so transparent and so manipulative. Obviously when he couldn't have me he moved straight over to her. I take a deep breath and exhale very slowly. Sophie will be really hurt when she finds out. I think about what he told her, about how he and Suzie were just good friends and that he was thinking of leaving. There is no way that Gareth will ever leave Suzie, I think angrily, and they looked bloody happy together if you ask me. I can't believe she fell for all that crap. Pure rhetoric, that's all it is. Poor Suzie. Those poor boys. All at once I feel quite weary, I don't want to tell her, I don't want Sophie to know that I was stupid and weak and that I nearly fell for his weaselly lines as well. I don't want her to know that I was nearly another notch on his bloody bedpost. And I want to spare her from knowing that all those romantic things that he says to her are just more lines, strung together to get her into bed. She has been my best friend for so long now, and even though I don't agree with what she's doing I don't want her to be hurt.

But then if I don't tell her about the night in the car park, then aren't I just as bad as I thought she was? Isn't that what makes this so much worse, that she kept it from me all this time? I can't believe that she hadn't trusted me enough to tell me. To think that this has been going on for five bloody months now and I didn't have a clue. Maybe if I tell her what I know, then she will just finish with him and nobody will get hurt. I think of how desperately sad Simon would be if he found out and then I start to think of how devastated I would be if I discovered that Pete was seeing someone else and it is at that moment that I know. I have to tell her, I am just not sure how.

Chapter 10

Simon

'Sometimes with secret pride I sigh,
To think how tolerant am I;
Then wonder which is really mine:
Tolerance or a rubber spine?'
Ogden Nash

I think Sophie is having an affair. My Sophie. My wife Sophie. I am not sure how I could have missed the signs, how this could be happening. How I could have become this complacent. I keep seeing snapshots of our life together, they flash before my eyes like a sordid film show, all the happy moments and memories suddenly seeming sour and unreal. The feeling of betrayal is knife-sharp. Most days now I have a physical pain in my chest and it hurts to breathe. In fact it hurts to think or do anything at all right now. I just want to go and lie down somewhere and not get up for a very long time. It came to me all of a sudden at Suzie and Gareth's house, a tiny niggling doubt initially, a tiny spark fanned and then fuelled by the secretive looks between them, little things at first, like the way she couldn't take her eyes off him, as if he had mesmerized her, and then when he smiled at her the tell-tale blush that her fair skin is incapable of hiding. The secret smiles, and the overly lingering touches. By the end of the afternoon, it was as if I had this rage burning inside me that had built up and up, an accretion of anger, protectiveness and helplessness, jealousy and sadness. I swear I would have hit him if we had stayed. And it is not just because he has managed to seduce her beneath my very nose, not just because of the way she looks at him, but because of who he is. Ever since I left school I have worked in a bank, a shining edifice resembling stability and equity, yet inside the doors, on the trading floors broking and dealing are the type of men who give the rest of us a bad name. I've seen them at lunch, swaggering in and out of bars, full of alcohol and their own self-importance, bragging about their latest conquests in the same breath as their latest merger and acquisition. Sex is like sport to them, as meaningless as a game of squash or golf. They have it all you see, the good looks and the easy-going charm and confidence. To them it is all too simple. Easy come and easy go, they wouldn't understand what it's like to spend six months trying to find enough courage just to speak to a girl like Sophie, to feel every day that somehow you will never be the person that she wants you to be. Maybe that's it. Maybe I just didn't cut it.

I can't believe she has been taken in by him. I agonize over how long this could have been going on. And then I think that maybe I am imagining it. Perhaps they are just good friends – after all, they have to work quite closely together. But then I think of him strutting across the lawn, of his bluster and cool arrogance and most of all the way that he looked at me. It was all he could do not to tell me. I swear he was laughing at me. When I think about it now, I should have realized. I should have thought it was strange that she has never mentioned him. Since she has worked at that office Sophie has always told me everything, I could probably recognize everyone she works with just from her descriptions. I know where her desk is and what kind of coffee is in the machine, I know what kind of food they serve in the restaurant and on what day, and where the safe is. I remember her telling me that Gareth was due to start work, I recall her being quite nervous that he might shake things up a bit. But then nothing. I remember asking her and her response was evasive to say the least. So here I am. I am supposed to be on a flight out of here but my departure time has long since gone. I can't seem to get out of the car, it is all just going round and round in my head. I desperately need a plan. I feel like I'm going mad.

I keep thinking back to all the times that she has been out lately, shopping trips with the girls, trips to the spa, painting lessons and aerobic classes. I think of all the times she has needed to work late and I feel sick. Sick at her and angry at me. I feel as if she has taken an eraser and effaced all the happiness from my memories of us. I feel cheated and hopelessly deluded by the only person I think that I have ever loved. For so long I felt we had this unshakeable partnership against the world, I loved the fact that when we were together it didn't matter what happened, it felt like we were invincible. I thought she loved that too, our partnership, that bond we had, instead she has tainted and desecrated everything that we had: that trust, our love. I run my hands over my face and realize that I am crying, actual teardrops. I lower my hands and stare blearily, unthinking, at the water on my fingertips. I can't remember the last time I cried and for a while I just give into it. Then I realize I need to know more, I don't know what I'm going to do yet but I need information. I mean, does she love him? How often do they meet? What is Amanda's role in all this, does she even know?

I drive home, slowly meandering through long since bypassed villages. This is the scenic route, however the countryside scenes slide seamlessly into each other today, merging into an undefined blur. I glance up and become conscious that I have been operating completely on auto pilot, just habitually going through the motions of driving, my mind elsewhere. I drive on, past picture-postcard houses, and gently nodding daffodils in ditches. The spring sunshine creates a pale golden haze that lies low over newly sown fields and collects hazily on the horizon. I look around me and find that I am astounded by the assiduous diligence of the world and everything in it. People are still going to work and children are at school, dogs still bark and it will still get dark. Only my life seems to have come to a standstill. I know that I need to keep going too, somehow. I need to keep on doing what I have always done, and perhaps by some twist of fate my life will become normal again. I start to feel a resolve building somewhere deep inside me and I take a cleansing breath, encouraged by the strength I am beginning to feel. This won't last for ever, I tell myself. I watched him at the party, he was constantly on the lookout for the next piece of skirt, a natural flirt, constantly preening and posturing. I tell myself that Sophie is just a quick thrill for him, a quick bit of entertainment until the next one comes along. After all, Sophie and I took vows, that must mean something, surely? I think sadly that I cannot imagine my life without her. Can I live with her infidelity though? How do I do that? How do you even start to forgive someone this? But then if you look at it logically, without any emotion at all, she definitely wasn't a virgin when we met, was she? I mean, she had kissed some frogs before and that didn't put me off. So does it really matter that she has slept with someone else? Even if it is that louse? Isn't it just my pride that is hurting? Then suddenly it all becomes clear. I just need to wait and bide my time. Of course he will get bored and when he moves on to the next one I will be there to pick up the pieces. And you never know, maybe this is some kind of wake-up call for me. Maybe I haven't been as attentive as I should have been. Perhaps this is an opportunity for me to try again.

I pick up the pace and drive faster, homeward bound. I

feel lighter as I now have a purpose. Maybe I will just tell Sophie that my meeting was cancelled and perhaps I will cook her something really special tonight. I could light some candles and maybe we can really talk for a change. The miles fly by as I plan my romantic evening and before long I am pulling into our street. I start to slow down out of habit but then as I get closer I spot Sophie's car on the drive and all at once I am concerned. Maybe she is ill? What could be wrong? Shouldn't she be at work?

And then as I drive closer I see it.

A low slung, sleek, black car is parked on the driveway. Gareth. On my driveway. I park indignantly, a little way off and switch off the engine. Think. My first instinct is to get out of the car and let him have it. But then it hits me. She has brought him here. She thought I would be away so she brought him here. To our house. The world feels as if it shifts slightly on its axis and I feel as though my heart is being gouged out of my chest with a blunt instrument.

Wounded and deflated, I fall back against the seat and feel the hurt radiate around me like waves. So this is what it feels like to have your heart broken. Can you die of this, I wonder? I lean forward and bang my head against the steering wheel in an effort to feel something real, something solid. I just sit there, not quite sure what to do, and when I next look up nearly an hour has passed and he is still there. A huge part of me wants to drive away and never come back. I fantasize about ramming that pompous, ostentatious vehicle off my drive. Who the hell does he think he is? Then I find myself getting out of the car. I look back and give it a cursory glance to check my parking and then I press the lock on the key fob, wait for the reassuring bleep and walk towards the house. I feel as if there is an imperturbable silence around me. The air all of a sudden seems heavy, humid.

When I look back at this moment in the future it is with a kind of bewilderment. They say that shock and jealousy can make you do crazy things. The French have a fantastic term for it: *crime passionnel*. In the 1800s in France I could have committed murder now and most likely have walked away scot-free, I think wryly. A crime of passion. I used to smile at the idea that a fit of jealous rage or heartbreak could excuse one from carrying out the most despicable of crimes, but now, as I walk towards the house, I am filled with an icy rage, a detached sense of purpose. Perhaps I am having an out of body experience, I think, as I keep walking in the direction of our house. Our house. A ripple of anger shoots through me and lengthens my stride. It doesn't take long and then I am there. I am standing outside my own front door, where I have stood so many times. I feel as if everything is moving much more slowly than normal. I gaze at the flowers in the planter to my left. The colours appear to be brighter than normal; I stare and stare until they unite and fuse somehow. I reach in my pocket and instead of my keys I find my old faithful, trusty penknife. Perfect for all those little jobs around the house. How did that get there, I wonder absently? That would have been great at the airport, security would have loved me. It feels solid, comfortingly heavy. I weigh it in my hand and switch out the knife attachment. And there I stay, as if turned to stone like some wretched man from ancient Pompeii, frozen in time, unable to take my eyes off the blade in my hand. Somewhere nearby a child is singing and I am snapped back to reality. I manoeuvre the sharp edge back into its carefully designed slot and slip it back into my pocket. I find my keys and in one movement I open the door. I am tempted to call out to tell Sophie that I'm home, to give her a chance. But I don't, because before I can say a word the sounds coming from the kitchen stop me in my tracks.

Straight ahead is the lounge with French doors leading to the garden. I look straight through the open doors out to the open beyond, as if in a trance. I am transfixed by the noise. The recurring, almost metrical breathing, and the whispered voices. As if attached and pulled by an invisible thread, I walk towards the sounds. The beige carpet beneath my feet seems softer than normal and there is a faint smell of something cooking somewhere. The unmistakable sound of sex, the cadence of lust. It's as if I am standing on a precipice and one more step is all that it will take. But then, the noises increase and become more frenzied, I feel sick. I need to get out of here and quickly. I don't think I am feeling so well, the room seems to be spinning, a mass of toffee and beige, and I lurch sideways. Then, from somewhere close, there is a clatter and something falls. I am suddenly more awake than I have been for a long time. I can feel every nerve and fibre in my body and my face feels taut, like it might just crack with the pressure. What am I doing? I take one more step and in my peripheral vision I catch nightmare glimpses of naked flesh and tangled limbs. I can't remember starting to run, but before I know it I am outside scaling the back wall of my own garden, sprinting away from the house as if the devil himself is behind me. I don't look back. I don't know if they saw me and I don't really care. Back in the car the shaking starts and it doesn't subside for three days.

Chapter 11

Sophie

'We cross our bridges when we come to them and burn them behind us, with nothing to show for our progress except a memory of the smell of smoke and a presumption that once our eyes watered.'
Tom Stoppard

I am sitting here staring at a small white plastic stick with a tiny window about half-way down. I can't remember how many times before I have stared at similar plastic sticks, all of which boast 97 or 98 per cent accuracy. Three minutes, that is all it takes. Somehow this time it all feels so different and for the first time I am unsure what positive would mean.

Nausea and vomiting, tender breasts, and feeling so tired – no, make that exhausted – that I feel as if I have run a marathon. All the signs and symptoms that I have craved and hoped for, all this time. I used to lie awake praying for morning sickness. How could I not have seen the signs, after waiting so long?

And I am reading but not really taking in the instructions. Two pink lines mean I am pregnant, one pink line means that I am not. How can time stretch itself out like this? How long is three minutes, for goodness' sake? God, I feel sick.

I glance again at the now clammy paper in my hand:

'When you begin to experience pregnancy symptoms, you will want to take a pregnancy test to confirm whether or not you are pregnant. When a fertilized egg implants in the uterine wall, it starts to secrete the pregnancy hormone human chorionic gonadotrophin (HCG). This is why it is recommended that you wait until the first day of your missed period, about two weeks after conception, to take a home pregnancy test.' I know all this, I must have read every book I could find about conception and fertility but just now, it doesn't seem to make much sense at all. I shift position and wait some more, willing the hands of the clock to move faster.

I know that if you wait too long to read these home tests you can get an incorrect reading as a line may start to appear that could be read as a positive result. The line turns out to be an evaporation line created as the urine on the test-strip dries. I know this because this is what happened to me last time I sat in this very same spot waiting for a line to appear. When nothing happened I just kept waiting, willing a line to magically materialize. And then it did. I thought my prayers had been answered and that somehow a miracle had occurred. The kind and patient doctor's explanation had been difficult to comprehend as the realization slowly dawned on me that my yearning for a child appeared to have manufactured this incorrect result. I remember the doctor's pitying looks and feeling so stupid that I just wanted the earth to open up and swallow me whole.

So this time I have set a timer as well. When the ringing begins I find that, instead of staring unblinkingly at the plastic stick, I have focused my gaze on the base of the bathroom light so when I try and look at the result I find for a moment it is hard to focus. I start to get flustered and check the time on the clock once more. Definitely three minutes. I blink and then blink again and then I see them. There they are for the entire world to see, two unwavering, pink, parallel lines. I shake the stick but they do not move or bend or

113

disappear. All of a sudden I realize I can't breathe very well and then I throw up.

I always thought I would cry with happiness if it ever happened, if I ever fell pregnant. You see, I had given up trying, given up thinking that it would ever happen to me. Instead I had started dreaming of a different type of life, an alternative ending to my story. Instead of children, and then grandchildren, I had us down for a life of exotic travel, to places that you can never really imagine going to. Perhaps even dangerous destinations like Columbia or the Middle East. Perhaps we would find somewhere so desperately beautiful that we would even buy a second home there. We could revisit every year and then when the time was right we would breeze off into the sunset and retire. It would have to be near a golf course, so that Simon could play, and I would need some decent shops, but apart from that my only other requirement would be that it would have to be somewhere truly stunning. I would be permanently suntanned from our travels and we would own sports cars. No people carriers for us or expensive school fees. And I always thought that my plans included Simon, my wonderful, dependable, charming husband. But when I examine my dreams more closely, I'm not sure if it is actually Simon – there is a man there, definitely, but I can't make out his features. Was this always the case? Was it ever Simon or did I just want it to be? I wonder whether this is some kind of omen or some strange pregnant fancy.

Pregnant, a small shiver of excitement wiggles up and down my spine. I place my hand over my flat tummy and try to imagine it swollen and round. I splay my fingers, a wordless caress to my baby. I stand up and look at the test again, this is really happening. I wonder absently if I should repeat the test, but this time it's all different. I feel different. I feel pregnant! I lie down on the bed and smile; I force myself to stop thinking of nurseries and delivery dates but of perhaps more pressing issues like who the hell is the father?

114

I can't remember when I last used contraception, I came off the pill years ago to try and conceive but recently I had begun to think that Simon wasn't ever going to get me pregnant. Things kind of happened too quickly with Gareth for either of us to be responsible. Risky, I know, but it's not as if he sleeps around. So really it could be either of them. The experts say that pregnancy can happen if you stop wanting it so badly, they tell you to relax and it may well happen. Maybe that is what's happened; maybe it could be Simon's. Maybe it was the acupuncture? Surely, though, it is more likely to be Gareth's? We have been having unprotected sex for five months now and we know that he is fertile, he already has two kids. And there would be no way of knowing, even when the baby was born, not from just looking, as both Simon and Gareth look pretty similar: they both have blue eyes and brown hair and they are both tall. Gareth said we would have amazing children, I think excitedly, and I know it's not ideal as neither of us have actually made the decision to leave as yet, but we have talked about it enough. Suddenly, I can't wait to tell him. I stretch out on the bed feeling happy and comfortable and, yep, pregnant. I feel bad, though, when I think of Simon, who would be just over the moon to know that I am pregnant. I think of my in-laws, who have always been so kind and generous, never putting pressure on us or dropping baby hints. They would be beside themselves at the thought of another grandchild. Why is life so difficult?

I hear a familiar tune and search around for my phone. I smile as I see Gareth's number, I have it saved under Amanda2 just in case. I press the button and take the call.

'Hi sexy.' Even the sound of his voice sends shivers up and down my spine.

I curl up comfortably. 'Hello, I'm missing you, where are you?'

'Very close, actually. Do you want to meet?' he asks, purring.

'Would love to, can't be long, though – Simon's due back home tonight so I really need to be here,' I say.

'Perfect, wear those pink knickers, the ones I like,' he says.

I giggle and promise that I will and tell him that I have something to tell him when I see him. He tells me that he is looking forward to it. We agree to meet in an hour. We hang up and I stretch and look at myself in the mirror, and decide on a quick shower. I discard my clothes on the way and can't resist looking at myself naked. I run my hand once again over my tummy and stand sideways for a different profile. No, absolutely no sign of anything at all. I sigh and hit the shower.

I get to our meeting point surprisingly ahead of time. I knew I would be here before Gareth because he is always late, you can rely on it. But I can't help smiling when I think about seeing him again. We have started meeting just outside town, near the start of a rambler's footpath. There is a tiny pub close by and it is remote and quiet, perfect for a clandestine rendezvous. It is really quite a pretty area and today even more so than usual as loads of bluebells are in flower. They sway together prettily, a sea of blue and green under the shady parapet of the trees all around. It seems to me that this mass of flowers seems to have appeared overnight, or maybe I just didn't notice them before. I stare riveted, hypnotized by the tranquillity of the scene and drinking in the fresh clean air. Maybe I will call the baby Bluebell if it's a girl, I think dreamily, and a bolt of excitement whizzes through my system again. It is that time of the year when most of the leaves are brand new, only recently unfurled, and tiny delicate green stubs still cover the branches, a promise of even more new leaves to come. The bright new greens are lit up, the sunlight accentuating and highlighting each leaf and picking out the embroidery of delicate veins within. I stare up towards the sky, wondering at the detail and beauty around me and basking in the afternoon sun. I walk for a bit, thinking about the last couple of days. Simon has been away

116

for four days now and I don't think we have spoken once. We have exchanged messages but every time I have called he has been busy, he then returns my call at odd times when I have either been out or busy or once even when I was asleep. It isn't like him, I think with a frown. He is usually so good at getting the timing just right, working out the time differences to make sure that we manage to talk. I took all four days off. I just wanted a break. Gareth managed to pencil in some fake meetings so we have been together nearly the whole time. Slowly over the last few months we have got to know each other more but the passion hasn't diminished at all. I check my phone for missed calls. I have been waiting for a call from the police.

Four days ago, in fact it was the first day that Simon was away on business, Gareth came round. It was strange at first to have him in the house, and we kind of tiptoed round each other like strangers for a while. It was surreal, when I think about it: he made polite noises about our décor and I showed him various pictures of my family, pictures of my life, the part of my life that he only usually hears about. I took him up to the bedroom, expecting him to ravish me there and then, but he moved on quickly, we ate lunch in the garden and then much later, after several bottles of wine, we made love in the kitchen. Everything was amazing, I think we both felt strange being in the house together but we had all of this pent-up sexual energy. We had left the door open as it was such a nice day and then all of a sudden, with us both near naked in the kitchen, there was the most almighty crash and then both of us saw someone run past the kitchen door. It all happened so quickly that I couldn't tell you anything about him except that it was a man. We couldn't even chase after him because we were both undressed. In his haste to do whatever he had come to do (and probably in his surprise to find us home) he had knocked over our wedding photo-graph, the one in the ornate glass frame. It had shattered into what seemed like a thousand pieces. It took us ages to get all of the pieces out of the carpet. Even now when I vacuum I am still finding tiny fragments of glass. We presumed he must have been trying to burgle the place; it was really scary.

Gareth and I talked about it and decided that we should call the police. He said that he was very worried that it could have been some weirdo targeting me and that he wouldn't rest unless he knew that we had reported the incident. Gareth thought that we would be able to convince the police to keep an eye on the house for the next few days while Simon was away. He was really sweet. He made tea and suggested we lay out some work on the kitchen table to make it look as if we had been doing something respectable. We made out that Gareth's reason for being at the house was to drop off some work that he wanted me to look over. I had a look round to see if our intruder had taken anything (frankly he could have taken half the house without us noticing) but I couldn't see that anything was missing. Even so I just couldn't stop shaking. I think the whole idea of someone being in your house is just so weird, especially because of what we were doing. He must have got a right eyeful.

The police were really efficient and were with us within twenty minutes of our call. A young woman, PC Turner and an older man, Sergeant Cleary, turned up. The woman seemed really nice; she had very sensible, shiny black shoes. Where do they go to get shoes that sensible, I wonder? Are they issued with the uniform? Does she swap them for stilettos and go dancing sometimes? Anyway, they were as sensible as their shoes would have suggested, professional and well organized. PC Turner took notes while Sergeant Cleary walked around looking at the broken photograph and spent some time looking around the garden. From time to time he spoke quietly into a dictaphone. Then he examined the lock on the front door for signs of breaking and entering and checked for exit points in the garden, as that was the way the suspect disappeared. Every now and again he would walk back in and ask a question, then he would nod and disappear again. I made a statement so that they could make some enquiries while Gareth made tea. PC Turner explained that they would probably speak to the neighbours to see if anyone saw anything and to be on the safe side they would drive around a little more often as Simon was away. PC Turner asked if I had a friend who could stay over with me and I said I would think about it, all the time not daring to look at Gareth. I'm sure I must have blushed, though. After a while the older man came back in and said that in his opinion it was probably an opportunistic thief who had wandered in through the open French doors on the off-chance. He had probably been wandering around for a while looking over fences, looking for windows or doors left open. PC Turner noted that the suspect probably got nervous when he heard noises and in his rush to leave knocked over the picture. I was given a victim of crime leaflet and a contact number to call if I didn't hear anything, and then they left. They told me that they would call if there were any developments.

There is something about the police; they make you feel guilty even if you are the victim. Gareth laughed when I told him this and said it was just my guilt complex and that Sergeant Cleary was hardly Columbo. This made me smile but I do wonder if they were fooled by our 'just working from home' line.

I glance again at my watch; I am bored of waiting and looking at bluebells now. I am starting to get agitated thinking of all the jobs I still need to do before the weekend, before Simon gets home. Where is he? Gareth is nearly ten minutes late now, and I am fed up of wandering up and down the same part of the lane, no matter how picturesque. Maybe I should be late sometimes, play a little harder to get. That would bamboozle him, I think with a smile. But the truth is I am hopeless at that kind of thing. I am definitely not your natural coquette, playing games has never been my forte. Somewhere in the distance a flock of birds are suddenly flushed out, and they are still squawking disapprovingly when they fly overhead. In a cloud of dust Gareth's car circles and comes to a standstill. The black paintwork, normally gleaming, is layered in a film of brown sandy earth. I stand beside it and absently draw a heart in the grime. Gareth leaps out of the car and without a thought for anyone around (although there is no one) pulls me to him and kisses me hard on the mouth. He sets me back down on my feet, grins and grabs my hand.

'So, do you fancy a shag in the woods before we have a drink or after?' he asks with one eyebrow cocked. He has a glint in his eye and he smells gorgeous. I am sure that he knows that I find him irresistible.

I laugh and lead him by the hand into the woods, looking back over my shoulder with what I hope is a come hither expression. 'You hussy,' he says throatily and I roll my eyes. We walk and talk for a while, enjoying the close proximity of each other. We come to a natural clearing and pause, again there are bluebells growing in every available space. Even the grass looks new, dainty slender shoots that have been hidden from view by the mass of flowers. The air is completely still in our clearing and we sit close together on a huge old tree trunk felled by a storm, long ago. I pick at the bark with my fingertips and it crumbles dustily in my hand. I brush my hands together and tidy my hair then I just do it.

'I have something to tell you,' I say, importantly. Suddenly I feel scared, really scared, I kind of wish I hadn't started but now Gareth is looking at me expectantly. He is grinning inanely at me and the words that I had practised die on my lips.

'Are you OK?' he asks. Concern has chased his smile away and now he is frowning ever so slightly, his eyebrows moving more closely together.

'I'm fine,' I say. He looks at me quizzically, and starts to smile at me again.

'I'm pregnant.'

I watch his smile freeze and disappear. He looks at me warily, as if there is something more left to say.

'I'm pregnant.' I say it again just in case he never heard properly, just in case I only imagined that I had said it.

'What? How? What?' Each word is louder than the one before.

'Shush. Be quiet. I don't want everyone to know,' I say. I am agitated now. I laugh nervously but this was not the romantic scene I had envisaged.

And he is looking at me with the strangest expression on his face, and he seems to have gone a funny colour. He appears to have turned almost the colour of beetroot and he is walking around muttering, 'This can't be happening, this just can't be happening.'

I try and catch his arm but he shakes me off roughly.

'You stupid, stupid cow. What were you thinking of?' he bellows.

I am so shocked that I stumble away from the log, away from him. I am fighting to keep the tears back now and I am stifling sobs in my throat. My mind has gone blank. This has got to be some kind of nightmare.

'It can't be mine, it must be his, in fact it could be anyone's,' he seethes.

I am so completely stunned by this last statement that I almost think I misheard so when I slap him it is a delayed reaction and takes him completely by surprise. He doesn't retaliate, he just stares at me with hate and mistrust and confusion in his eyes. I feel as though I have been kicked in the teeth and to my horror, I dissolve into tears before him. Before long I am sobbing uncontrollably, big hiccupping noises and snot and everything.

Flabbergasted by his reaction and my outburst I sit back

down on the log, tears coursing down my face as I watch him fume. And he just ignores my distress; he continues pacing up and down, running his hands through his hair and swearing under his breath. Somewhere in my grief I am hoping that he is just reacting like this through surprise and that when he calms down he will put his arms around me and tell me that everything will be just fine.

I feel as though I am crying for an age, then he finally comes over, hands me a handkerchief and strokes my hair away from my snotty, tear-stained face.

'Why do you think it's mine?' he says again, but quietly this time, as if that will soften the blow of his words.

'How can it not be yours?' I splutter. 'I've been trying to get bloody pregnant with Simon for three years now and nothing has ever happened and then a few months of shagging you and all of a sudden I'm up the duff. Work it out, Einstein,' I spit.

'So you haven't slept with anyone but me and Simon?' He asks this almost incredulously and for a minute I think I might actually murder him.

'No I bloody haven't, you complete *and utter* BASTARD!' I yell.

'OK, OK, look, I'm sorry all right? I was just checking, that's all.' He backs right off now, aware that he has over-stepped the mark. When he thinks I have calmed down slightly he tries again.

'Look, it still doesn't necessarily make it mine,' he says gently, and I can see the beginning of hope creeping into his tone. 'After all, you have been sleeping with both of us.' I notice that he has started talking in an exaggeratedly soft voice, slowly enunciating the syllables of each word, as if all of a sudden I have turned into a lunatic or a wild animal that may attack him.

'I can't believe you don't want me.'

'Of course I want you, just not a baby, not now. You could

have an abortion,' he says. 'It's really easy, I don't even think they keep you in hospital nowadays, and it's not painful at all.' His words are coming faster now, almost in an effort to say his piece before I start to cry again. 'I'll come with you if you want,' he adds for good measure.

I just look at him, at his recently whitened teeth and perfect hair and feel appalled at what I have done and at who this person is. In fact I am not sure I know who he is any more. I just keep staring at him. I feel disgusted by his cowardice and horrified that after all the time that we have spent together he knows nothing of me either. Or perhaps he just hasn't listened, not heard a word I have said. All that pillow talk, maybe there is some kind of vortex, a black hole between us into which our spoken words have fallen. I think of all the times that I poured my heart out to him, told him about how I longed for a child, that sometimes I could think of nothing but how much I wanted a baby. Was this really just sex for him, was I really just a quick shag?

'You complete and utter bastard,' I am shouting now, not able to control the grief and anger inside me any longer. 'Did you not listen to a word I said? Do you really think that a baby can be disposed of so easily? Do you think I can then just replace this child with another when the time is right, when it is convenient for you? This is not a bloody tin of beans we are talking about, it's a baby. For goodness' sake, it could be your baby.' I can hardly speak now, I am so upset. I cannot believe that he could be so heartless, I am staggered and really quite frightened by his attitude. What the hell am I supposed to do now?

Then he looks at me and he looks as though he has aged several years in the minutes that we have been here. 'I have children,' he says tiredly, 'I have two boys. What am I supposed to do? They are still children,' he says.

I am exasperated now. 'How nice for you,' I spit. 'So, if you are so damn happy with your life and your children, what was

123

all this about? Was this just sex, am I some kind of mistress?' I am struggling to speak now as it dawns on me. I am exactly that. I have become his mistress, a plaything to be picked up and put down whenever it is convenient for him. I feel sick.

'You never had any intentions of leaving, did you? I was just a quick shag, something to brag to your mates about. Amanda was right all along,' I say bitterly.

'What has Amanda got to do with this?' he asks and I can tell he is annoyed. So I tell him. I tell him all about Amanda's friend and what Amanda thinks about him. I don't know what he was expecting me to say, but he actually looks visibly relieved.

'I can't believe you told her about us,' he sits down heavily and runs his fingers through his hair. He looks decidedly nervous. 'I thought we agreed. This is exactly why I wanted to keep this whole thing a secret to stop stuff like this happening. Honey, you know me, don't take any notice of anything Amanda says. I'm sure she's just jealous. Look, I wasn't going to say anything but I am certain that she fancies me, a couple of times she has flirted and made it quite obvious that she wants me, it has all been really quite uncomfortable at times,' he says. 'I wouldn't hurt you for the world,' he sighs, trying to get hold of my hand.

I just look at him, waiting to see what else he comes out with.

'Don't look at me like that,' he says. 'I promise I am telling the truth. Every time it's happened I've made it clear that I am not interested. She is just jealous,' he says, shaking his head sadly from side to side for effect.

I think about this, no longer sure of anything any more.

'Of course I am going to leave some day, but we both agreed to wait,' he wheedles. He gets up again and paces up and down in front of me. I know he is still angry because his voice has risen an octave. 'I do love you but I can't just leave my wife because you got pregnant. How can I leave my children when I don't even know if the baby is mine or not? At least I know those boys are mine. Trust me I would leave tomorrow if I had some proof,' he says.

I continue looking at him as if he is a new specimen or creature that has just been introduced to me. I never noticed how hairy his eyebrows were before, I think, as I wait for him to start talking again.

'Can't we get some kind of paternity test or blood test done? Please be reasonable, you can't expect me to leave my family to raise some other bloke's kid.' He is pleading now, imploring me to listen. But all I can think is that none of this should matter. If he loved me, really loved me, he would find a way.

'We can't have the test done until the baby is a year old,' I hear myself say. My voice sounds remote and distant even to my own ears. I know when the test can be done because I have already checked. I spent nearly an hour about a month ago researching this just in case I ever did fall pregnant. I remember surfing the various sites in boredom, never thinking that there was ever really a chance that it could happen. It all seemed like a game then. But it would seem as though I am not the only one with this dilemma as there are now hundreds of companies out there who will do this kind of testing now. A simple blood test will do it, or a sample of cheek cells taken on a swab from the inside of the baby's cheek. Both Gareth and I would also need to supply a sample and then it is just a matter of waiting for the cells to cultivate. Apparently it is more than 99 per cent accurate. In Hong Kong there is a new method that can determine paternity at twelve weeks into the pregnancy using non-invasive testing methods, but that won't be available in this country for a few years yet. There is one pe-birth test available here. It can be carried out at mid-pregnancy. Cells from the baby are collected via an amniocentesis test and then cultivated. An amniocentesis is almost a routine test on mothers older than

125

thirty-seven to test for Down's syndrome or other abnormalities. But there is a one per cent chance that the test may trigger a miscarriage. This is not a risk I am willing to take so I say nothing about this more dangerous procedure. Instead I watch the man that I thought I loved trying to work out what to do so that his life isn't too inconvenienced by my news. Tears are welling in my eyes once more, and I hiccup when I try and and hold my breath.

'So, let's get this straight,' I say. 'Am I supposed to just hang around waiting for you to make up your mind? Put my life on hold until you deign to make a decision? What if I had already had children, what would you have done? Would you have left then? Would you still have shagged me if I was a mother already? Or do you only sleep around with women who don't have children?' I yell, crying again, but tears of frustration this time.

'There is at least a fifty per cent chance that the baby is yours,' I say, trying to sound as rational as I can. He comes over to me looking sympathetic and sincere.

'I still think you should consider an abortion,' he says. 'No wait. Listen to me. After all, if you got pregnant this time you could get pregnant again in the future, and it is just a heap of cells right now. We could always start a family when we are together. I mean, it is ridiculous to think it could work at the moment. If you have a kid you won't be able to work and I will end up supporting you and the kid plus my own family. We would end up living in some dive somewhere and hating each other and the baby,' he says. His voice is smooth and syrupy and all the time he is looking at me for some sign of acquiescence, a look of conciliation and pleading in his eyes.

But when I look at him, all I see is the consultant, the broker that I work with every day, and I marvel at how I managed to overlook this wheedling, manipulative side of him. With complete clarity now I realize why he is so successful.

126

Suddenly a dog bounds past, a Dalmation, a beautiful animal that makes running appear effortless. Shortly after he is followed by a blonde girl, about twenty-five, running to keep up. She looks pretty, fairly athletic, carefree and happy. And I watch Gareth watch her. He is captivated; I may as well have disappeared under the nearest rock like some kind of hairy toad. He snaps out of his reverie as she vanishes ahead, all long legs and flowing hair. But it is too late, he has been caught in full lech. He looks down at the ground, at least with the grace to look embarrassed. And I just stare at him. How could I have got this so wrong, how could I not have detected this side of him before? I make a show of looking at my watch and tell him that I have to go. I want to run and run and not stop for a long time. But we walk politely side by side back to the cars, both lost in our own thoughts. Before he drives away, he tells me not to do anything rash, and mentions that perhaps we can talk again on Monday when we have both had time to think things through. He tells me that we have a 'really good thing going'. And that we wouldn't want to screw that up. I look up at him unseeing, feeling wooden and impotent. I get in the car and start the engine and look as if I am ready to drive off. But instead I watch him go, overtly rubbing away the heart that I drew in the dust on his car and then finally leaving in a showy storm of dried earth. I sit long enough to watch it filter its way back down to the ground, tiny particles swirling down, collected and examined momentarily in the sunny shaft of light. I just sit and stare. I feel so stupid, so stupid and so alone. I garner all the thoughts and feelings I have right now and inspect each one. Mentally, I turn them over looking for clues. I reach back into the hour gone by with velvet gloves carefully handling each spoken word between us. I search for hidden indicators and explanations that may help me make more sense of this. I sit and let the hurt take root. I torture myself slowly, looking for any small gaps when I could have done or said something

127

differently. I recall with shock the way that he ogled the girl with the dog. I know men are made like that, I know they are designed to look constantly for females to impregnate. To sow their wild oats. But if ever there was a wrong time for a man to look, an inappropriate time to ogle, I guess it was today. I try and remember ever seeing Simon tentatively or openly watching women when we are together. But I can't think of any time at all.

I pick up the phone, turning it over in my hand, and speed-dial Amanda. She answers in her best business voice, I guess she is in the office and I ask her how things are going. She sounds busy and as I listen to the normal everyday noises of our office and her clipped professional voice, the tears start again. Before I know it I am sobbing into the phone and I can hardly speak to tell Amanda what is wrong. She sounds horrified at my very obvious, very naked distress and tells me to stay put, that she will come right now. She sounds mystified when I tell her where I am.

'What the hell are you doing out there?' she remonstrates. And then, 'Oh my God, you haven't been attacked or something have you?'

I snivel and tell her no, that I am fine.

'I'm pregnant,' I say.

'What? You're pregnant? But honey, that is wonderful!' She sounds overjoyed for me, this is the person who knows me better than anyone in the world. She has watched me obsessing over fertility dates and helped me through my various hysterical moments. She has named my fluctuating moods my 'babymania' and has never once told me that she is bored or fed up with hearing about it.

'It is quite normal for you to be weepy,' she says, an indulgent tone in her voice now. 'You had me really worried for a bit then, I thought something awful had happened.' She sounds relieved now. But the tears are still rolling down my face.

'Simon must be overjoyed, what did he say?'

'I haven't told him,' I say.

'What?' Amanda sounds confused now.

I take a deep breath. 'I don't think it's his,' I say and then I sob again.

'Look stay where you are, I'll meet you in about twenty minutes,' she says. The phone line dies and I wait, nervous and tense. The thought of explaining all of this sends my stomach churning. I am going to have to admit how wrong I've been about Gareth. I sigh and sink down further into my seat. How could everything have gone so wrong?

Within fifteen minutes she arrives. She must have broken all land speed records, because it should have taken her more like thirty minutes. I smile weakly when I see her. She is looking glamorous in a smart, business-woman kind of way. She is wearing killer heels and an expensive-looking navy blue suit. She is wearing her favourite diamond stud earrings and a single diamond on a chain around her neck. She has a firm, concerned look on her face. This makes me smile as I have seen this expression so many times before. Usually, though, it is worn to difficult client meetings, when we have to tell it like it is, knowing that the truth is not going to go down so well.

She picks her way across the car park gingerly in her beautiful shoes, avoiding the many pot holes and any particularly dusty patches and gets into the car with me. We couldn't look more different. She is so perfectly made up and all calm and collected and I have two rivers of eye make-up sliding down my face, to go with puffy eyes, swollen lips and snot. My fingernails, normally polished and buffed and beautifully shaped, are bitten and the cuticles sore. I am wearing jeans and what I thought this afternoon looked like a casual but sexy top. Now it just feels sleazy. I feel cheap, used and stupid and I look like hell. My life and all my plans seem to have shattered around me. Brief glimpses of my dreams

129

appear to glitter ominously, taunting me from the shards, along with the memories that I had so recently accumulated and coddled. They are all there, lying around me, broken and in ruins, distorted and twisted by the embarrassment I feel. I look at Amanda and the first thing she does is just hold me, and she doesn't say anything she just lets me cry and waits for me to explain.

I don't really know where to start so I just talk and then can't seem to stop the words rushing forward in a torrent, out they spill, falling over each other. Every now and again, when the tears strangle the words, she waits, holding my hand and stroking me. I tell her about the pregnancy test, and how amazed I had felt then. We talk briefly about how I feel physically and I realize that for the last few weeks I have felt run down, like I had some kind of virus in my system that was going to turn into a coughing, sneezing contagion at some point down the line. I tell her about the tiredness and that I have just started to feel a little sick and she nods sagely at me. She asks about Simon and I tell her that he hasn't got back from his trip yet. I tell her, though, how wonderful the last few days have been. My days with Gareth, that is. I try and explain how special our days together have been, playing house and just spending time with each other, not worrying about deadlines and alibis. I describe how caring and supportive he had been when the intruder thing happened. She looks quite shocked and I reassure her, telling her that it was probably some opportunistic thief. All the same, she offers to come and stay with me should Simon be delayed. We hug again and then I tell her about today, when I told him. How he reacted, the loathing odium in his voice and the way that he had moved as far as possible away from me, as if all of a sudden he found it insufferable even to breathe the same air as me.

Even as I speak it doesn't seem real, I am struggling to reconcile the Gareth I have come to know with the heartless, callous person I met today. I remember the ensnared and bitter look on his face, resentful that I had ruined what could have been a nice afternoon, a quick blow job, no doubt, and a pint before we went back to our real lives. I recounted my shock and astonishment that he had actually asked for a paternity test and had insinuated that I could have been sleeping around. Unbelievable. Amanda sits and listens but I can tell that she is getting angrier and angrier. Her foot has started to twitch and she keeps staring crossly ahead. I watch her eyes flash irately every time she looks back at me and her lips are now a thin pink line, drawn taut with emotion.

'Maybe he'll come round,' she says. I look down at the floor and then back at her; I take a deep breath then and tell her. 'He asked me to get an abortion.' I say this as quietly as I can, as if by whispering it, maybe it will just fade off into the atmosphere and I can pretend he never said it. Repeating it, that awful word, just seems to make it all very real and I start to cry all over again. I cry for my stupidity and for the innocent child protected and cosseted deep inside me.

'After all this time of praying every day that I would get pregnant, he wants me to have an abortion. I wouldn't have believed that he could be so obtuse and insensitive.' As I speak I lay my hands protectively over my tiny baby and, without realizing, I have lowered my voice to save the little mite from hearing that his father may be a monster. Perhaps, though, your daddy is not that nasty man, I think, absently wondering whether Daddy perhaps works in a bank. 'Perhaps Gareth hasn't got anything to do with my being pregnant after all,' I wonder out loud. I mean, if Gareth is right and he is not my baby's father then maybe it would be for the best.

'I don't really know how pregnant I am, I guess the doctor will be able to tell me that stuff. I think I must be around two months, it just never occurred to me that I could be pregnant, after all this time,' I say, blowing my nose noisily on one of Amanda's tissues.

'I can't believe I fell for him, I can't believe that I thought this was something special, I never want to see him again,' I cry and then: 'Oh, God! I'm going to have to leave work.'

'Of course you won't,' Amanda remonstrates. 'If any one should leave it should be him. Why the hell should you go? You haven't done anything wrong. I just knew he was trouble even before what happened,' she snaps angrily.

'What do you mean?' I start to feel confused, and she looks anxious. Amanda fishes about in her handbag (which matches her shoes perfectly) and goes to light up. 'Oh, sorry, I can't do this in here can I?' she asks. She doesn't wait for my reply as she knows my answer, so we get out of the car and she leans against it, looking out towards the trees.

'Look, I wasn't going to say anything because I knew how much you liked him. I didn't really want to tell you. I didn't want to upset you and I wasn't even sure that you would believe me. The last time we talked about this you got all angry and we ended up having that stupid row,' she says. 'I think it happened before you were together, anyway.' She takes another drag and blows the smoke impatiently into the air where it furls and dips and disappears. She keeps looking at me nervously and I feel a creeping sense of foreboding, but I am weary, bone-shockingly tired all of a sudden and I am not sure how much more I can take today. I sigh and ask her what happened, all the time not really sure if I want to know or not.

'I kissed him,' she says. 'It wasn't a big deal, it was way before Christmas and you were on some course somewhere. Well, we went for a drink and it just happened and I left straight after. It wasn't until the next day that I heard from Sue at McCallister's that he had this really terrible reputation. I tried to tell you. Honey, I am so sorry.' I let her hug me again but in her light embrace I feel crushed inside. I am so stupid, I think for the hundredth time. How can you get to this age and be such a monumentally bad judge of character? As if reading my mind, Amanda then tells me that I wasn't to know, and that from all accounts Gareth has this down to an art form. I'm not sure if this is supposed to make me feel better or worse.

'So, what are you going to do? You are going to have to tell Simon sooner or later. This is not something you can hide too easily.' We smile at each other and again I run my hand over my abdomen, thinking of my little one nestled warmly inside.

'I just know that Simon will forgive you, he adores you and he will love the baby, even if it is Gareth's. And if he doesn't then you still have your friends. Lots of people bring up children alone nowadays.' Amanda says this in a practical, sensible kind of way, all very matter of fact. But I look at her aghast.

'You don't really think I should tell him now, do you?' I say. 'After all, why should I upset Simon by telling him now, when it's all over? He doesn't need to know, does he?' I question.

Now it is Amanda's turn to look aghast. 'You don't really expect to pass off another man's child as Simon's, do you? And it must be Gareth's, I mean, after all these years of trying with Simon ...' her voice trails off into silence as we both know where her thought process is taking her. 'It just seems a little unethical, don't you think?' She says this last sentence with an incredulous tone in her voice. And I just stare at her. Because to me this now seems like the only way to go.

'What you're forgetting is that the baby could be Simon's,' I say.

'But it might not be. And Simon has the right to know the truth, you can't keep this from him. And what happens if the baby looks like Gareth? Or, even worse, what happens if he finds out somehow?' Amanda really looks concerned now.

'How is he going to find out? Only you, me and Gareth

133

know. And I'm not going to say anything, Gareth has made it clear that he is only too pleased to be shot of the problem and then that leaves only you. Amanda, I need you to promise me that you won't say anything,' I plead.

'You want me to lie for you?' she asks.

'Yes. Well, no. Look, not really, not like an out-and-out lie. I just don't want you to say anything,' I say, but we both know it's the same thing at the end of the day. I try and convince her that it is just a minor manipulation of the truth, and that it is for the best of reasons so this tiny person has the chance to know a father. After all, isn't it my job to protect this child, whatever it takes?

I look over at her as she visibly wrestles with her conscience. Her face softens and she looks back at me. 'Well, I guess the chances of him ever asking me are pretty non-existent, and I guess you are not the first woman ever to do this. But before you do anything go home and get some rest, you have had an awful day and you look shattered. Don't even think about making any decisions until you are thinking clearly. No one needs to know anything just yet. Go home and spend a nice evening with Simon, and try and forget it all, at least for this evening.' She clasps my hand and looks at me and I know that I can always depend on her.

I hug her again and we go our separate ways. As I drive through town watching people go about their everyday business I start to feel much better. After all, I am pregnant, I think, and with a small bubble of excitement I decide to pop into Mothercare on the way home. I give my face a quick scrub and fix my mascara and pop some lip gloss on. Still awful, but at least I won't scare anyone now. There is nothing like a little retail therapy to cheer you up. I walk through the doors with my head held high. I have a bona fide right to be here now. I walk through the aisles swinging my basket and before I know it I have passed a whole delightful hour and my basket is full of tiny embroidered babygros and a beautiful baby blanket. I add a tiny rattle designed to fit snugly around baby's wrist and head to the checkout. I suddenly realize that even though I know I can officially be in here now, nobody else does. I haven't told anyone that I'm pregnant. What if I meet someone? I'll have to pass this stuff off as a gift, I decide. I pay as quickly as I can and shoot back to the car. I pick up Simon's favourite Chinese food for supper and start driving towards home.

My phone starts to ring, so I pull over and forage around until I locate it in my bag. I glance quickly at the screen. Gareth. I press ignore determinedly, and continue driving. It rings four more times on the way back until angrily I stop again, turn it off and lob it into my bag. I carry on resolutely but in the back of my mind I wonder if maybe he is phoning to tell me that he does want us after all. I shake my head to dispel such a ridiculous notion and hurry home. It's nearly 6.00 pm now so I chuck the food in the oven to keep warm and dive into the shower. I lay the dining room table with our wedding silver and china and I am just lighting candles and admiring the overall ambience when the phone rings. Without thinking I pick up. Gareth.

'Don't put the phone down, we need to talk,' he says. I am sure he is speaking through gritted teeth. He sounds upset and uptight. Good, I think churlishly.

'What the hell do you think you are doing calling the house? I thought we had an agreement,' I snap.

'What am I supposed to do when you won't answer your mobile? I just wanted to say that I was sorry and that maybe I overreacted. Just don't do anything rash until you have had a chance to think,' he says evenly.

'So you are going to leave, after all? Does this mean that you do want the baby?' I say coldly. 'No? Well, perhaps you were ringing me to tell me about your little tryst with Amanda in the car park? How could you ever think that I wouldn't find out? You are a lying cheating bastard and I never, ever want to see you again. Got it?' I hear him trying to get a word in but I don't care any more. 'Just leave me alone and move on to your next little conquest or perhaps you should concentrate on your wife and family, now that will be novel for you. And don't phone me again. I don't want to see you or talk to you ever again.' And then I put the phone down.

And almost as soon as I put the phone down it rings again.

'Don't put the phone down on me,' he says coldly.

'Which part of "go away" don't you understand?' I retort.

'Stop being so unreasonable,' he says. 'Surely you must understand things from my point of view; I can't just leave because you are pregnant. How would we live? We need some time to think things through. Look, call in sick on Monday and we can get together and work something out,' he says.

'Goodbye, Gareth,' I say.

'No, wait, please? Meet me at 4.00 pm on Monday,' he says, an air of desperation in his voice now.

'Look, I'll think about it. OK?' I say, more in an attempt to get rid of him than anything else. I put the phone down and concentrate on getting ready for Simon's arrival. I check my appearance again and light some more candles. I swear that hell will freeze over before I ever see that maggot again.

By the time Simon arrives, there are no signs left at all of the turbulent days before. The house is clean, warm and tidy and the food is ready in the oven. I have opened a bottle of wine and put some music on. He looks tired and pale at the door and I am overcome with emotion. I hug him tightly to me, strung out from the stress of the day and tearful as the enormity of my actions hits me. I stand with his arms around me as the guilt and sadness flow over me. As I look into his kind, tired eyes I feel as if I just want to tell him everything. How could I have ever thought this was wrong or not good enough? I just want to stop feeling so bad, to end this self-reproach, I want to be able to look at him without this feeling of shame. I know I need to find some kind of absolution, and as I stand here wrapped in his arms I feel all at once safe and secure. Maybe Amanda is right, maybe I should tell him.

Chapter 12

Gareth

'Life being what it is we dream of revenge.'
Paul Gaugin

I have had such a crap weekend. Just my luck Sophie bloody well went and got herself knocked up. All this 'I'm sterile' crap. I reckon I've been stitched up like a bloody kipper. Apparently Simon has been trying to get her pregnant for something like three years and not a thing. Then, as soon as I turn up and shaft her a few times, bingo. And now the silly cow has put two and two together and thinks that I'm the father. Unbelievable. I wonder how many other blokes she's been shagging. After all, if she came on to me like that, I mean, I have never seen a bird drop to her knees that quick. She must be a player, obviously out to trick some poor bloke into getting her pregnant, you hear about it all the time. The kid could be anyone's. If she thinks she's going to get any money out of me she is going to have to prove it's mine and I told her as much as well. Suzie will go ape. If it is mine I'm going to have to set up a secret account or something to pay for it. I can't believe she is being so selfish. What is she thinking of?

We had a great thing going. I just can't believe she would want to ruin things by having a baby. No chance for a quick afternoon shag with a baby in tow, is there? And an abortion is so easy, a quick in and out and all for under £500 and then everyone can just get on with their lives. I really do think she is being quite unreasonable.

There were no real signs either. We had this great afternoon planned and instead of a warm, wet blow job, she gets me into the woods and hits me with the 'I'm pregnant' line. She then gets all stroppy when I don't seem over the moon about it. What was she expecting? That I would throw a party and leave Suzie and the boys there and then? She just hasn't thought this through, dim bitch. I mean, how am I supposed to support them all? I will be working until I'm ninety. I shudder at the thought. Suzie would get the house and it's a great house, I think resentfully. I have worked bloody hard to give us a nice life and what am I supposed to do? Leave it all just because some tart from work starts hearing her biological clock tick? God, we wouldn't even be able to afford a bloody holiday. I get up and walk out of the kitchen door into the garden and look around with satisfaction. I survey the house, remembering the various improvements we have made over the years; there is even a tree house in the garden for the children. All boys should have a tree house, I think, and my thoughts go to my boys. They're just kids, I couldn't leave them, and I don't want to leave them. No, this is my life, this is what I've worked for; the baby is probably not even mine anyway.

But I guess I was a little hard on her. After all, their hormones play havoc with them when they are up the duff. Worse than normal. She just wouldn't stop crying. Why do they do that? I must admit she looked pretty awful, and I felt a bit of a cad, so when I calmed down I tried to phone her back, you know, play the gentleman. Ask if she is OK and reassure her a bit. The last thing I need is her getting all hysterical and calling Suzie or something. But she wouldn't even answer the phone. Very annoying. I think it was important that I stood my ground though, I was right to manage her expectations early before it all gets out of hand. Anyway, then I phone her at home and I still can't get any answer, I think maybe she has gone out and so I try again. I know that she has to be home some time, because sensible Simon is due home. I know that she would want to be there when he arrives to play the good wifey and all that.

When I phone again she is as cold as ice. OK, maybe I was a bit harsh earlier, but what does she expect? Anyway, on top of the snow queen attitude I then get a whole barrage of abuse, as if this is my fault or something. It is so like a bloody woman to try and make you feel like you're the one in the wrong. Unbelievable. So I do the right thing and try and apologize and still she's giving me a hard time. I can't believe she is being so juvenile. So unreasonable. And she seemed so nice, so sweet and uncomplicated. I can hardly get my head round how devious she is being. It just goes to show that you never can tell.

Then to make matters worse it looks like Amanda has opened her big trap about me snogging her in the bloody carpark. For God's sake it was before I was even with Sophie and it was only really a peck, it's not as if I shagged her, for goodness' sake. Bloody Amanda, she really picked a great time to open her trap. She is such a bitch, landing me in it at this time. As if the whole pregnancy thing was not bad enough. I know her type though; Amanda has just been waiting like a big snake, just biding her time, waiting for her moment to strike. Hell hath no fury, they say. Well, she hasn't heard the last from me I can tell you.

Sophie and I are supposed to meet today to talk things out. She didn't turn up for work this morning so she is obviously planning to see me. Hopefully she has taken some time to think things through, maybe she has even made arrange-

140

ments to have the abortion and just get rid of it, I think optimistically. I've been home all afternoon just stewing on the whole bloody mess. I must say I will be glad when I know it's all over. I couldn't even concentrate on the golf on TV this afternoon I was so distracted. I had a meeting this morning and how I got through it I just don't know. Bloody women, they just mess up your head. I did think about going in for a bit this afternoon but I really didn't feel up to it. Better to sort this muddle out.

I walk back into the house and up the stairs. I walk into the boys' rooms, they are calm and tidy and it seems strange being here when the house is so quiet. Suzie is at work and the boys are at school. I wander in and idly run my hand through a box of toy soldiers. A whole mixture of miniature men are crammed into a Tupperware box. There are soldiers cast in army greens, nestled in with desert rats and dozens of cheaper soldiers, neatly cast but formed from a single coloured plastic. All of these are then mixed up with more elaborate, more expensive knights from the Middle Ages. Each knight is armed with a miniature joust and has a colourful painted shield. Plastic plumes fly in fixed directions from their helmets and their mounts wear bright standards and elaborate headwear. I glance around the room, up at the cabin bed with the metal ladder, and down at the desk beneath. I gaze at the stacks of puzzles and games and then at the framed certificates on the wall. I think again of Sophie, of last week and the time we spent together. Overshadowed by the news, those halcyon days seem now to be so long ago, a dream almost.

I smile at the memories, though, of afternoons entangled in bed together and long evenings just talking and caressing. And we had discussed children, and I do think we could have really sweet kids together. I obviously have really good genes so she could do a lot worse. And I do love a baby. I really enjoyed it when the boys were tiny. I think she would be a great mother too. I start rethinking, remembering how much fun the boys were when they were small and how great it would be to live with Sophie, perhaps to marry her one day. None of this skulking around anymore. We could go where we want to without worrying about who might see us. We could shag all day every day and I could get a blow job in the shower every morning. Then I think of Suzie and how much it would cost to divorce her and realize how ridiculous and expensive too much sentimental thinking could be.

Maybe we should just talk things through today and see what happens. We have both had some time to think now, so hopefully she will be seeing things a little more clearly and a little less selfishly. I dash downstairs and tug a jacket on. Suede in just the right shade of brown and a sky blue shirt to bring out the colour of my eyes. I have my favourite pair of jeans on, they are glorious. I don't think you can ever pay too much for a good pair of jeans. And these look fantastic. I check my appearance in the hall mirror, and satisfied, step outside and into the car. I had the car cleaned over the weekend so it is looking pristine again. I notice that while I was upstairs there must have been some rain, as the ground looks damp and there is a slight haze on the road. That suits me perfectly; hopefully it will have dampened some of the dust over where I meet Sophie. It is a great place, really secluded, but the dust there plays havoc with my paintwork.

I put some tunes on and off I go. Despite all this baby crap, I am still excited to see her. There is no way that she is going to throw all this away for some baby, and there is nothing like absence to make the heart grow fonder, I think. I park up in the car park of the King George and turn off the engine. There is no sign of her yet and I am around five minutes early today. Very unusual for me, just shows you how much I must be worrying. It is unheard of for me to be anywhere early. I watch a couple of rabbits eating their way through the foliage surrounding the car park. It is late afternoon now and the pale yellow sun is fighting a whole bunch of grey rain-clouds overhead. I start making some phone calls and before long I realize I have been waiting for around 30 minutes. Annoyed, I try Sophie's mobile but it is engaged so I dial Luke's number. It will be good to get his take on all of this before she gets here, I think, and I could do with some light relief. Maybe Sophie is throwing up or something. Another reason to just get rid of the bloody problem. I mean, why put yourself through all that crap? Luke picks up on the fourth ring and sounds delighted to hear from me. We slip into the usual repartee and then I tell him. He is understandably shocked and asks all the obvious contraception questions. His comment that 'she has done you up like a kipper' I don't find particularly helpful and I tell him so, even though I know he's right. Realizing I am actually quite stressed about all this, he turns a lot more serious.

'Are you sure she hasn't done this on purpose?' he says. 'You know, like chosen you to impregnate her?' This is all a little too sinister for my liking and I shudder in my seat. The rain-clouds overhead are moving in at pace, throwing shadows over the trees and chasing sunlight into fast moving patches as I re-adjust my position.

Luke asks me what I'm going to do but I still don't know so I can't tell him. I describe just how badly Sophie took my abortion suggestion and explain that I reckon she would have changed her mind now, especially now that she's had the weekend to think it over. I glance at my watch, where the hell is she? I have been here a good hour now. He asks me whether I'm going to tell Suzie and I ask him if he has gone mad. We both laugh out loud at this as we both know that there is no way on earth that I'm going to tell Suzie. I mean, why would I?

We talk some more and Luke reckons that if Sophie has gone out of her way to trap me into impregnating her, then she will hardly hang around. 'Mark my words, she will be off like a shot. I mean it's not as if you're planning to leave Suzie or anything,' he says laughingly.

'God, no,' I say. And he's right. I just need to extricate myself from this mess as soon as possible. Surely Sophie didn't really ever think that I would leave?

We say our goodbyes and I try Sophie's phone again. Nothing. She obviously has it turned off now as the phone goes straight through to answer machine. I am bloody angry now. That bitch has stood me up. I can hardly believe it. She must be with Amanda, I think, and I dial again.

Amanda answers almost straight away in that annoying clipped telephone voice. I don't even bother with politeness. I'm as hacked off with Amanda as I am with Sophie. I can't believe she told Sophie about that kiss.

'Is Sophie with you?' I spit down the phone.

'Oh, hello to you as well Gareth, can I help you?'

'Cut the crap, where is she?' I repeat.

'Oh, haven't you heard? She took the day off today, she and Simon have gone out to the coast today for lunch, to celebrate,' she says. Her voice is sugary and mocking, and I walk straight into it.

'Celebrate what?' I ask. Suddenly I feel as if there is a massive joke here and at my expense.

'Oh, hang on a minute,' she says again in that irritatingly sweet voice. 'I've got another call coming in. Call you back in five,' she says and then she is gone. I stare at the phone, not quite believing it. I chuck it in frustration back into the central car well and wait. Every few minutes I stare again at the phone, willing it to call. I pick it back up and try Sophie's number again. Still no answer. They are a pair of bitches, I think blackly. I imagine them laughing at me, conspirators in some kind of revenge plot. Bloody witches. I grind my teeth and I am still grinding when there is a knock on the window. Some old hag is standing there. I blink at her as if she is some kind of illusion. I don't even know where she has come from, she seems to have just appeared, materialized out of nowhere. We stare at each other and I realise that she is trying to get me to wind down the window. I press the button and the window slides down. This woman must be at least seventy, she has gnarled, veiny, arthritic hands, and she is covered in age spots. She has thin, wiry, grey hair and paper-thin bluey-white skin. I stare at her, trying to will her to disappear. She is wearing a dress that looks like it is made out of curtain fabric and old lady slippers with pink fur and flowers. This can't be happening. I become conscious that she is talking to me and I try to follow what she is saying. All the time I am thinking that she must have escaped from somewhere, maybe there is an old people's home nearby or something. Why doesn't she just vanish back to wherever she came from? I think impatiently. They really should try harder to keep these people in. I look at her again and realize she has quite piercing blue eyes and she is starting to look angry.

'Can I help you?' I say.

'I was going to ask you the same thing, you see this is a private car park for pub patrons only,' she says, and she seems to be speaking very slowly, as if I'm the one who is mad.

'And?' I persist. I am irritated now, who is this old duck and why hasn't bloody Amanda phoned back?

'I'm the landlady,' she says with an amused smile, 'and unless you're drinking I'm going to have to ask you to take your car somewhere else.'

I realize now that she has probably just trotted over from the pub. I mean, how was I supposed to know? Normal people don't go walking around in bloody slippers. And am I really doing any harm parked here? It's not as if they've got a rush on.

I try and give her my most winning smile.

'I was waiting for someone,' I say, 'but it doesn't look like she's going to turn up. Can I just wait a few more minutes and then if she doesn't turn up I'll go? I promise,' I say flashing her my business consultant of the year grin. I am not sure why I am trying to get round this old lady but there is something about the look in her eyes that demands respect. She nods in agreement, smiles and walks back towards the pub. She obviously thinks that I am some sad loser who's been stood up by some bird, I think furiously.

I pick up the phone and as I go to dial it rings again. Amanda. I press the green answer key and before I can bark down the phone at her she is speaking in that pretentious, sickly, client-friendly voice again.

'Oh, I am sorry. Client, you know, had to take it. Now, where was I? Oh yes Sophie, well, she's gone to the coast with Simon,' she says.

'I know, you told me that,' I answer through gritted teeth. I swear my blood pressure is about to go through the roof. I have a real headache now as well, just across my eyes.

'Yes, Simon was so thrilled about the baby. Oh, but, of course you knew about the baby, didn't you? I forgot,' she trills. 'So anyway, they both took the day off and went to celebrate. Everyone is so delighted for them. They have been trying for ages now.' She finishes and for a moment I can't say a word, I sit frozen to the spot not actually hearing what she is saying any more.

'She told Simon the baby was his?' I say, not quite able to believe what I'm hearing.

'Sorry, Gareth, must go. Money to make, clients to see, you understand. See you tomorrow,' she finishes cheerfully and then the phone goes dead.

I'm not quite sure what to do now; I am seething, frustrated, angry and perplexed. This is what I wanted, surely? I think. God, I need a drink. I get out of the car and walk over to the pub in a dazed fashion. The old woman greets me cheerfully and points me towards the bar.

'Oh, cheer up, son, there are plenty of other fish in the

sea' she says. I smile in acknowledgement and order a large gin and tonic and ponder my predicament.

What is the matter with me? This is the best outcome all round. Simon and Sophie have always wanted a kid and now they have one. I definitely didn't want any more and Suzie would have gone ballistic. God, she might have even chucked me out. Then she would have ended up with the house and I would have ended up living in some B and B with Sophie and a screaming baby. I would have become one of these saddo fathers with limited access, probably only able to see the boys in some fast food joint at weekends. And I shudder to think what Suzie would want in maintenance, it would have cost me a bloody fortune. It could all have been very grim indeed. I swig back the gin and tonic and once again thank my lucky stars. Lucky escape, that. Lucky escape indeed. I pay for my drink and walk out into the rain. I guess it's all over with me and Sophie now though, I think ruefully. Shame really, she was a great shag. Fantastic tits.

Chapter 13

Simon

'Strength does not come from physical capacity. It comes from
an indomitable will.'
Mahatma Gandi

I am sitting in a room full of family and good feeling. The sun
pours through the windows and lights up the faces all around
me and I remind myself once again of how lucky I am. It is
such a warm, happy day but I feel cold. I can't remember
being this congratulated since I completed my degree or
perhaps since our wedding day. I feel like I did when we
married, my face aches from all the smiling and I just want
everyone to go home so that Sophie and I can be alone.

The women are all crowded around Sophie cooing and
fussing, discussing when the baby will be due and guessing
the sex. We are thinking the baby may be born in early
November, just in time for Christmas. However, we have
started receiving gifts already; in fact, almost as soon as we
announced 'our news' the presents started arriving. We have
been thoroughly inundated with good will and con-
gratulations from just about everyone. They are all so pleased
for us. None of them have any idea that I feel such a fake. I
have told no one. I mean, who on earth would I tell? What

148

would I say? Somehow it is just easier to be carried along with it all, to play my part.

Sophie has been shopping for England. Already she has ordered a whole nursery full of furniture and fripperies and just this morning she bought more clothes, a steriliser and a playpen. I have never seen her this excited. Later this afternoon my father is coming round to help decorate the guest bedroom a suitable nursery colour (pale yellow, I think) and Sophie tells me that various women (even our next-door neighbour, who we only really know to say good morning to, and my Aunty Glad, who I haven't seen for ten years) have started knitting stuff. I didn't think women still did that. And of course we are grateful. I am grateful. We are surrounded by a hive of good intentioned activity and it is impossible not to get swept up in all that frenzy of planning and expectation.

It would seem that a whole new world opens up to you when you get pregnant and we seem to have appointments coming out of our ears: we have NCT (which is some kind of baby group rather than a car park), ante natal and scan appointments. We have to attend special breathing classes and parenting classes, we have to sign up for kinder music classes and tadpole sessions. We (or perhaps just I) have a lot to learn, it would seem.

All of a sudden we are contemplating baby locks on cupboards, even though we have months to go before the baby is even born, and we are having conversations about whether we should get a baby monitor with CCTV facility. Sophie and I no longer spend time frivolously, nowadays we are found discussing whether children should be given dummies and what schools we should sign up for, about whether breast or bottle is best and how many times a day you should feed. It seems that there are a multitude of different options for consideration and everyone has an opinion they need to impart on how we should do things. It really is quite mind-boggling. But pregnancy suits her; she looks amazing, breathtaking even, and completely unfazed by what is to come. I find that I am quietly in awe of her. The sickness and the tiredness don't seem quite so bad now either and I have got used to seeing her and bump in a variety of different maternity clothes. She looks at peace somehow. Happy at last, thank goodness.

I take a walk outside, warmed by the summer sun and glad to be away from the circus for a while. The garden is at its best now. For the last few months I haven't felt so sociable so I have been reading a few horticultural magazines and getting stuck into the gardening. I have discovered a kind of peace out here working in the soil, watching the flowers grow. I stand and admire the majestic spires of delphinium, and the towering pink hollyhocks. Verbascum and foxgloves grow together adding height to the back of the border whilst geranium and nasturtium add some interest to the front. Apparently this is a winning combination, recommended by some of the best English gardeners. It is not as warm as it should be yet but the heady scent of summer washes over me. I have planted roses, lavender and sweet peas near the windows so that these sweet, innocent scents will fill the house as well as the garden, giving me something new to think about when I'm inside, anything to stop me dwelling on what went on before. The garden isn't now as planned or as ordered as Pete designed. I have added to his planting, finding solace in the random harmonious blocks of colour, and riotous tumblings of blossom. I have spent hours pouring my love into training rambling roses and nurturing the soil. There is nothing like a garden to heal the soul, they say.

Our house backs onto a much larger garden. This is a throwback from times before, when houses were built with the right amount of ground around them, when space was not at such a premium and the cost of land was not as prohibitive. If you stand on a small wooden stool and look over our fence you see a rather forlorn orchard surrounded by long, lush, green grass. I have been able to identify apple, pear and plum trees, all looking fairly sad, definitely not tended or pruned; all in all it is a beautiful garden just wasting away. Almost abandoned. Last weekend I went to have a chat with the guy who owns the land. An old man now, but he used to be responsible for most of the railway this side of London. We spoke for a while of trains and the days of steam, and of gardens and the importance of family. We got on like a house on fire and ended up talking for most of the afternoon. He obviously loved his garden as a younger man and he walked me round, explaining what he had planned to do and what had grown where. Sadly, neglected flower beds and outlines of vegetable plots were now all that remained. I haven't told Sophie yet but I have made him an offer on the piece of his garden that lies directly behind ours and he was more than pleased to accept it. I think it had all become a little too much for him. I plan to keep it as an orchard and perhaps grow some vegetables over there as well. There is a big old walnut tree in the far corner, a beautiful majestic tree that houses a family of squirrels in its gnarled branches and lends gentle shade to the corner. It is a great tree for children to climb, I think. Children need space to run and trees to climb. I stand and try to imagine our son or daughter running around and I wonder if he or she will be blonde or dark. I wonder who he or she will resemble. I think that I'll put in a swing set over on the other side for when the baby gets older, maybe even a slide. I picture the grass mown and some new borders as well; just right now I need such dreams.

I stand and survey and think back over the last few months. It's just easier to be out here right now rather than in there, making small talk and keeping up the pretence of the proud father-to-be. I still shudder when I remember back to that dreadful day. I don't think I will ever forget it. I remember that I just went charging and crashing headlong through the garden, oblivious to the plants or the state of the soil, just desperate to escape from what I had seen. And even though some months have passed now, I still feel sick when I think back. And of course I know I need to just forget all that now and concentrate on the future, I mean, God only knows we have enough to keep us busy right now. But as much as I try to put it all behind us the memory still haunts me. I find that at the most inopportune times my mind will just slip back, and then I find myself forced to regurgitate the whole sorry episode again and again and again. When I think back now, back to the time before it all happened, it is as if I was a different person then, and that somehow this whole infidelity thing has changed me. I struggle to recognize the easy nature that went with the person I used to be. Somehow I feel so much more serious now.

Straight after jumping the wall I just kept running; I must have looked ridiculous dressed in my suit and city shoes haring down the street as if the very devil himself was after me. It wasn't until I stopped that I realized how strange I must have appeared. I remember one of my neighbours stopping to talk to me and asking me if I was OK. I have probably never spoken more than two words to her in my whole life before. I think it's like that now. We each live in our own cocoons, side by side, unaware and disinterested in the lives, the troubles or the passions of our neighbours. I had to walk back probably four streets to find the car, sweating profusely and feeling as sick as a dog. I must have looked as though I was about to have a heart attack or something. By the time I got back to the car my shoes had rubbed blisters into my feet and my back hurt but I just got in and drove and then kept on driving. I ended up in a hotel several hundred miles away, a huge sprawling mansion, once someone's home, now used primarily for conferences. The place was huge, all chintz and flowers and wildly expensive. But I didn't care; there was something reassuring about the orderly anonymity of the place. The first night I was there, I spent the whole evening doing lengths of the pool. Up and down without stopping, swimming until my lungs felt that they might explode and my neck felt as if it might snap. I swam until I was too tired to do anything but sleep. Tired beyond thinking, tired beyond dreaming.

Waking up the next day I almost thought I had imagined it, but then, even before I was truly awake, the reality and clarity of what I had seen came flooding painfully back. Sophie and him. Images of what I had seen in the kitchen. And, if that wasn't bad enough, what I hadn't seen I then imagined. Pictures of him touching her, kissing her, undressing her would fill my every waking moment. I learnt that jealousy has an unrestricted imagination and absolutely no pity or compassion. I was held hostage by my pain, frozen and immobile by constant strangled images of them caressing or making love or perhaps even just laughing together. Over and over again I tormented myself, knowing full well that all the while I sat in that flowered, pillow-strewn room they were together, in my house, in our bed even. Now, with hindsight, I think it grated even more because I could see so clearly the type of man Gareth was, and what I couldn't understand then and still don't understand now is why she couldn't see through him.

Most of the next day passed in a blur. I slept fitfully for most of it, trying hard to blank out the pictures in my head, too tired to move, exhausted by grief, too worn out even to be angry any more. Looking back now I think I was still in shock. At some point I think I must have decided to drink and I drank a lot. It is not big and I know it's not clever but sometimes it is the only way to get through.

I'm not proud of those few days. But sometimes you have to hit the very bottom before you can work out a way back up again. I wish I could tell you that I had a plan when I left there. All the way home I kept thinking that something would come to me, some divine intervention would show me where I should go or what I should do next.

I have no idea what time I arrived home. But it was like walking back in time. There were flowers in the hall and food in the kitchen. Sophie looked tired but relieved to see me and for a while I thought it had all been a dream. She complained playfully that she had been unable to contact me and I just went along with it, said that it had been a busy trip, that I hadn't had time to call. She told me that there had been an intruder in the house and that she had called the police and I remember making all the right husbandly noises. All the time scared to say too much in case I gave myself away. It turns out the police were clueless, thought it was a random attempt at burglary.

There was a part of me that was just so relieved that everything seemed to be back to normal again, that I didn't want to disturb anything. I have never really been one for confrontation. Of course there was a part of me that wanted to tell her that I knew, and moments that first night when I wanted to scream at her that I had seen her and that wanker together. I think there was a part of me that wanted some kind of retribution even, maybe I wanted to see the shock on her face when she realised that I knew, perhaps there was a part of me that felt as though I wanted to hurt her as I had been hurt. But I suppose I must be stronger than that, stronger than I ever thought I could be, because the evening went on. We ate and talked and even laughed together. I could see that she was trying so hard to make the evening work, to dispel any unease between us. So I made it easy for her. We talked about old times, about when we met and how innocent we had been then. And then when we went upstairs she held me so tightly I thought at times I may be unable to breathe. After she fell asleep I lay there, puzzled and bewildered, trying to work out what could have happened in

154

her world to warrant such a change. After lying awake for many hours, scared to move in case her arms fell from around me, I decided that her affair must have ended, and I think I even dared to hope that it would all be all right from then on. And so at last I fell asleep, only to be awakened shortly after by her sickness, retching that went on and on until the sun came up. I went in to offer my help, to assist her somehow. I sponged her face and kept her hair out of the way. And when she'd finished I popped her back into bed and cleaned up the bathroom. I knew then before she even told me. I remember wondering if this would be when she would tell me about her affair, I remember hoping and praying that God would give me the strength to know what to say.

I think at some point that morning, when I watched her, pale and sick and sleeping, that I knew what I was going to do. I knew that no matter what she had done I couldn't live without her. And it didn't really matter who the father was, did it? After all the baby would definitely be half hers, so right there was one rock-solid reason never to leave. I remember reading somewhere that anyone could father a child but not everyone could be a father. And surely it would be the person who supported that child and cared for that child who would be important at the end of the day. Perhaps the baby would never need to know. I mean, why would you complicate things? I recall working the whole thing out, surmising that there was a very good chance that it had to be mine anyway. I figured she must have used a rubber with him. Surely she wouldn't have been so stupid, in this day of STDs, to have shagged him unprotected. It was then that I made my mind up. I took a deep breath and walked back into the bedroom with a cup of tea for her and then I asked her straight out how far pregnant she was.

She just smiled at me then and held my hand. And then we both cried, the tea growing cold on the night stand as we hugged and tentatively made plans. I told her that I would always love her and that I would do my very best to be the greatest dad in the world. I remember the way she looked at me then and told me that she knew now more than ever that I was the only man she would ever love. And I felt strong again, strong enough to cope with anything, whole and invincible, jubilant and triumphant, after all it was obvious now that I had won.

But then winning is not always straightforward and sometimes bittersweet, and after the initial exaltation disappeared I was left feeling almost cheated, tricked somehow into thinking I was wholly victorious. What if the baby was his? Would that change anything? Does it matter if I am a cuckold, nurturing another man's child, like the bird who warms the eggs a cuckoo has laid in his nest? That will be me then, the Cuckold. And I have researched it. I needed to understand this; I needed to know how many other men go through this. Isn't this the way we cope with things nowadays, isn't there always an answer on the internet somewhere? Hundreds of websites exist where like-minded people can get together to explore their inclinations. And there are actually people out there who encourage their wives' infidelities and get off on being humiliated in this way. Apparently, in certain circles, a cuckold is a consummate voyeur who derives pleasure from seeing his partner serviced by another male. Right now I think that sticking red hot javelins in my eyes would be preferable. Cuckold. I hate this title, this new description of who I have become. There is a whole suggestion around it that I am weak, that somehow I have become a laughing stock. But surely if no one knows then it will be my secret? Something I need to come to terms with in my own time. The Portuguese use the term *corno manso* to indicate those men who, although cheated on by their partners, come to accept such infidelity as a fact of their lives. Maybe that is more like me, stoic, resolute even. It seems like a much more forgiving term. It sounds romantic somehow, strong and supportive, rather than feeble and walked over.

I am not really a religious man but they say that there is no such thing as an atheist on the battlefield of life. And perhaps most of us need to feel that there is at least some hope of divine intervention when things are looking bleak. I find it hard to believe that we are just here to muddle through unaided. So at first I found myself praying for strength, for some kind of confirmation that I was doing the right thing. I would even look for signs. Nothing too heavy you understand, not visions of angels or pictures of Christ in puddles, more like evidence of tranquillity at home, in simple things like Sophie and I being able to sleep and laugh again. Signs of a conscience at ease maybe. If I had made the wrong decision it would be apparent, surely. I would feel a palpable unhappiness, or Sophie would be uptight. There would be that nervous tension that lived between us before, a marked and constant underlying rigidity. I have heard it said that we are never really given any more than we can cope with, that in times of stress and hardship we all find a strength that we never knew we had. Maybe that's true, because now, when I look at my Sophie with that baby growing beneath her heart, I know that I am easily strong enough to do the right thing by her and the baby, whatever its paternity. As time has gone on I haven't dismissed the chance that the baby might be his. But then life never works out as you planned, and sometimes things aren't perfect. All I know is that we, Sophie and I, are going to be parents and that to me is all that matters. After all, if we had gone to a fertility clinic we might have ended up having to use a donor, who knows? If we had adopted, the child wouldn't have been our biological offspring but we would have loved it just the same. I am now decided that it really makes no odds. I will love this child because he or she will be part of Sophie and if there is any of me in there as well, then let's hope it's the good bits.

Things are getting better and we are getting stronger every day. Surprise, surprise, she has given up the weight-lifting classes and painting lessons and we spend each night and each weekend as we always did, together. We are back making plans but now instead of holidays we plan for the birth of our baby and speculate about how many more children we should have in the future. Every now and again I see her frown when her phone rings, she will glance at me and redden and immediately press the ignore button. When this happens I just pretend to look the other way. I do sometimes worry about what would happen if they got back together. In the early days I was tormented daily, every time she went to work, in fact, as I knew that he would be there, probably trying to wheedle his way back into her affections. But I have to learn to trust her. There are times when I have thought about revenge, of course I have. Everything from slashing his tyres to having him taken out by some shady hitman. But at some point you have to let it go. Otherwise it just eats you up inside, it controls you, it stops you eating and you don't sleep. You spend your whole life watching and waiting. I know I can't live like that, don't want to live like that. But I do believe that what goes around comes around and I think fate has ways of dealing with the Gareths of this world. So for now I will just watch and wait. Who knows – if it gets too bad in the future maybe we could emigrate. I have heard that Bermuda is quite nice.

Chapter 14

Amanda

'A lie told often enough becomes the truth.'
Lenin

Thank goodness Sophie and I are out to see a client this afternoon; I can't bear another minute in this building with that lying, posturing toad.

Just looking at him makes my stomach turn. Poor Sophie, I can't even imagine how difficult this must be for her. I can't believe he has had the gall to keep working here, I thought he would at least ask for a transfer. He should have just left the company. Does he have no conscience at all? No modicum of decency? I watch him hypocritically talk of honesty and sincerity to our clients, knowing all the time what he has been up to. Deceitful and disingenuous to the core. I find myself scrutinizing him as the words spill out of him, an unending spew of lies. He just can't help himself, he lies without thinking about it, everything he does he embroiders, he lies about his life, his past and his work. I am sure that he has been lying for so long now that he hardly knows where the truth begins. He is a fraud and a phoney and he has got to get caught out sooner or later. I'm sure of it.

I look over at Sophie but she seems to be completely unaware of the way that he is staring at her. It is just plain creepy. All the time he is trying to get her attention. It must be so hard for her. She has told him and told him again that she wants nothing more to do with him but he is so persistent, she told me that it has become like an obsession with him. He makes me sick now to look at him. But I can't help myself, I find myself watching him, determined to catch him out. I am fascinated by his behaviour, the way that a spider with a fly would fascinate, or a cat with a mouse. It is a fiendish, moreish attraction. As soon as he thinks that no one is looking he starts flirting outrageously; he really has a problem, ogling and eyeing up any poor female who steps into his radius. He is a complete lech. The worst thing is that Sophie and I have to be seen working and socializing with him, otherwise the rest of the team are bound to get suspicious. It is a nightmare. Sophie has been amazing though; you would never know that anything had happened at all. I am just so relieved that Simon never found out, he seems over the moon that Sophie is expecting and he is so sweet and protective with her. I can't remember Pete ever being like that when I was expecting. I can even remember when I was about eight months gone, him asking me to get a crate of beers out of the garage. Typical.

I must admit that I wasn't happy at all at first. It just all seemed so wrong. I couldn't believe that Sophie was actually going to brazenly pass the baby off as Simon's and not even mention the affair. I know it's the easy way out but that doesn't make it right, does it? I can't imagine that in the same position I would make the same choices and I don't think it's fair to take away a person's right to choose. Maybe I know that in the same situation Pete wouldn't even blink an eye. He would be out of the door in a shot and wouldn't look back. I know that he loves me too much to watch me love another man's child. He couldn't spend every day watching the baby grow up and resemble someone else that I had loved. He would always be looking for the differences, the reasons why the child wouldn't fit, always overlooking the likenesses. I don't think he would think it fair on the child either. After all, doesn't everyone deserve to know who their parents are? At uni I studied psychology, the big nature and nurture debate, whether you are born with your personality or whether you develop and become the person you are by learning from the people around you. Behavioral geneticists study five constituent human traits when looking at the nature vs nurture question: openness, conscientiousness, extroversion, agreeableness and neuroticism. So under openness they study the individual's emotional development, they look at how adventurous they are, for instance. Under conscientiousness a study is carried out on the individual's tendency to show self-discipline, act dutifully and their aim for achievement. Extroversion is all about energy levels, positive emotions and the tendency to seek stimulation and the company of others. Agreeableness is probably more obvious – the tendency to be compassionate and cooperative rather then suspicious and antagonistic. And finally neuroticism. Here psychologists look at whether an individual has a tendency to experience unpleasant emotions easily, such as anger, anxiety, depression or vulnerability. If you look at these traits, assuming of course that they are inherited rather than learnt, and also assuming that the baby is Gareth's, the differences are going to be colossal. I mean, both Sophie and Simon are stay-at-home introverts. They are both self-disciplined and ambitious, hard-working and even-natured. Gareth, though, is a reckless extrovert, he is antagonistic and without compassion, he is lazy and moody. I just don't see how Sophie is going to get away with it. How can you turn a blind eye to such negative personality traits? I pray for the sake of that poor child that he inherits Sophie's traits rather than Gareth's.

Surely this child will look around him one day and notice the differences, surely he will wonder why he doesn't really take after anyone he knows? Won't he wonder why his personality is so dissimilar? What if he starts to feel as though he doesn't really fit in? You hear of adopted children who constantly feel as though they can't succeed, that they were never really what their parents wanted. It could easily happen. Because, if he is Gareth's child, he definitely wasn't designed to be brought up by Simon, was he? And Gareth is just refusing to let go, he is still phoning several times a night and hanging around her all day long. What if he tells Simon? What if he turns up at the hospital declaring his undying love, and the baby to be his. Simon shouldn't find out like that, it is just not fair. It is adding insult to injury. Sophie needs to take responsibility for this and just come clean. At least that gives Simon the option to be involved in whatever they tell the child. Simon should know that he might be about to bring up another man's child.

I worry about Simon's parents as well. Can you imagine falling in love with the idea of a grandchild, maybe even the child itself, only to find out that he is not your flesh and blood after all? They will be heartbroken. I am desperately trying not to judge Sophie, not to act as some holier than thou umpire in all of this. But every time I see Simon I get an attack of the guilts. He is such a good man. I think he deserves to know. And I think the baby has a right to know who his father is.

I think Simon loves differently as well, differently to Pete that is. He has always placed Sophie high up on a pedestal, no, pedestal isn't quite right. Maybe an ivory tower or minaret, tall and protected. I think he would love her no matter what she did and I think he would definitely have the capacity to love another man's child, even Gareth's. There is no way that he would leave her.

So maybe Sophie's right, maybe he doesn't need to know.

And perhaps he won't see the signs; he might just think that the baby is his. Maybe his love for the child, his love for Sophie will blind him to any apparent dissimilarities. Who knows? Maybe I am completely wrong and by some fluke of fate the baby is his after all.

I read somewhere that something like fifty per cent of women have said that if they became pregnant by another man but wanted to stay with their partner they would lie about the baby's real father. Fifty per cent! I find it shocking that such a high percentage of women feel themselves capable of such deceit. That they could blindly ignore and blatantly disregard what is morally correct to protect themselves and to provide their child with a father. Not the correct father, you understand, but a father anyhow. Maybe you just get used to living a lie. Perhaps if you wake up every day and say the same words day in and day out then after a while those words start to become the truth. And if you say something long enough then maybe you start to believe it yourself, especially knowing that if you were to deviate for even one second from this well-rehearsed verse, it would mean the lives of the people closest to you would be devastated just because you changed your tune. How could you ever then just stop? How could you reveal all one day and watch all those carefully tuned and honed words smother and choke the people around you? Anyway, maybe if you raise a baby to be a child and a child to be an adult, then you deserve the right to be called its father. Maybe it's just a word after all.

Chapter 15

Rebecca

'Only enemies speak the truth; friends and lovers lie endlessly, caught
in the web of duty.'
Stephen King

It would seem that for as long as I have loved Luke I have
hated his best friend Gareth. You may think that hate is a
strong word, perhaps unnecessarily dramatic, but there it is. I
wish I could tell you that time had reduced or nullified my
passionate abhorrence. But it hasn't. If anything this anger at
him, at what he does again and again and again, is kept
gently simmering. Occasionally, when I witness the start of
another indiscretion I boil over, in fact Luke has stopped
confiding in me now as he knows how furious the whole
situation makes me. Countless times I have watched him lie –
and brazenly too, without any regard at all for the people
closest to him; he respects no one, not his family, not his
friends. Over the years I have watched him deceive and
betray all of us, his wife, his children, his friends and even his
mother. For him it is all part of the game. He cheats and
swindles those closest to him and all the time with that
polished smile plastered on his face. Every time it happens I
am told to bite my tongue and keep my silence. So I listen,

fuming and livid, as Luke does his best to mitigate his friend's 'indiscretions'. We have even been his alibis. The problem with a lie, though, is it never really dies, it is like dropping a stone into a pond, the ripples created encircle forever, widening continuously, expanding until everything on the surface is touched. I detest the way that we always end up inexplicably drawn into his games. Sometimes it is as though we become guilty purely by our association, he mentions us and we become linked to his crime. I have put up with him for years now and I must say I dread his phone calls and am revolted by his escapades.

And it all seems to be happening again. I couldn't wait to get out this morning, I can hardly look at Luke I am so angry. So I have come to the beach, always my refuge. I can be here in less than fifteen minutes depending on the weather and the traffic. And this is my time. The children are with our nanny and so I get this time alone with my dog just to breathe. It never ceases to amaze me how different the beach looks every single day. Sometimes when the weather is bad, I stand and stare in awe at the crashing crescendo of water that seems to boil and seethe with an energy all of its own. Hard to conceive, I know, on days like today, when the water seems almost too lazy to find its way continuously to the shore. I watch as slow undulating curls topped with gentle froth meander to the shore, hardly moving the shingle at all. And the sun is hot today, really hot. Too bright to look at as it sparkles down beatifically onto a million shiny facets on the water's surface. It is just perfect. The sun has enticed other people out onto my beach today as well. I smile and greet people as I pass, mothers with small children collecting things in buckets and a sprightly looking elderly couple with their arms looped together. Further away a young girl sits on the pebbles watching the sea. She is clutching a mobile phone to her ear and I watch her laugh every so often. I smile contentedly, feeling the warm sun on my back and my arms as I watch my loopy Retriever run in and out of the surf. She is a big dog, and I watch as she lopes along, her paws slipping on the large smooth pebbles that make up our beach and for a moment I forget all about how vile Gareth is and I feel like the luckiest woman alive.

When we moved out here, all my friends thought we were mad. They couldn't understand why we would possibly want to live so far away from the city. But for as long as I can remember I have wanted to live by the sea. I have no idea why, all I know is that I feel at peace here. I wanted my children to have this kind of childhood. I wanted them to have the opportunity to learn how to swim and windsurf, and learn how to sail, not on some man-made inland lake, but on the open sea with all the adventure that goes with it. I wanted them to be able to play on a beach whenever they wanted and not have to breathe in the fumes and the smog of the city. And the air is so clear here. It has to be better for them. I want them to grow up with happy, carefree memories of their childhood. When we moved I did wonder for a while whether I would come to take it all for granted, the beautiful house and the beach so close by. I wondered whether the novelty would wear off and I would no longer feel this compulsion to be by the sea. When we lived in London I am ashamed to say that I stopped going to places like the Tower of London, the Tate gallery and the waxworks. I felt like I had seen it all and done it all before. But here, the sea calls to me, I think. It wakes me up and invigorates me if I am tired or hung over and celebrates with me when I am just happy to be alive. I smile as I look over at my daft hound. She is lying in the surf now, her light golden hair coloured a shade darker by the water, and her face relaxed into her sunny, happy dog smile. Her own personal spa treatment, I think. And as I walk I think again for the umpteenth time that morning how lucky I am and how glad I am that I am not Suzie.

I met Suzie years ago; it must be ten years ago now. A

long time before I had the children. Luke was really good friends with Gareth (why, I have no idea, they couldn't be more different) and over the years we have become quite close. She is one of these women who puts everyone before herself, she really will do anything for anyone. She works really hard as well, irregular hours at the hospital just so that she can be around for those boys. I have known her to work nights and not get the chance to sleep just so she can watch them play football or take them to the park. Sometimes she sounds so tired I almost have to order her to get some rest. Boys are tough as well; they just have so much energy. You really do have to run them like dogs to get any peace. And she puts up with so much from Gareth; all I can think is that she must turn a blind eye for the children's sake. Why else would any woman put up with that kind of treatment? I can't believe she doesn't know, doesn't see the signs. She is an absolute saint.

But then Gareth had me fooled at first, I was taken in by his smooth charm and easy humour. And he is a charmer, he has the ability to look into any girl's eyes and make her feel like the only important person in the room. But he is nothing but trouble. One Christmas Luke and I had a party and Gareth and Suzie came along. He met a few of my girlfriends and although he didn't try it on that night, he went out of his way to contact each one shortly after. He was systematic and literally called every one of them. I mean, how embarrassing. And just awful for Suzie as well. One of my girlfriends, Michelle, went out with him for about six months. I couldn't even warn her because Gareth told her to keep it a secret. He had fed her this cock and bull story about not really getting on with his wife when all the time Suzie had no idea at all and was at home by herself every night coping with the boys and juggling work. She was completely unaware. It was horrible. He is utterly egocentric and he seems to have an unquench-able appetite for sex. You read about these men who book themselves in for rehab because they have a sex addiction and you don't really believe it, at least not until you meet someone like Gareth. And now it's happening again. I have to do something, I have to stop it. There is a part of me that wants Suzie to find out what he is really like, to have him exposed as the cad that he is. But then there is another part of me that doesn't want her to get hurt. I feel so bad for her.

It all came to a head last night. I must have fallen asleep on the sofa but about 10.00 pm I was woken up by Luke talking on the phone. First of all I thought it was just one of his local mates but then I heard Suzie's name and got curious. I couldn't help but overhear. Luke was in the next room so bits of the conversation were a little nebulous but I am quite sure that I got the gist of what is going on. I lie very still just listening to Luke talk. Gareth is seeing someone again, someone called Sophie. And this time it's even worse, this Sophie is pregnant. About five months gone, from what I could make out. Gareth is a complete tart, he is totally feckless and entirely irresponsible. What is wrong with him? He has a beautiful wife and two gorgeous children. What more can he want? I just couldn't believe what I was hearing and Luke was oblivious to me listening. Normally I sleep so heavily nothing wakes me. Luke must have thought it was safe to talk as I was sound asleep. So I just lay there incredulous, and getting angrier and angrier every time I thought of poor Suzie.

I spent most of the night worrying about what to do, trying to work out whether I should say something. After all, if it was Luke I would want someone to tell me. What kind of friend am I if I don't say anything? For most of the night I have been wracking my brains, the name sounds so familiar. When we went to their Easter party there was a girl he kept talking to there. But her name was Amanda, definitely not Sophie. She had a little boy, I remember. For a time I thought something was going on with her but it turns out that they don't actually get on. They work together and Gareth hates her apparently. However, I can always rely on Luke for some information. He won't volunteer anything but if I'm right he won't try to lie to me. I remember asking him about Amanda on the way home. I asked him outright if Gareth was sleeping with Amanda and he just laughed and said that I was completely off the mark that time. Since then I had almost forgotten about it all, and I can't blame Luke really, I suppose he is in a difficult position as well. I mean, what is he to do if Gareth confides in him?

It wasn't until this morning when I was preparing breakfast that it came to me. I think Sophie was the blonde girl, Amanda's friend. She seemed quite harmless, not the type of girl you would imagine would run off with your husband. If anything, I would say she seemed a little naïve, she definitely didn't appear to be any kind of femme fatale – obviously there is more to her than meets the eye. I remember meeting her husband as well; I think he was a banker or a lawyer or something. A really nice guy. Why on earth would Sophie risk her marriage for someone like Gareth? She has to be completely demented. I keep thinking that maybe the baby is her husband's but it doesn't sound as if it can be. Luke spent ages talking to Gareth about what he should do, about whether or not he should come clean and tell Suzie. I have always known that Gareth is horrible but to think that he could do this to Suzie is a real shock. Someone has to stop this. How can I just stand by and do nothing? As I walk with the dog back to the car I realize I should telephone Amanda; after all, we got on quite well that day and I did put her in touch with my father.

By the time I get home it is around 10.00 am. I make the kids a mid-morning snack and pick up the phone. I still have Amanda's business card. My father is on the board of a large computer company and I passed Amanda's details to him, just in case his firm needed a new adviser in the future. It turned out that he called her and they got on really well, so I

169

am going to use this as an excuse to phone her. I just knew that Gareth was up to no good that day; he had that sharp, shifty look about him that I have got to know so well, always a precursor for trouble ahead. I can't believe I didn't notice him flirting with Sophie; they must have been playing it cool. When I think back to that day, I get so cross that he could have so little respect for Suzie that he just calmly invited his mistress round for the afternoon. He has got to be stopped.

I dial Amanda's mobile number and wait. After around four rings she picks up. She sounds genuinely pleased to hear from me. We talk for a bit about the weather and her work and I ask about her boy, Max. We talk for a bit more and I can tell she is becoming curious as to the reason for my call. I compose myself and then get right to it.

'I think your friend Sophie is having an affair with Gareth;' I say. I exhale slowly and wait.

There is a resounding silence on the other end of the line and for a moment I wonder whether she has hung up or whether we have been cut off. I can almost hear her thinking.

'Look, this isn't easy for me,' she says tentatively. 'Sophie is my best friend,' she says.

'I know, but Suzie is mine,' I say defensively. 'And she doesn't deserve this.'

'I don't know what you know or who has told you what, but it's all over now. There was something going on some time ago but Sophie finished with him a couple of months ago,' she says. I can tell that she is struggling with this, but still I press on. I am doing this for Suzie.

'But isn't she pregnant?' I persist.

There is a sharp intake of breath now and I realize that I have hit a nerve.

'Look, it isn't what you think. The baby isn't Gareth's,' she says.

'Are you sure?' I ask. I am confused now, trying to reconcile the conversation I heard Luke having, with what

170

Amanda is telling me. 'I think Gareth thinks the baby is his,' I try again.

'He can think whatever he likes,' she spits angrily. 'He has done enough damage and he should just leave her alone,' she continues. 'I know Suzie is your friend and everything but it really has been all over for months now. Sophie is really happy with her husband again and they are both excited about the baby. Sophie just wants to forget all about Gareth.' Amanda says this in hushed tones and I realize that she must be in the office. I know this is difficult for her, but I can't leave it alone; how can Sophie know that it is definitely her husband's baby? Could this be some kind of cover up? I try again.

'Look, I know this is difficult for you, but I heard Luke talking to Gareth last night. Gareth is sure that the baby is his. Is there any chance that it might be?' I persevere. 'I just think that Suzie should know if it is, and maybe someone should tell Sophie what kind of man Gareth really is. That's all,' I say.

'Oh my God, this is getting so out of hand. Look, it could be Gareth's, who knows? But I promised that I wouldn't say anything. So many people could get hurt if this gets out. I don't see why Suzie needs to know. Sophie has stopped seeing Gareth now and her husband thinks that the baby is his. What is the point of stirring things up further?' she finishes.

And I can see her point, but I still feel as though I need to do something. Surely as a friend I should tell Suzie. So I ask Amanda. I ask her what she would do if she was me, but Amanda is adamant that Suzie shouldn't find out. She tells me that she thinks that Sophie was completely manipulated by Gareth and that Sophie is fundamentally a good person. Amanda tells me that she thinks that someone like Sophie was just not equipped to fight off someone like Gareth and so it all just got out of control. We leave our little chat with me somehow agreeing that I won't say anything to Suzie for the time being, and Amanda promising me that if the relationship kicks off again she will tell me and we will then think about telling Suzie. And then, if Suzie has any sense, she will divorce Gareth and clean him out in the process. That ought to curb his desires somewhat.

Chapter 16

Sophie

'Keep five yards from a carriage, ten yards from a horse and a
hundred yards from an elephant, but the distance one should keep
from a wicked man cannot be measured.'
Indian proverb

Nearly lunchtime, thank God, I am absolutely starving, I
must get something to eat soon or I swear I'll expire. I have
just ten minutes to go until I can leave and get some food. I
check my list of things to do and realize that I really must
chase the police again. I know they are busy, but if we gave
our clients the kind of shoddy service they dish out we would
soon be out of business. How much effort does it take just to
telephone someone to keep them updated? I think, fuming.
I don't expect that they have found our intruder for a minute
but they could at least call and tell us that. I phoned them
about a month ago and was told that someone would
definitely get back to us and that they would try and locate
our file but we still haven't heard anything. Nothing at all. I
just want some closure that's all. I still feel a little nervous
every time I hear a noise at night or I'm home alone. And
what with being pregnant I guess I just feel vulnerable at the
moment.

I sort through my drawer and find the business card that Sergeant Cleary left me and dial the number. I have a reference number so I patiently read out the number to the operator and ask for Sergeant Cleary in person. Perhaps if I speak to him personally he will be able to tell me something. At least he won't be able to say that he doesn't know anything about it. After a short wait he comes to the phone. He has a great telephone voice, I think, he makes me feel safe even though he is some twenty miles away. We exchange pleasantries and he asks how I am. I can't resist telling him about the baby and he congratulates me. We talk for a bit about babies, late nights and nappies and then more seriously he informs me that he is unable to update me any further. He tells me that our file has been taken to be reviewed by a team working on a series of burglaries on the other side of town. He says that he will check out our case again when the file is returned but he thinks it unlikely that any progress would have been made. He tells me that he doesn't personally think that our intruder fits the profile that the other team are looking for and that he still thinks it was opportunistic. He explains that these occurrences are seldom repeated, especially in our case when the would-be thief must have got quite a shock to find us home. I agree with him, blushing quite red at the memory of what he must have seen. We talk some more about security generally and he gives me the number of a local security company. He also suggests that we get a dog and I thank him again, whilst he apologizes for not being able to help any further. He says he will contact me if there are any developments, but I'm not holding my breath.

I grab my handbag and dash out to find some lunch. Just lately I have started walking the ten minutes into town at lunchtime rather than grab a sandwich at the restaurant at work. The walk will do me good, I think; I have become quite addicted to cheese and pickle sandwiches lately and there is a

174

deli in town that serves the best sandwiches ever, with pickled red cabbage on the side. I just can't seem to get enough of pickled red cabbage at the moment. I'm getting through a jar a day easily. I wonder whether that means that I am carrying a little boy or a little girl. It feels like a girl, I think fondly and look down at my gently rounded tummy. I am twenty-three weeks pregnant now and reaching this stage is a big relief. My baby measures just 42 cm currently but with modern technology, it should be able to survive outside the womb now, if, God forbid, I was to have her early. There is still a risk, of course, but, according to my obstetrician, she now has an eighty per cent chance of survival in a special baby care unit. And her chances of survival become greater each week that goes by. Every night I read my mother and baby books and find out what new development to expect at each stage, and I can't help but feel as though we have bonded already, my baby and me. I am happier than I think I have ever been. I sail through each day knowing that I have this glorious secret growing inside me. Simon and I chose not to find out the baby's sex, because we really don't mind one way or another. We just pray she is healthy. And I really do think it's a girl. Simon, on the other hand, swears that I'm carrying a boy and has already started looking at football kits and Scalextric sets. Apparently the baby is now covered in something called vernix, a greasy white protective film which will protect her soft skin. She even gets hiccups now and I hold my hand to where I can feel the tiny jumps, mentally telling her not to worry. After all, it must be quite scary to hiccup for the first time ever. I have started playing soft classical music to her in the evenings, and I talk constantly to her as well now, getting as close to my bump as my new shape will allow. I'm sure Simon thinks I am quite mad as I babble away, I talk about the weather, what I'm doing or just how much I love her. Apparently she can already recognize my voice. I never cease to be amazed at this miracle growing inside me and I know that I've become a real baby bore. All these years I have taken my body so much for granted but now I know that this is what we are here for, I now realize that I was born to do this. Designed especially for reproduction. Amazing that I never thought of my body like this before. I have always viewed myself as something that was never quite right, always too fat or too flabby, not long enough here or too big there. It was just a glorified rack to hang clothes from.

Every day of my life now I thank God for my baby and, as her due date gets closer, I pray that it will all be OK. And I am so relieved that she will grow up with both a mother and a father. All the fears I had that I could one day just leave my baby and walk away now just seem ridiculous. I know now that I am not my mother, and I will do whatever I have to do to make sure my baby always has two parents. I know that Amanda still questions my decision not to tell Simon about the affair. But I know I have done the right thing. Simon is the most loyal and responsible person I know and he would never leave us alone (unlike Bloody Gareth, who would be off after the first piece of skirt that comes close). No, Simon is as committed as I am to providing a secure and loving home for this child. Why on earth would I do anything to jeopardize that? I promise silently that my baby will never have to sit and wonder where her parents are. She will never have to lay awake night after night, wondering what it was that she could have done that was so wrong, so bad that it made her mother leave. No, I think determinedly, this baby will never feel isolated or desolate like I did. And why should she have to grow up knowing that her father could possibly be a man that didn't even want her to be born? I don't care what lies I have to tell or how many people I have to mislead, it has to be different for her. I continue through the park, heading towards the shops, I still have a good five minute walk before I get there but I am tired already. I nod and smile at people walking past, trying to concentrate on the

176

lunchtime world around me. Lately, I have become quite used to complete strangers striking up conversation with me, asking me when the baby is due; I have even had a few complete strangers try and touch my tummy, so now I try and head for one of the bistros, less chance of any interruptions, I think.

I have decided to play it safe and give birth in hospital – if anything goes wrong there are trained medical staff on hand and some of the best technology. I know the whole childbirth thing is so safe now but I still feel nervous when I think about it. I'm getting really tired now as well. The trouble with this job is that I need to follow Amanda around to different clients for most of the week. Maybe I should stop travelling so much now; the last long journey we did made me so tired and my feet were swollen all evening. The last thing I want is to end up giving birth in the back of Amanda's car along with the discarded cigarette boxes and Max's toys. I also find that I am in a bit of a daze most of the time. I think I'm the only mother-to-be at the NCT classes who takes notes. I am sure the rest of them think I'm a bit strange, but I really am struggling to concentrate right now.

The NCT classes are held in an enormous conservatory that looks out onto a sweeping lawn edged all around by old trees. The conservatory was built as an addition to a private nursing home and each week when we arrive we are greeted by a horde of elderly patients eager for an update and a chat. We sit each week, looking out over the lawn and drinking tea, whilst learning about correct breathing and the different stages of labour. I have been going to the classes since I first found out that I was pregnant and I have met some really nice girls. There are four of us who are first-time mothers, the rest of the women already have children. One lady who goes is on her fourth; I am sure she only attends to get some peace from her other children. You wouldn't think you would need the classes after doing it three times before. One

177

of the other first-time mothers is a single parent and I cringe every time I see the other girls go out of their way to be nice to her. She is taking her mother with her to the birth as the father is just not interested. Every time I see her I think that it could have been me. If I had taken Amanda's advice and come clean to Simon, it would have been me being pitied by the other girls and coming to terms with bringing up a child alone. I shiver just to think of it and know without a doubt that I have done the right thing. I am not that strong. There is no way I would have the strength to bring a child into this world and then cope with that child alone.

I have told the company that I will return to work after the baby is born. In reality I am not sure what to do. Sometimes when I get called into the office to discuss handing my workload to the admin department or maternity leave dates I have to stifle a fit of the giggles. The whole thing still feels surreal, like some weird fantasy. On days like this I rush home and sit in the nursery, touching the tiny clothes and piles of nappies, reassured by the tangible evidence around me. Work have been really good about me attending all my appointments. And I must say I was surprised at how good the care is, even though the system is totally unorganized. I have had to take the whole morning off work for each visit. And each time I go it is with trepidation. I have read all the books so I know kind of what to expect but there is still the fear of the unknown. The midwives are excellent, and they take a real interest in how the pregnancy is going, but the doctors are so efficient and impersonal you leave feeling like a piece of meat. Every time they examine me I get scared, and when they walk towards me clutching their sonic aid to listen for the baby's heartbeat I can't help but panic. I am so anxious all the time that everything will be OK. And they don't actually tell you anything, they just look at the test results you have had to date, and write more notes. After waiting all those hours to see them you expect to be told something about the baby at least. And while they write, you sit waiting, feeling the paranoia creep up your spine, wondering if all pregnant women turn into raving hypochondriacs.

And I wonder about Gareth. I know he wants me back and I see him watching me. Surely he must wonder about the baby? I can't help but feel sad that he has just thrown this all away.

Simon has been a real sweetheart and tells me that we can manage on just his salary. He recently got a promotion so we have a little more money now anyway. I wonder whether I can do pension and investment admin from home. Perhaps that way I can work around the baby. Everyone tells us that our whole lives will be turned upside-down. They tell us how this baby will change everything for ever. As I sit here in the sunshine with another fork full of cabbage I smile ruefully to myself, my days of having long lunches by myself are probably numbered! I find that, as my time comes nearer, I am consciously building myself up to expect the worst, just in case. I try and work out strategies whilst I still have time to think. I plan how I will cope with a colicky baby or perhaps one that doesn't stop crying. I have booked into a first-aid course as well, just in case, and I am sure the local pharmacist thinks I fancy him as every day I seem to buy something else to go into our medicine cupboard. We now have a plethora of teething aids, nappy rash cures, cradle cap cream and Calpol. You can never be too prepared, I think.

Last week I had my twenty-three-week scan. Nowadays these amazing machines can see all the visible features of the baby: its heart, brain, kidneys, stomach, face and limbs. The whole scan was just magical, I got to lay down with my stomach in the air while they sent high frequency sound waves bouncing off the tissues and bones of our baby which then magically turned into a picture. Even Simon got tearful. The ultrasound technician left us alone with this real-time picture of our baby on the screen, and I swear we could have stayed all day, just watching our baby move around as if in space, moving her tiny hands and stretching out her legs. All the backache caused by softening ligaments (how scary is that?) and the cramps and constipation, the headaches and heartburn all become unimportant when you see this tiny picture.

I have started having strange dreams as well, and they are really wild, really vivid. I dreamt that I left the baby in the boot of the car when I went shopping and if that wasn't bad enough when I got home I realized that I hadn't fed the poor thing for a couple of days. In my dream I rushed outside and threw open the boot only to find Gareth sitting there and my baby gone. I woke up in a cold sweat feeling guilty and anxious all at once and the nicer Simon was to me the worse I felt. Another time I dreamt that the baby woke up in the night and when I went in to pick her up she had changed into Gareth. Always in these dreams Simon is there somewhere too. Perhaps standing on the stairs or eating toast in the kitchen. How random is that? I know that it is normal to have weird dreams but there is a part of me that wonders whether they could mean anything. Sometimes I wish to God that I had never laid eyes on Gareth, that I could just relax and enjoy this experience with Simon. All of a sudden a whole lifetime seems a very long time to feel guilty, and I wonder whether time does heal all. At the moment I can't help feeling that this baby is mine alone. I know that there is a chance that Simon could be the father but I can't shake the feeling that I need to protect her from everyone, it is as if no one could possibly have the same burning need to safe guard her as I do.

For the longest time when I first fell pregnant Simon seemed to go right off sex, I began to think that he had gone right off me. He would come up with a list of excuses why we shouldn't. He cited the fear that we may bring on a miscarriage, that he had a headache or that he was tired. I'm

180

sure he even faked sickness one night. I did everything I could to put his mind at rest. We spoke to the doctor and read articles. But then one afternoon he came home early, he kissed me passionately in the kitchen and with almost a look of resolve on his face took me upstairs. We spent all afternoon in bed. It was almost as if he needed to prove to himself that he could still make love to me, that I was still his. It felt weird at first and I felt kind of empty, but I think if someone is relentlessly good to you then you can't help but love them back.

I start to walk back to the office when I become aware of footsteps behind me. Nervously I clutch my bag to me, all at once feeling vunerable. I try and speed up a little, glancing around me nervously to check out where people are in case I have to scream for help. With the change in my centre of gravity and the additional weight I find that I am struggling to pick up the pace. As I glance behind me fearfully. I see Gareth striding towards me and a flash of anger passes through me. When he stands next to me he is so close that we could touch, and I feel claustrophobic suddenly and the air seems to become thicker, the chemical reaction that used to fold and combine us so easily now pooling thickly around us.

'You. Just leave me alone. I don't want you anywhere near me,' I say, my voice sounding strangled and distant.

'Sophie, be reasonable. I just wanted to see how you are. Just have a drink with me,' he asks, and I can see he is ill at ease, nervous of my reaction. I find it hard to look him in the eye, and he knows it. 'Look at me,' he says, 'look at me and tell me that you don't want me, tell me that you don't love me. You can't, can you?' he says, mocking me. And for a moment I can't, I am terrified of looking at him. I am scared that the moment our eyes meet that he will strip me bare, that he will be able effortlessly to discard my careful façade of casual indifference. That he will know how I really feel, and I will be unable to keep up this deception any longer, this pretence of aloof apathy. And I am suddenly panicked, flustered and fearful of this confrontation. He scares me to death now, I am so cautious of the hold my heart thinks he has over me, I am distrustful of myself and my carefully designed determination. And, as I look purposefully away, I can feel my heart thudding in my chest and I fight the impulse to get away. But then I think again of that day in the woods, of his cold heartless antipathy. I remember with painful clarity how I felt when he told me so cruelly, so unsympathetically, how I should get rid of my baby. I remember clearly how I felt when I realized that we, my baby and I, had become an inconvenience, a liability. I know that he is watching me, waiting for my response, looking for any chinks in my armour that he can exploit and abuse, manipulate for his own ends. And suddenly it comes over me, a cool, remote fury. And my body becomes strangely quiet inside. It is as if a stillness has taken over now, calming my hammering heart and strengthening my resolve. I draw my strength from the venom I saw in his eyes that day, and all the hateful, cruel remarks that have lain suppurating and festering inside me.

'For the last time, I don't love you and I don't want you and I wish I had never clapped eyes on you. Oh, and by the way, I'm pregnant, Gareth, so I don't do drinking at the moment, and even if I did you are the last person that I would want to drink with. If you ever even think of coming near me again I swear I will phone your precious wife and tell her everything.' My words are spiky and hard, spat out and shaped by the repugnance I feel, delivered in disgust. I turn around angrily and as I try to walk away Gareth grabs my arm, trying to pull me round to face him again.

'Get your hands off me. Just leave me alone.' My voice has risen now and I am starting to shake with anger. 'Let go of me or I start screaming,' I threaten.

'You wouldn't,' he says, but lets go of my arm just the same. I glare at him witheringly and turn on my heel.

'Why are you doing this?' he looks really quite pained now. But it is too late. Far too late. And so I walk away from him. I turn round once to glare at him once more but he has gone already. Submerged into the milling midday throng of shoppers.

This is not the first time I have had to do this. After I stood him up in the car park it was as if he refused to let me go, even though he knew I had told Simon that the baby was his. What was I supposed to do, wait around in case he changed his mind? He was so angry that I had told Simon without 'consulting' him. It was as if he thought me incapable of making a decision without his divine bloody guidance. I think that it galled him that he was no longer in control and that the balance of power had shifted. He actually had the audacity to say that I had no right to tell Simon, and then the nerve to lecture me about morals, insisting that the baby could be his. Amazing how, all of a sudden, he changed his tune. I couldn't believe that he was angry that I hadn't given him a chance, that I had taken away his right to decide after all that he had said. Well, tough. He should have thought about that before. If he had acted in any way pleased about the pregnancy I think I would have given him some room for error. But I will never forget the look on his face; I will never forgive him for making me feel so worthless, for making a mockery of my feelings for him. And every couple of weeks he tries again. He tells me that it is killing him imagining me with Simon. He tells me that he misses me and that he is sorry. Lately he has even started asking for a second chance. And every time he walks away, despite everything, I swear a piece of me goes with him.

Today, as I walked away, I thought I felt the baby kick. Instantly I feel guilty, and I am shamed at my outburst. I worry that my tiny innocent child is reacting to all those hurt and angry feelings whizzing around my system. She must know when I am unhappy, I think. Then I worry that maybe she is not just moving around idly, perhaps she is kicking me for pushing her father away. Why can't he just accept things as they are and let me be? I don't feel as though I trust my own judgment any more. If I am doing the right thing then why do I feel so bad? Why does it seem like every bit of me wants him to stay? I want to sink into his arms and just melt clean into him. I want to breathe him in, drown in him, and fall asleep next to him. I am exhausted by his absence. And no matter what I say to Amanda, at the end of the day there is no fooling my heart. Sometimes, when I know he is busy or in a meeting, I call him just to listen to his voice on the answer phone. And when I hear him speak, I sit very still, and track the hurt as it runs right through me, aware of every inch of its journey through my system. And then when I put the phone down I berate and chastise myself, knowing how ridiculous I am. But I can't seem to stop myself, like an addict I am pulled hopelessly along, desperate in my quest for fulfilment, dizzy and derelict in my pursuit of gratification and all the time fighting with myself, my better judgment heckling and screaming at me to listen, to pay attention and to focus. And I know I just have to wait it out, wait for when my longing for him fizzles out. I know that I have to keep reminding myself why I made this choice. I grit my teeth and steel myself. After all, I know that this isn't about me any more.

Chapter 17

Amanda

'A human being has a natural desire to have more of a good thing
than he needs.'
Mark Twain

It has been three weeks now since Sophie went on maternity leave and the office seems quiet without her. She must be relieved to be away from Gareth and all his disingenuous overtures. He still won't give up, though. How unfortunate for him, I think, that all that passion and pent-up emotion seems now to be so one-sided. I watch him, and he is like a dog with a bone, constantly worrying, consumed by remorse. Knowing that it is now too late and that she is lost to him, probably for ever. At one point his fixation (because that is what it has become) seemed to grow positively sinister and I was genuinely worried that he was stalking her. One day he even managed to take her car keys, break into her car and leave her a rose, and he has followed her on more than one occasion now, I mean, how scary is that? And the more she tells him to leave her alone the keener he is. I am sure he sees her lack of compliance as a challenge. Maybe it is just the thrill of the chase for him. Who knows?

I wonder whether, unwittingly, Sophie is sending out

mixed messages. Unknowingly confusing her signals. For the longest time she never said a word, about Gareth or about how she felt. And I never asked, knowing that the time would come when she would be ready to talk. And then one day, when we were having lunch, Sophie just broke down and everything that she had been storing up, all the pent-up emotion and regret of the last few months poured out. She admitted that she still loves him, that she was angry initially but that now she misses him. She told me that she grieves for him physically, that she dreams about him kissing her, that sometimes she even dreams that they are still together. The scary thing is that I think he knows that, knows how strongly she feels and it is as if he is just waiting until the right moment to step back in to her life. I have watched him watching her. You can see that he is eaten up with jealousy; I bet the thought of her back with Simon is killing him. I think he is regretting all those things he said when she told him that she was pregnant and now he has to watch her back with Simon, playing happy families and pregnant with what could be his child and he hates it. 'The injured lover's hell,' as Milton described it. When I think of Gareth, with his now unrequited love, I feel nothing but unease. I pray that he leaves her and that baby alone. No good can come of any of this.

Sophie only has a few weeks to go before the baby arrives and I have been visiting every couple of days to make sure she is OK. I know as her time comes closer she has more than the usual new mother worries. She is concerned that Gareth will turn up at the hospital and she is having recurring night-mares that the baby will so closely resemble Gareth that everyone will know. I try to calm her, and tell her that she shouldn't worry, that Gareth and Simon are so similar that no one will possibly be able to tell. I have not given up trying to convince her to do the right thing, to tell Simon, but she is adamant that he doesn't need to know. I have tried to persuade her that telling Simon may just ease her mind, that it will kill her safeguarding this terrible secret for the rest of her life. But it is all to no avail. She honestly believes she is doing the right thing. But still she worries. I think she is also trying to understand how she managed to fall for such a controlling narcissistic, lying womanizer when she is married to Simon (who she agrees is the nicest man on earth). She knows now that Gareth is no good but still she longs for their romantic interludes. I try and tell her that maybe she is in love with the idea of being in love. I tell her that even if they got back together, life with a new baby is hardly romantic. I know she loves Simon but in a different way, and it is going to take some time for her to completely give up the dreams she had made with Gareth and start to look forward to her new life with Simon.

I really do think that as soon as she has that baby in her arms she will feel so much better. At the moment she has too much time on her hands to contemplate and to worry. When the baby comes she will be so busy that she won't have time to think about that loser. Last time I saw her she told me that Gareth had started turning up at the house. So I telephoned him, told him to back off or he would regret it. But he just laughed at me. He was openly scornful of my attempts to protect Sophie and derisive and abusive when I threatened to tell Suzie. I was in a murderous frame of mind when I put the phone down and ended up calling Rebecca. We have become quite close over the last few weeks, united in our concern over the Sophie/Gareth affair. She still thinks we should say something to Suzie. She thinks that if Suzie knew she would go berserk and that would refocus Gareth's efforts. We have talked so many times about this now that we are both convinced that Gareth, despite his obsession with Sophie, still would not leave Suzie. Rebecca thinks she knows him very well after all these years and is absolutely certain that, if faced with personal discomfort, perhaps the loss of his house and large wardrobe space, he would turn tail and run the other way, leaving Sophie in peace. It all sounds great and believe me no one would want to see him suffer more than me, but by telling Suzie I betray Sophie. My best friend.

Someone once said to me to be careful as everyone has an agenda. At first I laughed at such cynicism but now I find this to be true. If you examine my own motives with this in mind, first on my agenda would be the need to keep that unfaithful, feckless creep away from my best friend. But I also can't deny there is a hint of personal vendetta in there also. Sad, I know, but he lied to me as well that night he kissed me. And I am fed up with being stuck in the middle, I have been their alibi (unwillingly) and their reluctant confidante. And all the time I have watched the effect their duplicity has had on the people around them. I have been shocked at the person Gareth has turned Sophie into. I have seen her lie without batting an eyelid to protect their secret and watched her take on an almost mutable persona, as fluid and as changeable as the wind. I wonder sometimes who she is now. I wonder if she knows who she is any more.

So I can't help but wonder about Rebecca's agenda. I know she is trying to protect her close friend and in turn Suzie's children, but is that it? Sometimes I am quite taken back by the strength of her annoyance. She really does become quite incensed by the whole situation. Maybe that is how it affects you. Perhaps having to watch a serious of lies play out every day of your life poisons your system and corrupts your thinking. And we always end our conversations the same way now, agreeing that we don't really know what we should do. Both of us conscious that we should do something but unwilling to become anything more than the spectators that we currently are.

I must admit that I told Pete today. Today is our day together. I love our Saturdays, but today I know that Pete has a really large job to do next week so Max and I have been roped in to pack up plants and shrubs and trees to be planted the following week. It has been a beautiful day and around lunchtime we stopped to get something to eat. No chance of anything even remotely healthy if Max is choosing so we ended up eating burgers and skinny fries under an arbour set right back in the corner of our garden. Afterwards we drowsed together in the dappled shade, enjoying what must be the last rays of sunshine before autumn sets in with a vengeance. It has been late coming but there is a definite chill in the air now. I look around the garden, as the leaves begin to turn, and only a few autumn crocuses remain in flower. For months and months while Pete was studying I would help him, desperate for him to finish the course. Knowing in my heart that he would be devastated if he failed. I did everything in my power to help him learn the sometimes indecipherable names of the flowers and plants that would be his trade. We would go through lists of them together and while Max had his list of spellings from school that would include that, there, their, through and thought, Pete would have a completely different list. Every night we would struggle together to pronounce and remember names such as nicotiana, achilleas, Thuja atrovirens and petro-selinum crispum. Patiently I would write such words on small brightly coloured pieces of paper and leave them around the house, stuck to mirrors and placemats. Hidden in his lunchbox even. They were there as a constant reminder, a colourful study aid.

And so, after four years of supporting him, I now find that I can recognize nearly as many as Pete. And as I gaze at the garden around me now, I know that all that effort was worth it. He does have a talent and he has created some amazing gardens. To my left there is a border and I can pick out mullein, and valerian, roses, lavender and rosemary. I breathe deeply, secure, fed and happy. Max is off now; bored with sorting out plants, he has disappeared with some thick

189

plastic sheeting to build a camp and so I snuggle closer to Pete, just enjoying the peace and quiet. I smile as I feel his arm snake around me, pulling me closer and I know that despite our ups and downs we are supposed to be together. Normally we talk about everything, we perhaps don't always agree but we don't really keep secrets from each other. And as he kisses the top of my head I sigh. I know that I shouldn't really have confided in him, after all, Simon is his really good friend and now he will just worry. But the whole thing was making me bad-tempered and grouchy and Pete is my best friend, I was sure he would know what to do. So earlier while we were sorting plants, I called him over and told him that we needed to talk. 'Right,' I said. And he looked at me with the beginnings of a smile. 'That always means trouble when you say that,' he said.

'Look, I have to tell you something.' And as I told him he just looked at me, nodding and looking suitably shocked as I explained the whole sordid affair. I glossed over my involvement, the times that I have been their alibi and I omitted completely the time that Gareth kissed me. But the rest, well, I kind of told like it was. But men are completely different from women. There was no excitement or gossipy exchange. At first Pete didn't really react at all. There was no real animation to his features or noticeable interest in my tale, just the initial disbelief and then his measured words of wisdom.

'Don't go getting involved. I know what you're like but this has nothing to do with us and Sophie has made her decision. It is not for us or anyone other than Sophie to tell Simon,' he said. He then made some manly noises about 'poor old Simon' and the subject was dropped. I am not sure what I was expecting really, definitely some sympathy for Simon but perhaps some reassurance for me? Men just don't seem to get as drawn in to things as women. I know women talk about their feelings so much more, so as a friend you start to empathise. But even though he really wasn't that much help I am glad I told him. I really believe that you shouldn't hold on to these things – all those angry, destructive feelings lying dormant in your system can only do you harm. And it is a waste of energy. All the time I am consumed with my worry and loathing, Gareth is still out there (shagging other hapless females, probably), completely unaware of all this time and energy I am committing to thinking about him. In fact, he is so vain that he would probably get off on the idea that people were spending time thinking about him. I shrug and thank God that Pete and I are so normal, and as I stand next to him, watching him label pots and check plants, I wonder once again why anyone would want to make their life that complicated.

On Tuesday we have a client day. This is basically an opportunity for us to reward our more loyal clients and at the same time provide our prospects with the opportunity to get to know us a little better. It works really well, as we only invite clients who are currently satisfied with our services (this makes it easier for us as well, after all, why would you want to spend the day with a load of miserable clients?) in the hope that they will then encourage the prospects to sign up. Today we are going to lunch at a rather nice hotel a few miles out of town, nothing too difficult this time. The last client day was a complete shocker, we took ten clients on an off-road day. It was very muddy, driving small jeeps around a saturated sludgy course. One of our guests, the financial officer of one of our prospects, was thrown roughly from the jeep on a particularly steep hill and ended up breaking her arm in several places. I have never seen anything like it, she was covered head to toe in mud so thick you could only just see her eyes. Funnily enough she never became a client.

Today should be a lot tamer. All the consultants are going and already Gareth is turning on the charm. I resolve to sit as far away from him as possible. The arrangement is that all the guests are to meet at our offices first, to become acquainted with each other and the rest of the team. I am talking to a tape-measure manufacturer when I notice a rather young attractive woman walk in. She is wearing killer heels and an Alice band, her long blonde hair captured and smoothed beneath it. She is poured into a pencil skirt and I watch her remove her jacket to reveal a rather low-cut, flimsy blouse. Predictably, she now has all the male attention. Very banal, men are so sad. Even the client I am talking to moves to get a better view and he must be over sixty. I find out that the token female is the CEO of one of the large pharmaceutical companies, a real high flyer apparently. I walk over to meet her and we get on, surprisingly, like a house on fire. Her name is Lucy and she is definitely a smart cookie and not as young as I first thought. I reappraise her swiftly, putting her dress sense down to personal taste. After all, she does look fantastic so why shouldn't she dress like that?

We leave for lunch in separate cars and meet up in the grounds of Whitley Manor. The manor is set in twenty-six rolling acres, where deer roam almost unhindered, safe from traffic and free and unfettered in the fields and woods all around. Closer to the house there are magnificent formal gardens where mellow brick paving gradually leads you from one garden through to the next, meandering around fountains and encircling sundials. We turn towards the house and we are greeted by a magnificent border. At the front I recognize alchemilla mollis and silver-leaved stachys flourishing in the dry light soil. The planting spills over the stone edging, completing the repetition of colour and texture at ground level. Ensconced cosily at the back, a magnificent yew hedge provides a dramatic backdrop to echinops. Further on you are tempted through ancient archways that frame the old house as it stands regal and dignified and adorned with ancient wisteria.

The dining room is vast, almost baroque in style, but

softened with chintzy seat covers and enormous vases of flowers. Thankfully I am seated a long way from Gareth. We have interspersed the female consultants up and down the table to stop the whole thing becoming too testosterone-driven and the atmosphere is relaxed but business-like. I watch from my end of the table as conversations are engineered and further meetings are arranged. Gareth has managed to get a seat next to Lucy, and I can barely contain my amusement as I watch him struggle to keep his eyes off her chest. But it is going well; she seems to be laughing with him and hasn't yet noticed the predatory gleam in his eye. After lunch we amble outside. There is a dark oppressive cloud overhead and the wind has started to pick up, but there is still some sunshine and our guests break off into comfortable groups, while the smokers take advantage of being outside and light up a postprandial cigarette. I could murder a cigarette myself, but I don't smoke in front of clients. I think it gives the wrong impression. So I wait it out, impatient now for the afternoon to be over. I am finding it hard to concentrate as well now and, as I talk about the future of the property market, I notice that Gareth and Lucy have wandered away from the group. Inwardly I seethe; I can't believe he is up to his old tricks and with a client! That is a sackable offence. Instant dismissal. I stand and watch him place his hand proprietorially on the small of her back, but she sidesteps neatly, dislodging his hold. She is still laughing though and I watch their body language in dismay. I sigh. I thought she was better than that. Will catches my eye from over the other side of the patio and rolls his eyes at me. Even the guys are fed up with Gareth now.

People are starting to leave when Lucy comes running back up the stairs. She has a face like thunder as she marches back into the dining room to grab her jacket. She notices my concerned expression and instantly her face changes, her features smoothing until she looks calm and refined once more. Gareth is still nowhere to be seen, though, and as the minutes go by, he is conspicuous by his absence. I can feel all the eyes of my team on us, all of them wondering why Gareth and Lucy didn't return together. I touch Lucy's arm in what I hope is a reassuring gesture, and ask her if everything is OK. She nods and smiles but I can see the tension in her eyes. I am tempted to ask her again, ask her if she is sure, but then she smiles, thanks me for lunch and says her goodbyes. We shake hands and then she is gone. And I watch her walk away from the house without a look behind her and wonder what Gareth has been playing at now. I wander over to the team, shrugging my shoulders to indicate that I am none the wiser, and we all adjourn to the drawing room.

We stay for a while, drinking coffee and swapping notes and generally relaxing together. Gareth slopes back about twenty minutes later, grinning widely and adjusting his tie. Before he even crosses the room he starts, unable to resist reverting to type, strutting exaggeratedly, bragging loudly to anyone who will listen about how Lucy had been asking for it, and how no one could blame the poor girl for trying, that she obviously couldn't help herself. God, he's got a problem bigger than his ego, I think, and as I look around the group I can tell from the raised eyebrows that I am not the only one who thinks so. I can't help but wonder if he really does have an ego the size of a planet or whether it is all bravado to hide low self-esteem or a lack of confidence, perhaps even a very small penis. I grab another coffee and overhear him discussing how he supposedly charmed Lucy. He stands in front of the fireplace, holding court, bragging about how Lucy couldn't wait to get her tongue down his throat. He says she stormed off simply because, after snogging Gareth stupid (that wouldn't take too long I think), apparently she had become annoyed and 'precious' when Gareth had refused to go home with her. According to Gareth she had begged him to shag her there and then. A likely story, I think, and I throw him a withering stare as he describes how she was 'panting for it'. As thick-skinned and as arrogant as ever he ignores me and just keeps going. He is as big-headed as he is stupid, I think. And I watch him continue with his tale, telling the team how Lucy pleaded with him to phone her, and how he might look her up and do her a favour some time. Because, after all, he adds, the poor girl will not know what to do with herself now she's had a taste.

Unbelievable, I know, but I can't help but be fascinated by his nerve, the sheer impudence of him, I watch him standing there with his hands on his hips, his conceit and vanity blinding him to the animosity of the people around him. Will is particularly stony-faced and sending waves of hostility Gareth's way. Lucy is Will's client and he doesn't look happy at all as he walks over to me and we walk back to the car park together. 'I have known Lucy for ten bloody years,' he says. 'I know her, she wouldn't fall for his crap. She's a really bright girl, she has a PhD in nuclear science, for Christ's sake,' and he says no more, just shakes his head despondently. We say our goodbyes and leave and I wonder once again just how Gareth gets away with it and what really happened in the garden today.

Chapter 18

Sophie

'Life is not measured by the number of breaths that we take but by the moments that take our breaths away.'
Anonymous

You can never really believe, all through the pregnancy, and even during the long hours of labour, that you are actually going to end up with a baby. I swear that it is enough to make even the most hard-hearted and cynical believe in miracles. I lie in a state of exhausted exhilaration in a hospital bed in a ward of four. The room is painted a nondescript cream and each bed is made with military precision, dressed in either a pink or blue bedspread. Bright sunshine streams through the large windows, caressing gently each of the four tiny Perspex cribs placed protectively beside each bed. The sunlight bounces off the clear plastic, reflecting haphazard beams of prismatic colours around the room. Each tiny crib contains its own unique miracle, each one just a few hours old. I notice that each cot has its own hospital-issue blanket, again blue or pink, but this time the colour denoting at a glance each baby's sex. I look back again to my own baby. I find I am too exhausted and sore to even sit up but somehow I just can't sleep. I glance around the ward, furtively eyeing the other new mothers around me, and I note thankfully that I am not the only one here that looks just a little lost. I know everyone tells you to sleep every time the baby sleeps but even though he is slumbering soundly beside me, I just can't rest. I feel like a child at Christmas. I don't want to miss even one minute of this.

I look over at him through the cloudy Perspex of his hospital cot, and I am simply blown away. My perfect, perfect baby. My son. All these months I didn't have a clue how dramatic and all-encompassing my love for him would be. I cry with it, laugh with it, I am consumed by it. I wonder at his perfection, at his tiny nose, at his perfect little toes. I swing between moments of absolute terror, when I think he may have stopped breathing, and absolute blessed relief that it is all over and he is here with me and healthy. The silliest little things seem to make me cry. I don't think that I have ever felt this humble or grateful for anything in my whole life. And right now I don't think I will ever get bored of looking at him. I try and etch each tiny feature, each moment of these days into my memory so that I never forget, so that when he asks me about when he was a baby I can recall everything, every little detail. The sense of relief is overwhelming. Straight away, he lay in my arms peacefully, just staring at me myopically with his little dark eyes. And now he is just three hours old and he sleeps. I realize that at some point this afternoon someone must have brought me tea and toast. When did that happen? I seem to be quietly oblivious to the outside world. I sit up, pick up the toast and nibble absentmindedly, watching him all the while. My son.

In his very first hour he seemed to look around his new world almost knowingly, with what seemed like years of wisdom in his eyes. Simon was with me all the way through, thank goodness. I really couldn't have done this on my own. And the whole experience has given us back something I thought we had lost a long time ago, or perhaps, if I am truthful, something I thought I had squandered. Before Gareth and long before I was ever unfaithful it was as if we had a kind of secret between us, Simon and I. We may never have had an earth-stopping orgasmic passion but we had an alliance, built on the carefully nurtured trust between us and bolstered by the secrets and dreams that we shared. In the early years we seemed to get stronger all the time. We were buoyed up by the exuberant eternal optimism of youth, and we never worried about tomorrow, living only for the day, every day. Our relationship became more and more robust by the experiences we had together and then, as we started to mature, with our plans for the future. I remember that I felt secure in us in those early days. Simon was always my rock. Our relationship was solid, and it was pure, somehow, unsullied. And then, one day, I wanted more. I thought that I wanted something edgier, more exciting, something more colourful, more ardent. And in my ceaseless quest for that something better I forgot how important it was to feel secure, and how rare it is to be loved by someone so infinitely patient and sweet. Scarily, I stopped viewing our bond as special. Quite callously I looked down at our life, the life that Simon and I had worked so hard to create, and condemned it as no longer good enough. I felt stifled by the security and bored by what I had seen as the banality of our routine. Inside I began screaming for a way out. And so I risked it all. I threw all my cards on the table and for what?

I look back over at the small scrap of humanity beside me and I know now with certainty that things happen for a reason. I am positive that we are pushed and tempted down different paths by fate for a purpose, perhaps to achieve some predefined and complicated endgame. Or maybe just because there are lessons on these paths we need to learn. OK, so Gareth turned out to be a number one louse, but I am sure that he is the reason I now have my son. A very good

198

thing has come from all of that bad, and both Simon and I now have the opportunity to be parents.

I sigh again and feel sad. I am sad for Gareth, who perhaps will never enjoy the present, because he is always looking for something better for the future. I see now that he is vain and shallow and for him life is just a game, the people around him just playthings to be manipulated for his amusement. I can only pity him now because he has thrown away the opportunity to watch this little boy grow up. In the pursuit of hedonism he has frivolously cast us aside. But maybe, with two children already, this wasn't so exciting for him. I look over at my innocent babe and shudder at the thought that anyone could ever take this for granted. It is beyond my comprehension that anyone could become blasé and unmoved by the innocence and wonder, the sheer possibility of each new life born into this world. But I feel sad for me as well, that something must be missing or be very wrong inside me too. I wonder why my whole life seems to have been this futile quest for true love. Surely that isn't normal? I sigh and stretch out my limbs. It has all become so complicated, so confused. Why is it that I never seem able to be satisfied with anything for too long? For some reason, what I have is never enough. Maybe I'm just as bad as Gareth after all. I close my eyes and pray again. I pray for the health of my son and for the wisdom to be satisfied now that I have my baby. I look up as Simon is walking into the ward. I realize it is visiting time, and at his heels are three other fathers, the third helping an older looking couple who I guess must be grandparents.

Perhaps it was the whole childbirth experience, that whole reliance on another human being to get through a physical feat, that has brought about this new closeness. Simon looks at me now with concern and love and pride and I look back and smile he doesn't have to say a word, but, despite smiling, I appear to be crying again. This seems to happen a lot lately, we look at each other and we just cry, sometimes we cry with happiness, sometimes in wonder but every time with relief. Nobody tells you how overwhelming this is and how romantic as well. We did this together. There were moments when I didn't think I could do it, I am sure there were moments when Simon didn't think I could do it but he never let on. He just kept on encouraging me, holding my hand and helping me breathe correctly, even (very annoyingly) singing at one point to keep my spirits up. I know that I couldn't have done this without him. Our baby is just 6lb 3oz and only I know that he may not be the fruit of Simon's loins. There are no physical indicators that could give us away; I have left no clues to catch us out. He has dark blue eyes but then so do all babies. He has a smattering of dark brown hair, a tiny mole on his tummy and long toes. I watch our sleeping son curl his fingers around his Daddy's finger and know with certainty that neither of them ever has to know. We have decided to call him Benjamin, for Simon's grandfather. He looks like a Benjamin somehow.

The ancient Greeks used to believe that we should beware of feeling too happy, too proud or too in love or the Gods would look down upon us and in a jealous rage, destroy our contentment. At the very least, in their envy they would meddle and interfere, they would perhaps throw us stumbling blocks and obstacles whilst all the time observing us from the heavens, laughing and discussing our endeavours for their after-dinner entertainment. I know this, and as a fatalist I believe also that our future is ordained by a higher deity, yet I defiantly bask in my delight and joyfully and ecstatically tend to my son. If I give any thought to the Gods at all it is in thanks and I am so caught up in my bubble of love, and the disorder that a new baby brings, that I forget to guard against obstructions and complications. So, on day three, when I am introducing Benjamin to his paternal grandparents, I am quite shocked when another group of visitors arrive. I lay my now sleeping son down and try to prepare myself. They arrive excited and with much banter and I am suddenly confused as my in-laws depart and I am surrounded by a sea of friendly faces and presents for the baby. My team from work.

I have had no time at all to prepare and I suddenly feel vulnerable and off guard. I run my hands through my hair to smooth it and pray that my unmade-up face doesn't look too scary. They all crowd round and there are suddenly a million questions and kind words. I give Amanda a hug and she squeezes my hand in support. Amanda. She must have been in four times already and I am so grateful for her help and her friendship. I smile at her and look around the group clustered around my sleeping son. It is then that I see him. He is standing apart from the others and is just staring at me. Gareth.

I can't say anything. I study his face hungrily, drinking in every detail of him, I feel my insides melt under his gaze as we just lose ourselves in each other. The world around us seems to recede and all of our history vanishes, I am lost once more in the here and now, deafened to any reason by the thudding of my heart in my ears and blinded to sense by the look in his eyes. I drink in the sheer size and strength of him, the way his hair effortlessly falls into place and how beautiful his hands are. Once again I am suspended between disgust and pure need. I want him to go, I know that it is wrong for him to be here, but I can't seem to speak. My mouth has turned dry and I am hot all over. Amanda picks Ben up and passes him to me. Automatically I clutch Ben to me closer, trying to hide him from this man who could hurt us. And as I fight for control, he just keeps staring. I feel as though my insides have turned to liquid, even my poor battered feminine parts respond, betraying my heart and my soul. I feel myself throbbing for him, and we stare at each other again, unaware still of the crowd around us. I feel Amanda dig me in the arm

201

with her elbow and the world floods back. I shake myself mentally and, startled, we both look away guiltily. The spell is broken and reality comes reeling back. I look down at Ben again and steel myself physically.

For the rest of the afternoon I go out of my way not to look at Gareth at all. And after the initial shock it is easier than I thought it would be; I calm down a little as I get drawn effortlessly back into the world of work, my life before Ben. I am humbled by the mountain of gifts and good wishes. All is going well until Kate from accounts unknowingly passes Ben to Gareth. I feel sick and glance around quickly, searching for Amanda, my ally. I see her but she is oblivious to my attempts to contact her. She is standing very still, hardly breathing in fact, just watching them together. Gareth and Ben. I follow her glance back to Gareth helplessly. There is no way I can rush over and tackle my baby away from Gareth without raising suspicions or looking like I have completely lost it. And I must admit he looks comfortable with him. I try and work out whether Gareth is studying Ben for clues to his paternity, whether he is examining the shape of Ben's little thumb or the contour of his nose for any similarities. My heart contracts painfully watching them together and I have to remind myself that his finesse with babies has come from years of practice rather than some uncanny blood link. After all, the reason that both Simon and I look so clumsy with Ben is that we are still new to this. Gareth reclines Ben easily onto his forearms, cradling his head very gently, and then talks to him very quietly. Ben looks up into Gareth's eyes adoringly and I smile despite myself. Ben loves anyone at all who talks to him. I watch his little fists wave up and down in silent but enthusiastic response. I can't hear what Gareth is saying, but I relax a little all the same. I try and listen with one ear whilst looking attentive to the admin team who are dying to fill me in on the office gossip. I just want them all to go now, to stop talking so I can take my fill and watch them together. And then, just when I think that my poor heart will surely stop with the tension and the emotion of it all, Amanda efficiently plucks Ben from Gareth's arms and he is back with me. He is back in my arms and safe. I glance up to look back at Gareth but somehow he has managed to slip away.

Chapter 19

Amanda

'I was not lying. I said things that later seemed to be untrue.'
Richard Nixon

It is 6.00 pm and I have come home and hit the streets already. Despite my vices; my smoking, my love of junk food and more than the occasional tipple, I am a runner. Most people are shocked when they find out, I mean, my body is hardly a temple, I can't stand vegetables and I can only tolerate fruit if it is juiced and mixed with vodka. But I run. I can't tell you why but somehow it is in my blood. When I was young it was something different, atypical, which was great as I was never one to follow the herd. My friends all played hockey and netball but I was never really a girly girl. I have never thrived in the competitive female environment and I was just not a team player. So I took to running and it was a great diversion, it helped me keep my weight consistent, cope with exams and manage my hormones. But now I run for different reasons. I run because it has a way of soothing and calming my overactive mind and chasing away my demons. I am convinced that it makes me a better person as well, less of a perfectionist and less obsessive, which can only be a good thing, and if I am more relaxed then I'm easier to be around. I tend to demand less from my friends and I am more patient with Max. Running makes me kinder. I know I can be difficult, I am not naturally maternal and I can be ambitious and highly strung. But running helps somehow. I play music really loudly from a playlist that includes Nirvana and The Clash and, well, anything that is loud and fast. And then I just run, I find my rhythm and I lose myself. And then somewhere along the way my head clears and the knots in my subconscious untie and I become human again. I love the euphoria of the runner's high and the elation I feel when I finish. I run if I am angry, depressed or frustrated and usually by the time I get home I am happy, peaceful, passive and non-violent again.

Sometimes when I'm tired or I have smoked or drunk too much I feel as though I never want to run again, but on nights like this I just want to keep going and never stop. It is raining now and I breathe deeply, steadily, relishing the cool, cleansing air against my skin and deep in my lungs. I am reassured by the constant pounding of my shoes as I weave through the streets, my legs strong, my pace steady. I run a familiar route, feeling my anxiety melt away with the miles beneath my feet. And I let my mind wander freely. I am a perfectionist. It is who I am. I like to give one hundred per cent to everything I do and every day I try and be better. I know that if I am not careful I set impossible standards for myself and sometimes for the people around me, so I try really hard to be more forgiving. And not judgmental. Definitely not that. I would hate to be seen as hypocritical, negative or, God forbid, condemnatory. But I saw the way they looked at each other, when he first turned up at the hospital. And I just knew then that it was all going to go horribly wrong, it was all going to happen again, it was only a matter of time. It wasn't even that they were close in proximity but they might as well have been. I didn't see them touch each other or speak but the emotion between them was palpable. And I knew when I saw the way that she looked at him that, despite all of her good intentions, all the hurt and all the history, that Sophie was lost as soon as he walked in. She just couldn't take her eyes off him. And I know that even though she denies it until she is blue in the face, I know that she is seeing him again.

And every day now I feel as though I am being drawn further and further into this human mess around me. I feel strung out and exhausted by the sheer effort of this pretence, inextricably I am becoming further entangled, unintentionally enmeshed deeper as I lie again and again to protect my friend. And I find that I am called upon often, a casual falsehood here, an alibi there. To protect the past, to maintain the present. To ensure that any unsavoury history, the months and months of betrayal, remain for ever undiscovered. To protect the lives of the innocent, the unsuspecting. But if this is the right thing to do why do I feel so awful? She knows this kind of stuff doesn't sit easily with me, so why does she keep putting me in this position? I feel dishonest and immoral by implication and I realize that I have become unwittingly and stupidly embroiled, all in the name of friendship. I recognize now that I am incapable of doing the right thing and, even worse, confused now as to what is the correct and right thing to do. So I stand and survey in frustration, adding reluctantly to the plot only when I have to, watching the whole bloody charade become more and more intricate as deceit layers deceit.

If you didn't know Gareth you might think that Ben looks a little like Simon, but I see Gareth every day and unfortunately there is no mistaking who is Ben's father. And as he gets older he just looks more and more like him. I am so surprised that no one else has noticed. It really is that obvious. When Gareth held Ben that day in the hospital the resemblance was unmistakable, uncanny even. And I am sure Sophie must see it, I am sure that every day when she looks at

Ben she sees Gareth. Perhaps that is why, after all that has happened, she still needs to be with him. I am truly mystified that love can really be this blind or this stupid. I have told Sophie that at work Gareth relentlessly flirts with anyone in his vicinity. I have told her in lurid detail about how he tried it on with Will's client, Lucy. I have updated her regularly on how he has been seen in numerous bars around town with numerous women. How he still talks about sex as if it is a sport, how he is constantly seeking his next conquest. I just can't see the attraction. Of course she has denied the rekindling of any romance, denied it categorically, but after all that has happened I just don't know if I trust her any more. Just this afternoon, when her in-laws were in the lounge, her phone rang. And I watched her blush and scuttle from the room, her phone in her hand, the door closing behind her to shield and shelter her conversation. We have been friends for so long, I know when she is up to something. As I run up the last hill on my route I realize that I am doing my best not to judge Sophie. But I am scared that I am starting to lose respect for her. And if you don't have trust and respect and faith in someone's integrity, I wonder what is left?

And we talked about this, about how she would feel when the baby came, whether she would be able to go through with her plan even if the baby looked like Gareth. We discussed endlessly whether she should tell Simon about the affair, about the fact that there was a strong possibility that the baby was not his. And although I wasn't happy I agreed to support Sophie, no matter what she decided to do. And I was so relieved to think that she had finally seen through Gareth, it almost seemed like it was all going to work out for the best.

And now I am so angry with her for making this whole confounded muddle worse. I watch Simon, so happy and so accommodating. He is up in the night feeding Ben and is just as proud as any man could be. If he sees any signs of infidelity or inconsistency he never lets on. But surely he must see signs? I feel sick when I think of how hurt he would be. And they have to be found out sooner or later. Surely Gareth's wife must be suspicious? Lately I feel as if I am about to witness a train crash, I can almost hear and see the whole thing picking up speed and momentum and I swear I am already starting to brace myself against the unavoidable impact. I have nightmarish visions of myself wandering through the wreckage, I see the inevitable broken hearts and lives all around me, I see the disbelief and the disappointment and I shudder involuntarily. I start concentrating again on my pace, I regulate my breathing and skip forward to the next track on my playlist, and as I head towards home, still feeling frustrated and angry, I can't help but wonder how far I will have to run to make myself feel better.

Today it just seemed so much worse than usual. I went to visit Sophie and Simon's parents were there. And like Simon, they are good people: honest, simple and adoring of their first grandson (they have two granddaughters). I watched them today and they are over the moon. I listened to them while they explained how happy they were, how pleased for Sophie and Simon. I watched Simon's mother become tearful as she confided that they had not dared hope for another grandchild as they were aware that Sophie and Simon had been trying for such a long time. I watched Simon's parents hold Ben and hold hands together, I saw the love and pride in their faces as they bonded with their grandchild and spoiled their daughter-in-law. I sat and watched them and felt sick. This just isn't right. Someone has to do something before it gets any more out of hand, I think, perhaps for the hundredth time. I am home now and I let myself in the back door and, without warming down or stretching, I reach for the phone. It is time someone intervened; it is time to give Rebecca a call.

Chapter 20

Susie

'Death is not the greatest loss in life. The greatest loss is what dies inside us while we live.'
Norman Cousins

Monday morning, 8.00 am. I stand at the door and wave goodbye to Gareth. Today marks our eleventh wedding anniversary. Eleven years and I just don't know where the time has gone. I think back all those years ago to our wedding day, remembering how innocent my expectations were, how exciting and romantic I thought it all was going to be. I couldn't wait to get married, to leave my job and have lots of children. I wanted someone to love and cherish me for the rest of my life and I could hardly think past my fluttering nerves and new matching crockery to take stock of the disapproval around me. My mother didn't trust him from the word go, and two of my best friends had slept with him previously but I was blind to all their concerns. He loved me and that was all that mattered. And this wasn't just a shag, Gareth was going to marry me. Surely that meant that I was different?

I watch him adjust his tie and sweep back his hair as he gets into the car. Some would call him vain, but I think it's great that he cares about how he looks. And we have worked hard to prove everyone wrong. Of course we have had our ups and downs, what couple doesn't? When the children were small there was never enough money and despite my dreams I ended up going back to work just to make ends meet. It was really hard. We never ever had the support of Gareth's family as he hasn't spoken to them for years. So any help we have had has come from my family, grudgingly at first, I admit, but then when the children came along they just got used to Gareth, I think. My Gareth is the kind of person you either love or hate, he is a bit like Marmite in that way. There is no in between. I think the problem is that people are intimidated by him. I mean, he is so good-looking and he just exudes confidence and charisma. And he has done really well for himself. We have a beautiful house in a really nice area and the children both go to private schools. We have the kind of life that most of my friends can only dream about. And he has a really good heart, I know he can be a little boastful, but he has every right to be proud of what he has achieved. I am proud of him anyway.

I shut the door and pick up the post; I will look at it later. Today I have taken the day off, I want to go into town and have my nails and hair done as Gareth and I are going out tonight. I think I may go to the gym this morning. I try and stay in shape for Gareth really; after all, I think it is important that we make an effort for each other.

As I go upstairs, trailed by my ever trusty hound, the phone goes. I decide not to answer. I am sure it's Rebecca again. I run my hands through my hair and sigh. I am not sure I have the energy this morning; she has left one message already. Talking of people who hate Gareth, Rebecca hates Gareth with a passion. She denies this, of course, but I know that she does. Rebecca is married to Gareth's best friend so it can get a little difficult. There is a real atmosphere between them sometimes. Rebecca claims she is looking out for me but I am beginning to think she has a problem. I know Gareth has a glint in his eye. But then, don't most men with a pulse? And I am fully aware that he is a flirt. I realize that women find him attractive but you can't live in constant fear of what may or may not happen. You would go quite mad. And there is a part of me that knows that he will always come home, after all he loves his boys too much. He loves me too much. In the first two years that we were married I caught him with a woman. And yes, I was shocked and hurt and all of my faith in my marriage – and, for a while, in all men in general – was rocked to the core. But then when you think about it, we are in this marriage for the long haul. We both took vows, for better and for worse, and that means something to both of us. We are both human and we both have weaknesses. Christ, I am not always that easy to live with. But that is what marriage is all about. For years and years I thought that it was my job as Gareth's wife to support him, and help him overcome this feebleness he appears to experience when in the presence of women. I was young and I thought he would just grow out of it. I remember honestly believing that my love would conquer all. But then it happened again.

She was a friend that time, a close friend and so I think that hurt even more. That time it was a full-blown affair and it went on for ages. In the end I couldn't stand it any longer so I phoned her husband. And that was the end of that. Gareth never saw her again. Even after she was divorced. I guess some of the attraction disappeared when she became available. By that time I had had the boys and I knew he wouldn't leave us. I am sure there have been a few others as well, one night stands, minor indiscretions. But he is a fit, active attractive male. And men are programmed to sow their seed. He has a high sex drive, even after eleven years, we still have sex at least four times a week every week. And now I am old enough and wise enough to know that his behaviour, the flirting and the occasional indiscretion, isn't a reflection on me as a wife, it isn't because he isn't satisfied. He just likes sex. And what if he is unfaithful again? I suppose I half expect that he will be. In fact, I am sure that is what Rebecca is calling for. She has obviously overheard something that has made her suspicious. So she is calling to drop hints again to warn me that she believes or suspects a further impropriety. And I know that it is her way of trying to protect me. And of course I listen, but for the sake of appearances I pretend not to understand her insinuations and intimations. And if Rebecca becomes less subtle in her inferences, I cut her dead. I have become good at this. I mean, what does she want me to do? What am I supposed to do? Am I supposed to throw him out? Divorce him? After eleven years and two children?

I think back to my mother, who lived in an abusive relationship with my father until I was seven and for many years before I was born. Even at that young age I knew when things were bad. I knew when to hide. But he was always sorry. It was like a sickness. And when he left my mother, she struggled for years. She struggled for money and she struggled to raise my brother and me. We never saw our father again. I know that Rebecca would say that I should think of myself, that I deserve to be treated better. But she doesn't understand. Even when Gareth is unfaithful he is the best husband and father anyone could want. He is always thoughtful and considerate, he helps out with the boys and he is fun to be with. And the upside of it all is that I get great gifts if he has something on his conscience. I mean, is it really that bad? It is not as if any of these women actually mean anything. He never flaunts his transgressions. I have never been publicly disgraced or embarrassed. And marriage is all about taking the good with the bad. I did not make my vows lightly and I am convinced that Gareth didn't either.

I put my gym stuff on and head for the door; the sun is shining and it is going to be a lovely day. I glance at the post and make a mental note to look at it when I get back. I notice several pastel-coloured envelopes in the pile that look like anniversary cards. See! And they never thought we would make it!

Two hours later and I have worked out every inch of my body, and am feeling relatively fit and toned. I am aware of subtle aches in my legs and my shoulders but I am gloriously relaxed. I am looking forward to a nice cup of coffee and bowl of cereal. I open the door and wait for the ecstatic furry welcome to subside. It doesn't matter if I have been gone for ten minutes or an hour, the greeting is always the same. I go down on my knees and hug Harry's wiggling hairy body. He is so happy that he just can't keep still and wriggles with delight. I scratch his head and tickle his tummy and then we make our way into the kitchen. I knock the switch on the kettle to the on position and grab a bowl and some cereal. As I go to get the milk I catch sight of the post, grab a chair, and start opening while the kettle is boiling. I discard an electricity bill, a party invitation for Tristan, and a circular advertising a local double glazing firm. Below this are several envelopes that can only be anniversary cards. I smile as I open the first one. It is from my mother. She would never be seen to forget, how ever much she disapproves; the second one is from my friend Cassie, who was my maid of honour. She has her own husband and four children now. The cards fall into a pile as I open the third. Although I am not so sure that it is a card now. The envelope and paper inside are heavy manila, and both are typewritten. I frown and wonder if it is from a solicitor. The letter is folded into itself and I get up with it and make my way over to the kettle. As I pour water into a cup I manage to shake the letter open and I scan the contents quickly. Is this some kind of joke?

213

Dear Suzie,

I am writing to inform you that your husband is having an affair. I know this will come as a shock to you, but the situation has been ongoing for some time now and has become serious as he has now fathered a son. His lover is a woman he works with called Sophie Bellinger. Her husband is not aware of the affair and believes the child to be his. I understand that your husband and his lover are making plans to be together. I apologize for this rather unorthodox method of communicating this news, however, this will obviously have certain implications for you and your children so I thought you should be informed.

Please be assured of my best intentions at all times.

Yours sincerely
A FRIEND

I dump the letter in disgust. What rubbish. I whiz around the lounge collecting old newspapers, discarded socks and numerous dog toys. I straighten cushions and smile as I find Tristan's beloved rabbit stuffed in a corner. And for probably an hour I tidy, trying to put the letter out of my thoughts. But it keeps coming back to me, unbidden and unwelcome. An annoying prod from my subconscious as I water a plant, an uninvited dig from my intuition as I sort magazines. What if he is going to leave this time? What if the letter is right? What if he has had a baby with this Sophie? I go to the bedroom and start looking for clues, I am not even convinced that I will find anything, but isn't forewarned better than fore-armed or something like that?

In the end it takes me less than fifteen minutes to find the evidence that indicates the end of our eleven years together. And what gives him away eventually is not something old-

214

fashioned or corny like someone else's underwear stuffed in a suit pocket or a packet of condoms hidden in his wallet. It is a whole series of photographs and emails on his computer in the study. I flick through the photos, they are in date order and organized as if this is the most normal thing in the world. I look carefully at the way that he looks at her, searching for clues. But then I see the pictures of the baby, pictures of them with the baby. And I feel as though my heart has broken. I switch to the emails. I look at the pages and pages of text; I am mesmerized and as much as I know that I should resist, I can't help reading them. I know that each sentence, each line hammers another nail into the coffin that will bury our marriage and that each statement of affection will take me to a new stage of pain, but, still I read, incapable of turning away. And it looks as though this has been going on for ages; I look at times and dates and realize that this has been going on almost since he first started at the company. I sit back on the chair and stare at the street. I wonder if the people responsible for email ever envisaged that this would become a whole new way to commit what must be the oldest sin. I can't believe that Gareth thought that he could actually keep this stuff here on our personal computer. It took me roughly three minutes to access all of this via his secret password. And I managed to crack it first time. Sophie. Nothing clever or too hard to decipher there.

I look again at the pictures of her, the pictures of them and pictures of their baby. I feel a little dazed, I know I need to find some strength from somewhere but I feel as though I have been punched in the stomach. I think back to the letter. 'the situation has been ongoing for sometime now', 'he has fathered a son', 'your husband and his lover' – the words swirl round and round my head and I try and work out what to do. I drink my coffee. It is cold now but the taste revives me. And I wonder who would have written the letter – 'they are making plans to be together'. I can see from the emails

215

that this could be the case. He is going to leave. I have started to cool down from my workout now and suddenly I feel chilled to the bone. I get up and pace up and down. I realize I am crying and I scrub my hands over my face angrily. I take a deep breath and tell myself to stop being so ridiculous. Crying never solved anything. I grab my jumper from the newel post and sit down with a fresh cup of coffee and the letter and read it again.

I am looking for clues. The language sounds professional, formal, almost old-fashioned. 'Please be assured of my best intentions at all times'. What is that supposed to mean? 'A FRIEND'. What kind of friend sends a letter like this? A shy friend? A mad friend? A friend of whom? My friend or Sophie's? I work out that the writer must be a female; no man would send a letter like this, that's for sure. From the pictures I realize that Sophie is that timid little thing from his office. Is her surname Bellinger? I struggle to remember but all I can recall is her insipid little face. What is he thinking? Gareth has had a child with her? I think of my boys at school and burst into tears.

At some point I drag myself upstairs into the bathroom. I feel as though I have aged a hundred years. I run a bath and empty half a gallon of bath salts into it. A cloud of perfumed mist rises all around me and I sit, balanced on the edge of the bath, staring into space, aware of the room steaming up around me. The dog sits patiently trying to work out what is required of him. I scratch his head absently as I try and think back over the last few months. I look for clues but find none. I can't think that he even mentioned that Sophie was on maternity leave, there was definitely no talk of a baby. But then I guess there wouldn't be, would there? How could this have happened? How could I have been so stupid? But even as I think it, I know that I am not stupid, I know that Gareth is good at this, practised one could say. I wonder when he was planning to tell me? After all, you can't hide a baby for too

216

long. I think back to Rebecca's message, 'we have to talk', and wonder if she knows, or rather how long she has known for. Rebecca must have found out from Luke. I swirl the bubbles in the bath tub angrily with my hand, I am feeling stupid now and angry. I can't believe that I could be the last to know and I wonder how I could have missed the signs and how he could do this again. But as I turn the taps off and grab a towel I realize this time it's different.

I don't know quite what to do this time. Maybe I should find this Sophie, maybe I should phone her husband. After all, it worked last time. I visualize this but feel sick at the thought of telling her husband that the son he thought was his is actually Gareth's. He is probably completely unaware of what has been going on. Unheeded tears slide down my face again, so I splash myself with cold water, throw off my clothes and get in the bath. I need to work out what to do next and I need to get a grip. Gareth is coming home early today so I need to have a plan of action before he gets home.

At midday I am done. I have blow-dried my hair and done my nails myself. Not bad if I do say so myself. I have put on some make-up and a suit that I keep for formal appointments and interviews. I make another coffee, take a deep breath and grab the phone and the phone book. I go through the listings systematically. It doesn't even occur to me that the number I am searching for may not be in here. And there it is, luckily there aren't too many people around with that surname, not round here anyway. I take a deep breath and dial. She answers on the third dial and for a moment I can't say anything. She sounds happy, as if she has been laughing at something.

'Is that Sophie Bellinger?' I ask.

'Yes, can I help you?' there is no attempt to hide but then I guess she has no idea that I was going to call.

'I understand that you are having an affair with my husband.'

Nothing. The silence seems to go on so long that for a moment I think that I may have lost connection.

'Who is this?' she says, not so confident now.

'I presume, unless you are having many affairs, that you know who I am,' I snap dryly. I am losing patience now and I visualize her simpering, snivelling little face and for a moment I hope she is as scared as she sounds.

'I just wanted to say that you are welcome to him, and I hope you are happy. You think you are the first? You are just one more in a long line of tarts that couldn't keep their legs closed. You are not the first and you won't be the last. He could never stay faithful to me and he won't stay faithful to you. But before you take him, make sure he is what you really want. Because I won't have him back this time.'

I slam down the phone and swig back my coffee. I go through the directory again and find the next number I want and dial again. The coffee and adrenaline have kicked in and I am positively buzzing with energy.

'Good afternoon, is that Sly, Weasly and Bobbit solicitors? It is? Good. I wonder if I can have an emergency appoint-ment this afternoon please. No, it can't wait. Yes, it is a matrimonial matter, yes. 3.00 pm lovely, thank you. I look forward to seeing you then.' I put the phone down and reach for the directory for the last time.

My next call is more practical. I find an emergency locksmith to come within the hour to change the locks and then I write myself a cheque for cash which just happens to equal the amount in our savings account. I put the cheque safely in my handbag until later. I can deposit the cheque on my way to the solicitors, I think, oh and I am nearly out of milk. I take my coffee upstairs and sip at it while I throw some of Gareth's clothes into a bag. I stuff the items in, not caring that they will become creased or confused. In it all goes: t-shirts, toiletries and socks. I chuck in a picture of the boys for good measure and throw the bag out of the window. I watch it land with a gentle thwump beside the drive. It lies at a precarious angle between two rhododendron bushes. I close the window and sit down again. I finish my coffee and decide on some light dusting before the locksmith arrives.

Chapter 21

Gareth

'The greatest of faults is to be conscious of none.'
Thomas Carlyle

It should have been such a good day. I got a fantastic blow job from Suzie this morning to celebrate our anniversary, I mean it was magnificent, I could hardly remember my name by the end of it. How could such a great day have gone so wrong? I shove my empty glass over to the barman and watch as he refills. Another whisky, that should sort me out. I need something for my bloody nerves. How the hell am I going to tell Suzie? She is going to kill me, that's for sure. Perhaps I won't tell her yet, I don't want to upset her on our anniversary. God, she will go ballistic and then she will go on and on about it like a broken record for the rest of the flaming year. Birds are like that, so bloody sentimental about stuff. Anyway, it might all blow over in a couple of days. I can't believe they could sack me just because of some fabricated harassment story. Where is their proof? She is not even my client. What are the chances, as well, that the only client I kop off with that whole day happens to know our top man? I can't believe that Lucy had lunch with our Chief Executive Officer, I mean the head of the whole bloody company. And

220

at some point between hor d'oeuvres and desert she just managed to drop into conversation that I had sexually molested her at some lunch thing we did a few months back. I mean, what a complete bitch. I can't believe she complained about me, she must have thought that she would get some kind of compensation or something.

I actually laughed when they told me. I mean, what is the world coming to? Surely you can feel a bird up without being sacked nowadays? Why put women in an office environment anyway? At the end of the day it is her word against mine. And it will be in the company's interest to back me, surely? After all, they can't risk it getting about that their consultants go round molesting their clients. They pay me to represent them, so they have to be loyal to me, after all, I'm one of the best consultants that firm has ever seen. They will be lost without me.

I have another drink and I find that I am actually starting to feel a little better. After the roasting that lesbian from HR gave me, it's not surprising that I blew things out of proportion a little. All that talk about assault, harassment and stalking, it's enough to give anyone the heebie jeebies. It's just like HR to make a mountain out of a bloody molehill. Now I have had some time to reflect I can see that they have to be seen to be taking these things seriously. OK, so I was a naughty boy. It's not as if anyone got hurt, it was just a snog and a grope. I mean she should count herself lucky. Frigid cow.

I knock back another glass and head for home, I was due home early anyway as I am taking Suzie to one of her favourite restaurants. I did think that time might be a little tight but, now that I have been suspended and sent home early, it has actually all worked out fine. Perhaps I will sue them when it's all over for defamation of character or something. Just the thought of all those mincing corporate do-gooders falling all over themselves to apologise to me, cheers me up immensely. I may even get a big fat cheque.

It is 4.30 when I round the corner into the drive. I check my appearance in the mirror before I get out of the car. Yep, still looking good. I run my hands through my hair and jump out of the car. I juggle my keys until I find the front door key and, as I am about to open the door, I suddenly realize that the lock looks different. I shrug, maybe it has always looked like that and I have just not noticed before. I try the key out but I can't seem to insert it. Maybe one too many sherberts at lunchtime, that will be it. Good job we are not going out until later. I try the key again. It's a different bloody lock. I stand back and stare at the thing, the whisky is starting to have an effect and I can't seem to work out why we have new locks. I search my memory; did Suzie tell me there was a problem? Was I supposed to have remembered something about this? Maybe there was a problem with it today? Perhaps she just forgot to tell me. And it is as I take another step back that I trip over a bag. What the bloody hell is that doing there? It's my overnight bag and it is just laying carelessly on the drive. Perhaps Suzie left it there by mistake? The bag is heavy; I open the zip and inside there are a selection of my clothes. A picture of the boys is on the top and haphazardly squashed between shoes and shirts are toiletries and socks, deodorant and shampoo. She must have booked us a surprise trip, I think. Perhaps she has booked us a room in a hotel somewhere to celebrate our anniversary. That is just so like her. I look back at the bag and frown, I really must have a word with her about her packing, though. I mean, looking at the way this lot has been stuffed in, she will be ironing for most of the time we are there. I pick up the bag and wander to the side of the house. There is a new lock there as well. Bloody great when a man can't even get into his own house.

I go back to the front door and ring the doorbell several times in succession. There is no answer but Suzie's car is on the drive so she must be close. I ring again and I am just about to start knocking as well when one of the upstairs windows open.

'At last! I have been out here bloody ages, couldn't you hear the doorbell? What has happened to the locks?'

'Go away, Gareth, just leave us alone. I am sure you have a key for Sophie's house, perhaps you can go there.'

I look at Suzie now, and realization hits me. She knows, she bloody well knows. I start to think really quickly. Keep calm, don't panic. Deny, deny, deny.

'Look, honey, you have obviously got the wrong end of the stick. Just let me in and we can talk about this.' I realize that I haven't seen her like this ever. She looks as if someone has taken all her soul away. She looks brittle, empty, cold.

'Gareth, you are a terrible husband and a dreadful liar and I never ever want to see you again. You will be hearing from my solicitor.' She says this matter of factly, as if she is tired. And she is looking at me without any compassion or feeling at all. I find that I am starting to feel nervous.

'Suzie, please don't do this, you don't understand, I love you.' I stop talking because I realize that I am not having any impact at all, she just looks straight through me. So I try again. 'It is not what you think.'

'Just stop, stop now. How can you stand there and lie to me? I have seen the pictures of you and her. I have read all of your bloody emails. I have seen pictures of your baby. How could it not be what I think? So don't stand there and lie to me any more. Just go.' And with that she shuts the window and draws the curtains. I wonder where my boys are, she has probably sent them somewhere for a sleepover. I can't even hear the dog barking. There's loyalty for you.

I sit down on the bag filled with my possessions, not really knowing quite what to do. But then after about five minutes I realize that maybe I need to give her some space. She will soon come round, and there are the boys to consider. I know her, if I promise never to see Sophie again she will be right as rain in a few weeks. And Sophie has been such a bore since she had that baby, maybe it was time I knocked it on the head. Perhaps Luke will put me up. I cheer up now as I think of the night ahead, Luke and I could hit the town, it will be just like the old days. I could even get lucky, and it wouldn't really count if Suzie and I are on a break, would it?

But then, when I call Luke, he tells me that he and Rebecca are out of town. Apparently they have gone away for a couple of days. Bloody unbelievable. I can almost hear that scheming bitch Rebecca in the background, and it sounded suspiciously as if she had a dog with her as well. I wonder if it's Harry. I don't think I have ever heard their dog bark before. Perhaps she has the boys too. That would be just classic. Just as I try and find out Luke tells me that he has to go and that he will call me later. Luke definitely sounded odd, so I guess he couldn't talk. Well, you know who your mates are at times like this.

So I drive to the woods where Sophie and I used to meet, park the car and listen to some music. I start to worry then; what if Suzie doesn't want me back? I try and call her but she just tells me to speak to her solicitor in the morning. She says she wants nothing more to do with me at all. Bloody hell! Surely she can't keep me out of my own house? I should never have kept those sodding emails and pictures at home. But then who would have thought that Suzie would ever have worked out the password? I mean, she is a great girl but hardly the sharpest tool in the box. What a nightmare and on top of it all, it looks like I will have to sleep in the bloody car. I phoned Sophie earlier, but she sounded too busy to even talk to me. She can't even fit me in for coffee until 3.00 pm tomorrow. I wonder whether I need to see how the land lies there, after all, it could be fun to shack up with Sophie for a while, maybe we could find some day care to put that baby in, at least that way we can spend some time in bed. It could be fun, I think, just until I can sort this mess out with Suzie. I wonder again what the hell is going on? Perhaps this is just some astrological blip. Perhaps Pluto has collided with Mercury in my chart or something. I make a mental note to read my stars tomorrow. I mean, a couple of months ago Sophie was gagging for a bit of me and now I have to make a bloody appointment. I close my eyes and go to sleep, sure that this will all seem better in the morning.

Chapter 22

Sophie

'There is no calamity greater than lavish desires. There is no
greater guilt than discontentment. And there is no greater disaster
than greed.'
Lao-tzu

It is Monday around midday and I am sitting in the lounge
still holding the phone in disbelief. After all this time, despite
all of the subterfuge and deception, Suzie, Gareth's wife, has
found out. And she doesn't just suspect she actually knows. I
mean there was absolutely no doubt in her voice. I think I
must be in shock. I have to sit down because I don't think I
can stand right now, my breathing seems very shallow and my
legs have completely gone to jelly. He must have told her.
Gareth must have come clean. I find that I am quite
astonished by this. Dazed even. There is a part of me that
never imagined that he would. He didn't have to or anything.
So why now? I think back to our last conversation, frantically
trying to remember anything I could have said that he may
have misconstrued as an ultimatum of sorts. But no, there
was nothing like that. And after all that has happened I
thought that I would feel differently. But somehow it feels
almost like an anti-climax. I try and work out tentatively how I

feel, prodding cautiously at my emotions like a tongue on a sore tooth, expecting some reaction. Something to prove I am not completely cold and heartless (or maybe even dead) and I find that there is something there, amid the shock. I probe it uncertainly, yes, I think it's relief. After all, isn't this what I wanted? At least now all the lies and the constant manoeuvring can stop. It really was becoming quite exhausting.

I look over at Ben asleep in his crib, and then all around at my home. Our home. I look over at the photographs on the mantelpiece and tables, mementos of our journey together, hard evidence that Simon and I did get married, that it wasn't just something I dreamt up. There are snapshots of holidays and pivotal life events, keepsakes and reminders standing shoulder to shoulder, jostling for space and attention. These are the pictures that Simon and I chose carefully together. Pictures that represent who we are, and to some extent our journey to get here. And I wonder sadly, what happens to these pictures now? Do you just bin them and start again? Do they get buried along with your old life when you start your new one? Oh God. Am I really contemplating starting again? Didn't I once think that things would be perfect when I got to this place? I mean, we have a good life, Simon and I. My God, we have a baby. All of my dreams have come true. I look again at the pictures of Simon and me together. Images of our life before Ben. We smile out at the camera confidently, carefree. And then there are our new pictures, taken professionally, recording our proudest moment of all, perhaps our greatest achievement. Ben. The shots are beautiful, tasteful and artistic, mostly black and white. A family at last. I look at the picture of Simon and Ben and try and imagine Gareth in his place. I squidge my eyes together, trying to blur Simon out of the image, but it doesn't work so I give up. This all seems so confused now. I wonder how my life became so complex, so difficult. Before Ben, my relationship with Gareth seemed so easy and so right. Gareth and I had developed an almost parallel life that I used to just slip in and out of. But now it all seems far more difficult, far less glamorous. I seem to be more the courtesan than the courted now. The whole affair has become seedy, grimy. We tend to meet here now, at the house, and I can never relax. Shagging Gareth in the laundry room while my son is asleep was never part of my dream of motherhood. And for the last few weeks I really have wanted it to end. I wanted to make my life with Simon. I don't know why I let this happen again.

I read recently that the reason that Crystal Meth could be the drug choice of kids in the future is its potency. Apparently this evil concoction creates 1200 times the normal amount of endomorphines that the body would normally come up with when happy, and who is strong enough to resist that? That is the only comparison I can think of to describe the effect that Gareth has on me. Somehow, when I am with him, I seem powerless to resist him, I crave the high that I get when he is near me. It is a force that is so compelling that I don't know how to even start to defy it. And it is not just about sex, it is something bigger, greater and brighter. But lately, after every hit, I just feel ashamed, shoddy almost. This feeling and attraction that was once my whole reason has suddenly became something more sinister. I have ended up feeling manipulated and dirty, shamed by my lack of willpower. It has got harder and harder to say no. And he was relentless. Constantly telephoning and turning up at the house, almost as soon as I got home from the hospital. In the end I just gave in, but all along I thought that I would tell him that it was over when I was stronger, maybe not so tired. I groan when I think of the mess that this has all become. And now Suzie knows. 'You are not the first, you certainly won't be the last,' that is what she said. And what was the other thing? Oh yes, something about me being one of many, one in a long line. What was she talking about? She was obviously delirious and understandably she was just trying to stir things up. The whole conversation was ridiculous.

I jump as my mobile rings and, before I even see the call display, I know that it is Gareth. I hurriedly turn it off and throw it on the table. I need some time to think. This is all happening too fast, and strangely I wish that Simon were here. I used to be able to talk to him about anything. He always had the answers and has always been cool in a crisis. I sigh and rub my forehead; I have a tension headache developing over my left eye. I groan and sit down again. Somehow I can't really see that Simon is going to be much help to me with this one. I look at the clock; I have probably another hour until Ben wakes up. How lovely to be so tiny and so innocent. To be blissfully unaware of anything but the most basic human needs.

I sigh and get up, I walk around the kitchen half-heartedly, I am still rubbing my eyebrow in an attempt to assuage the pain and my poor head feels like I have ingested a very large cloud that has become lodged somewhere between my eyes. I shake my head wearily. It would seem that since having Ben I have become a large woolly mass incapable of making a decision. Usually I sort laundry and tidy when Ben sleeps, but today all I seem able to do is walk around. I pick things up and put them down again. What am I going to do if Suzie tells Simon? I sit back down at the table and contemplate the unopened mail. I shuffle through the batch of letters uninterestedly. It looks like another round of bills. But then at the bottom I spot something a bit different. There is something different. It is a cream envelope, heavy and expensive looking. I turn it over looking for clues but there is nothing so I open it carefully. Maybe some rich relative has died and left me something. Or perhaps it's a wedding invitation. I frown, trying to think of anyone I know who might be getting hitched some time soon, but draw a blank. It is not often that I receive such fancy stationery. It must be something important, I think. I stop opening and check the address again just to make sure it is definitely for me. Yep, no mistake. The letter is artfully folded and so I unfold it and lay it flat. There is no address and the message is brief but to the point.

Dear Sophie,

I am writing to inform you that you are currently the victim of a serial philanderer named Gareth Banks. Mr Banks is a man of proven dubious character. He has been unfaithful to his wife on numerous occasions and is currently spending his time with several other women in your area. I understand that Mr Banks may be the father of your son and so I would advise you to proceed with caution in your future dealings with this man. I am sorry to inform you also that your colleague and friend Amanda Stearne has also been the subject of Mr Banks' attentions and I would therefore strongly urge you to consider this before making any further commitment to him. I apologise for this rather unorthodox method of communicating this news, however, I realize that this information will have implications for you and your son.
Please be assured of my best intentions at all times.

Yours sincerely

A FRIEND

I look at the letter in total disbelief. Will this woman stop at nothing? And after giving me all that crap about not wanting him any more. She obviously has some really serious issues. What a weird letter, and as if I wouldn't know it was her. She is obviously a complete nutter and Gareth is better off without her. But then I look at the letter again. How would Suzie know about Amanda? She has only really met Amanda a couple of times, if that, and Amanda wouldn't have told her about Gareth trying it on. It doesn't make sense. I look at the letter again. Amanda. It must be from Amanda! What on earth is she up to? She has really gone too far this time. She is just so jealous. She knows that I don't believe her stories about Gareth's supposed flirting; I mean, according to Amanda no woman is safe from Gareth. It is laughable. I can't believe she has sent me an anonymous letter. What does she think I am? Stupid? God what a morning. I appear to be surrounded by lunatics. I get up and grab the phone. As I pick it up it starts to ring. Bloody Gareth again. Well, he will just have to wait. I speed-dial Amanda and wait for her to answer.

'Hi, hon.' Hmm, Amanda actually sounds quite sunny.

'I got the letter,' I say. And while I am speaking I glance back to the letter. After the drama of the morning and all that stuff with Suzie it actually seems quite amusing now and I must admit the language is hysterical.

'What letter?' Amanda sounds genuinely bewildered. God, she's good.

'Oh, come on, I know it was you. Friend,' I say cryptically.

'Are you having some kind of post baby fit?' she asks. 'I really don't know what you are talking about, but anyway, have you heard about Gareth?' she adds breathlessly.

Suddenly I can feel pins and needles up my spine; she must have heard that Gareth and Suzie have split up. I hear her walking and know that she is heading towards one of the offices so that she can speak without being overheard.

'We have had internal audit in all morning, they are pulling the place apart,' she says. 'Apparently Will's client, Lucy, has complained that Gareth assaulted her when we had that corporate lunch a couple of months back, and now compliance has found some accounting issues. Apparently Gareth has been fiddling his commissions for months. On some cases he has been taking a commission and a fee without the client knowing. He is *soo* sacked.' I can hear the glee in her voice and I feel sick and confused. This is really serious.

'Are they sure? I mean Gareth wouldn't assault anyone and he is really successful. Why would he fiddle his numbers?' I realize I am stammering now.

'Oh wake up. Gareth will assault any thing moving in a skirt, I can't believe you still think he is so bloody innocent. Apparently he snogged Lucy and put his hand up her skirt! And on top of everything, Vicky from accounts says that if they ask her, she is going to tell them about what he said to her in the kitchen that day. All of a sudden all this stuff is coming out of the woodwork. It is unbelievable, he is never going to worm his way out of all of this. And this morning I had coffee with Will and he reckons that there is some woman on the first floor who has told HR that Gareth almost stalked her when he first got here. And you're never going to believe it, turns out that it's that girl who had the boob job, you know, the one with the blonde highlights. Everyone is talking about it. Anyway, he has been suspended without pay or benefits until his disciplinary hearing.'

I know that she is still talking but I can't really hear too well any more. There are big teardrops just sliding down my face and I am shaking so much now that I can hardly talk. So when Amanda gets a call on the other line we agree to speak later and I put the phone down shakily.

I realize that I still don't know whether or not Amanda sent the letter. But whether she did or not seems of little consequence now. What a nightmare! I wipe away the tears. I know without doubt now that all that creepy stuff in the letter was true. 'A serial philanderer'. I feel sick. Oh my God, I am such a mug. I know now without a doubt that Suzie was telling the truth as well. She must be thrilled that she has finally found someone to offload him on, I think gloomily.

And he is going to be unemployed! He probably won't ever work again. So not only will I be landed with a sex pest, he will be an unemployed sex pest as well. I have visions of Ben and I living in a run down apartment somewhere, with Gareth selling porn films from the back of his car just so that we can make ends meet. I mean, harassing women and fraud never looks great on your CV, no matter how you dress it up. What an idiot. I feel totally taken in. Why on earth could I not have just ended it that day in the woods? How could I have been so stupid, to start all this up again, to risk my life with Simon? And then I think about all the times that I have seen him since Ben was born. And I realize that it's a bit like a new coat. The first season you wear it all the time. It goes with everything and makes you feel amazing. When the summer comes it goes away, hidden with the rest of your winter wardrobe. Then when the weather turns colder, you go back to the coat. You put it on. But maybe it doesn't feel such a good fit anymore. It is still the same coat but the world of fashion has moved on and so have you. And that is exactly what has happened with Gareth. I have changed. I realize that now. I am no longer the unconfident, excitement-starved girl he met. I am a mother now and everything is different. I've changed. I take a deep breath because all of a sudden it all seems very clear. And I have to do what is right for Ben. It isn't just about me any more. I pick up the phone and speed-dial his number.

'We should meet,' I say.

'Sophie, thank God, I thought I was never going to get hold of you. I have been ringing all morning.' He sounds angry, petulant. 'You are never going to believe what has happened, I am having a complete mare. So much has happened, but it is so good to hear your voice and, darling, I have told Suzie. I told her everything and now we can be together at last.' This last sentence is delivered with much aplomb and I feel a little embarrassed.

'Mmmm, yes about that. Look, let's meet for a coffee, I can't do today, how about tomorrow?'

'But I really need to see you today,' he whines.

'I just can't today. I'm too busy.'

'But I could come round?' he pleads. I lie then and tell him that Simon has taken the day off, and that my only opportunity to get out is the next day. He seems satisfied with this and we agree to meet at around 3.00 pm.

He is obviously desperate for conversation and tries to keep me on the line, he repeatedly asks me to tell him that I love him but I tell him that I can't talk and put the phone down hurriedly. Oh God, what was I thinking?

I call Simon's mother the next day and ask her to sit with Ben, so that I can run an errand, and once again I am struck by how over the moon she is with my request. She gets to the house in under twenty minutes and without worrying about make-up or my hair I jump in the car and head to our usual coffee spot. I am there a little early but instead of ambling and looking in shops I stride purposefully towards my destination. When I get there I am shocked because Gareth is there before me. Not only is he early but he looks terrible; he looks as though he has slept in his clothes, and his usually glossy hair hangs greasily over his face. It doesn't even look as though he has shaved. Suddenly I find that I am not at all nervous, there are no butterflies when I see him and even when he touches my hand there is nothing. The relief is enormous. I am finally over him. I take a deep breath, glad that all this madness is finally over. And with this knowledge I say my piece.

'I have come to say goodbye,' I say. Better to get this over with straight away, I think.

'What? But, wait—' He looks completely perplexed and a little petulant. His eyes are red and his face is puffy but I feel nothing. Not even pity. 'But you have only just got here,' he tries to joke, but my words just hang in the air between us, their meaning plain.

'But, I have left her, I left Suzie,' he says. There is a look of mild panic about him now and he starts to look around him, agitated.

'Please don't go. We can be together now, you, me and Ben. Oh Sophie, I have had the worst day. Apparently some tart from one of Will's accounts has complained about me. Compliance are crawling all over my files and, God, I might even lose my job. I just want us to be together so we can put all of this behind us.' And to my horror he starts to cry.

'Gareth, stop, there is no us. This hasn't been right for some time now.' I try and say this gently but he is staring at me in abject horror. His mouth has fallen open and it is not attractive. I force myself to look at him again and continue. 'I am sorry that things aren't going so well for you right now but I have to think of Ben. And, to be honest, I just don't love you any more, I love Simon. Please don't contact me again.' I go to stand up and notice the waitress in a red gingham apron looking at us curiously. I make no eye contact but reach for my bag.

'You can't be serious? You are just going to walk away and leave me like this?' He is incredulous now and I notice that a rather unattractive bubble of spit has accumulated at the side of his mouth. 'You bitch! I left my bloody wife for you and now you change your mind?' He starts to laugh hysterically. And as I panic and try and get away from him he grabs my wrist roughly.

'Go on, run along, scamper back to your boring husband with your boring life and screaming brat. There are a hundred tarts out there just lining up to be with me. I don't need you. Just don't think you can come crying back when you need a proper shag.' He sits back down heavily and I stare at him in embarrassment, horror and contempt.

I realize that there is nothing more to say, so I walk away. I am stunned for a while, not quite believing that it is over. I sit in the car and watch life go by. I watch pigeons scrabble for crumbs and shoppers park. I don't feel anything but a quiet numbness. I wonder idly if I have had some kind of stroke but no, all my limbs do actually still move when I want them to. I wiggle my feet and wonder if I will ever feel anything ever again. Wearily I put the key in the ignition and as I turn on the engine I hear my phone. I don't recognize the number but I answer anyway.

It is Sergeant Cleary. My waterlogged brain springs back to life. There is something about the police that demands respect and instant attention and I snap back immediately. My first thought is that something must have happened to Ben. No, not that, I think, anything but that. Or maybe something has happened to Simon? But then, just as I try and speak, and try to ascertain which disaster he is calling about he tells me not to worry, that it is a routine call.

'Sorry,' I say, 'routine?'

I can't seem to get my head round this now. My life has become surreal.

'We were going through some files and I realize that we never did get back to you about your break-in.'

I sigh with relief and try to concentrate on what he is saying.

'Are you OK to do this now?' he asks. I confirm that I am and he continues.

'It seems that on the day of the break-in we did a neighbourhood sweep. You know, we spoke to anyone who might have seen anything. Anyway it turns out that three of your neighbours reported the exact same thing. It seems that your intruder may well have been your husband.'

'My husband?' I say this slowly, not really comprehending, not wanting to understand the ramifications of this.

'No, that can't be right. My husband was in Tokyo or Hong Kong or somewhere, he was on some kind of business trip.'

'Well, not according to your neighbours he wasn't.' His tone is almost jovial. 'Apparently your husband came out of

236

your house and bolted over your back wall, went like a bat out of hell by all accounts. The lady from number 47 said that he looked like he had seen a ghost; while a Mrs Turner said that she had never seen him move so quick. And in a business suit as well. Anyway I thought that I would let you know, so as to put your mind at rest. Seems like it was your husband all the time.'

He sounds cheerful and chatty, he asks about the baby and I tell him the usual, I tell him that he is happy and we are both well, that we called him Ben. But even to me, my voice sounds strange, almost disconnected, and distant. As we say goodbye he checks again that everything is OK, and then he confirms that I have no further questions and as I haven't I agree to close the file.

I feel sick. It was Simon. I am struggling to take this in, to assimilate this new information. All this time he has known. It was him that day when we were in the kitchen. He must have seen us. Oh God. I have to get home. I have to talk to him. I remember back. I remember being confused when he didn't call from that blasted trip. Oh God. I think back to when he got back from that Hong Kong or Tokyo trip. He looked terrible, so sad and so grey and I thought he was just tired from travelling. I feel so awful, I can hardly drive. I can't believe that I could have been so wrapped up in my own life that I can't even remember where he went, Tokyo or Hong Kong.

When I get home Simon's mother has gone and I am greeted by Simon. He takes one look at my tear-stained face and general pallor and hustles me into the house. All at once he is concerned and kind. He sits me down and puts the kettle on. He lifts up my feet and eases my shoes off. He puts my feet on the sofa and holds my hand. The nicer he is the more I cry. But he doesn't ask what is wrong he just holds me and lets me sob into his jumper.

How can I tell him that I am crying because of how sorry I

am, that I am crying because it feels as though my heart will break with the love I feel for him? That I regret ever being born at the moment. And I want so badly to talk but I just don't know where to start.

After a while he begins to ask gentle questions, he says things like, 'you know you can always talk to me' and then 'please tell me what's wrong', and even worse 'there is nothing that we can't get over together'. And so I sit up, I hold his hands and I tell him. I tell him through hiccups and whilst blowing my nose. My miserable story is peppered with grief and regret, punctuated with apologies. And he says nothing. He just strokes my hair. I try and explain that there are no excuses for my behaviour. And then I say all the usual things that people say in these circumstances, I tell him that it wasn't him it was me, that I understand if he never wants to see me again. I tell him that it is all over now, that I never want to see Gareth again. I finish by telling him that I know that he has known all this time. I explain about the police and the phone call and everything. I say this last bit slowly, and for the first time I look straight at him.

But instead of shouting, screaming or just walking out he looks down and strokes my hand. And it is my turn to listen. He tells me that he has known for ever, since way back at the barbecue. That he could just tell from the way we acted around each other. He explains that he thought it was just a fling and that he was sure that I would see through Gareth eventually. And then he tells me again the story that I love. He tells me that he loved me before he even met me, and that he spent months watching me before he could get the courage up to ask me out. He tells me that he knew straight away that I was the one for him and that life without me was never an option. And as he talks I realize he is crying, huge teardrops splash onto my hands, but still he talks. In haltering speech he describes painfully how seeing Gareth and me in the kitchen almost killed him. That he had

238

considered suicide. He apologizes for pretending that he was on a work trip when all the time he was holed up in a hotel a couple of hundred miles away. And he tells me that he doesn't blame me, and that nothing I can do can ever change the way that he loves me. And just as I start to relax he drops the bombshell. That he knows that he is not Ben's father.

He gets up and crosses the room. He has his back to me now so I can't see his expression, there is no way for me to read what is going on in his head.

'We don't know that,' I stammer, then 'there is every possibility' I say weakly, my words disappearing into the space between us. I look up into his eyes, and see beyond the pain. I see the kindness and the wisdom and the depth that is my Simon. The Simon who is always so cool in a crisis.

'Look, just stop. It doesn't matter,' he says. 'None of this matters. Do you think I would throw this away? You, me, Ben. This is our life. We are a family now. And it doesn't matter what has happened or who has done what. All that matters is that we are together now. No blood result could make me love Ben any less. And we don't need to know. Nobody needs to know. He will always be my son, no matter what, and he doesn't need to know. All he needs is us. Just you and me.'

He turns away from me and stares out into the garden. His pride and joy. It is dark now and I walk behind him and embrace him. We stare up at the moon together. It is a crescent, just a sliver of light, but enough to illuminate the whole of the sky.

Chapter 23

Rebecca

'Heaven has no rage like love to hatred turned.'
William Congeve

They would have received the letters by now. I posted them
on Friday so they must have got there. I could have written
great paragraphs devoted to his deceit and duplicity. But in
the end I kept each letter brief, factual and to the point.
Someone had to do something. I just couldn't stand by and
watch this happen all over again. Gareth had to be stopped.
Over the years I have watched him destroy marriages and
friendships, and deceive and devastate a whole string of
women, myself included. It all happened a long time ago but
the ramifications will affect my family for ever. When I heard
about Sophie, well something just snapped. And so now,
maybe because of my letter, Suzie has had enough as well.
And he won't get round her this time. Oh no. I hear that he
has lost his job too; well, it couldn't have happened to a nicer
person as far as I am concerned. I raise my face to the sun
and relax at last. I am at the beach, my favourite place, and I
look over at my son, a walking double of his father. My
beautiful boy with his shock of perfectly straight, shiny brown
hair and his big blue eyes. So different from Luke. I know just

by looking at him that he will break hearts one day. But hopefully not as many as his father. And in all these years Luke has never suspected a thing. But then why would he? After all, Gareth is his best friend. I did toy with the idea of telling Luke early on, but then, when you think about it, does anyone really need to know?